Racingbooks.org

ISBN. 978-1-9164910-8-3

A Fatal Addiction

Part 3

The Victor and the Vanquished

By

Max. M. Power

Introduction

A Fatal Addiction-The Victor and the Vanquished covers a much shorter time period than the previous two in the series: The Seduction of Speed, and The Triumphs and the Tragedies. The ten-year period covered in this book saw dramatic changes, not only in motor racing but significantly in the younger generation's attitude to life.

By the mid-sixties motor racing had begun to change significantly from the preceding years.

The advert of cheaper racing cars allowed opportunities to a much wider selection of young men, and a few women, to fulfil their childhood dreams and become professional racing drivers.

While the introduction of Formula Junior in 1959 had given the likes of Jim Clark and Jackie Stewart the opportunity to showcase their exceptional talents, the introduction of Formula Ford in 1967 opened the door to a much wider range of keen young people, desperate to promote their driving talents, and become professional racing drivers.

Advertised as "the £1000 racing car" Formula Ford quickly became a great success throughout the worlds racing centers, and especially in England.

In this story, the third and final part of the Cartland -Marshall family saga, both Cameron Cartland and Mathew Marshall attempt to progress their racing career through their early successes in Formula Ford racing cars.

Many Formula One Champions including, Emerson Fittipaldi, and James Hunt had learnt their race craft in this formula before, getting "noticed", progressing through Formula 3, Formula 2, until eventually becoming Formula One drivers.

The other significant development in motor racing, during this period, came with the introduction of the 3 Litre engines for Formula One in 1966. With Coventry Climax reluctant to invest the thousands of pounds needed to develop a engine suitable for the new formula, many teams desperately searched for a replacement.

Fortunately, by investing £100,000 in a company called Cosworth, Ford produced an engine that would become an icon in the world of motor racing; the Ford Cosworth DFV.

Just as Formula Ford had allowed young drivers to find an affordable way to get onto the first step of the Motorsport ladder, the availability of the Ford Cosworth DFV, V8 engine allowed aspiring team owners an affordable way into, until then, an exclusive club the world of Formula One.

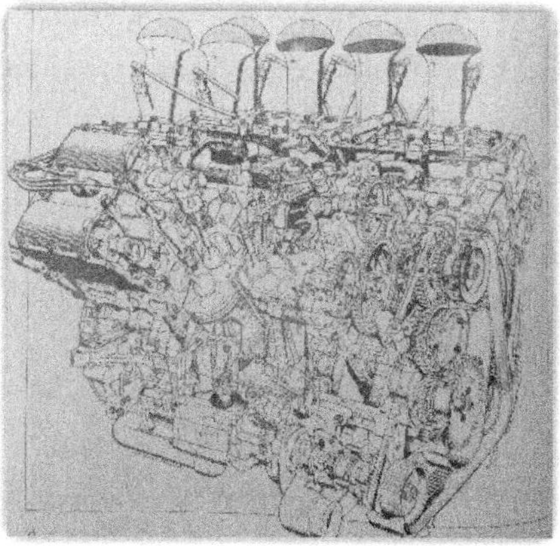

The introduction of this engine came at Zandvoort in June1967. For the rest of that year the engine was solely used by Lotus, this advantage helped Graham Hill win his second world championship. Until this time teams had to build their own engines or used the Coventry Climax engine. When, in 1968, the Ford DFV engine became available, at an affordable price, to a wider customer base, (much to the displeasure of Lotus owner Colin Chapman), new teams including McLaren, Williams, Tyrrell and Hesketh took full advantage.

Now they were able to join Lotus and build competitive Formula One cars, much to the disgust of some of the old establishment teams like BRM and particularly Ferrari. Enzo Ferrari was always particularly unhappy, calling the new young upstarts “garisters.'

Motor racing has always been a dangerous sport and the ten-year period covered in this book suffered more tragedy than most other periods. Between 1965 and 1975 at least one driver each year had been killed in Formula One races compounded by the tragic death of Jim Clark, who's fatal accident at Hockenheim affected the confidence of every driver.

'If it can happen to him it could happen to me.'

An accident at Spa which almost took the life of Jackie Stewart later led to the three-time World Champion, in the early 1970's begin persistent pressures to alter the approach to safety of team owners, drivers and the track owners.

A quote from Jackies' outstanding autobiography.

'Four established drivers had been killed on the same weekend of four successive months, but the season had to carry on...' Leaving home to race at Spa or the Nurburgring we all thought, *'will I survive to see home again.'*

Of course, all successful racing drivers are inherently selfish. To win at the highest level in any professional sport requires complete dedication and a single-minded obsession.

It is the impact the consequences of the actions taken by these drivers have had on their families and loved ones that I have tried to express in the story that follows.

By the end of the period covered here, in 'The Victor and the Vanquished', the original famous old circuits of Spa, Nurburgring, Monza, Silverstone, Le Mans and Zandvoort had been dramatically altered, many say castrated, with the introduction of speed reducing chicanes, or in the case of Spa a major alteration to the layout.

Sometimes the actual racing events in this period were so dramatic and unlikely that there was no need to dramatise them. The incredible year when the rivalry between Nicki Lauda and James Hunt, recorded in the excellent film 'Rush', still seems like it must have been fiction.

This has been a long journey through three generations in the 'A Fatal Addiction' trilogy is a fictional account of events as they unfolded over the years.

Chapter 1

Farewell to Frank Cartland

5th November 1965

Death had been a constant shadow for three generations in the Cartland family, and now, once more, it had become a reality.

The cold winter wind circled the bell in St Mary's church tower. Its mournful, lonely toll reverberated among the family and friends of Frank Cartland who had gathered for his funeral. There would be no fireworks in the village of Burlham that year.

Lady Mary Marshall shivered on the cold black oak of the Cartland family pew. Death always causes regrets for those still living, she thought, sitting with head bowed. Here to bury her father, Frank Cartland, now all the "I will, I can...and maybe next week" suddenly became "I should have, I could have and ...never."

Her father had always been an essential part of her life until William Marshall had entered her world and stolen her heart. The longstanding Cartland and Marshall family conflicts had saddened her continuously. Now, without her father, memories brought tears as Mary felt an overwhelming sense of loss.

Sitting in the pew directly behind her eighty-eight-year-old Doctor Howard Jones uncomfortably shifted his massive body. He slightly shook his bald head, thinking how could this beautiful, elegant woman could be the scruffy oily-handed little girl I used to know?

He had sat in this place many times for the weddings and funerals in the Cartland family. Sadly, there are far more funerals than weddings. The last time the bells had rung for Frank Cartland, it had been a joyful peel to celebrate his marriage in 1920. Howard was the only one of more than one hundred people crowding into the church who had known Frank as a boy. What a life; I never expected years ago that such a skinny, battered, and bruised little boy would have packed so much into his.

Among the congregations in that overflowing village church were the living results of the life of Frank Cartland. In the group were his three remaining children, Mary, Peter, and Emily. All his grandchildren, including Mary's son Mathew and daughter Florence, Peter's son Cameron, his only child, and Emily's four, whose ages ranged from ten down to a restless two.

Cameron and Mathew were now strapping teenagers; their grandfather had been delighted to encourage both these lads to follow his motor racing passion. Howard knew Frank had nurtured ambitions for someone in his family to become a world champion, a dream which had eluded Frank. Not that these boys needed any encouragement; both were determined to be Formula One World Champion racing drivers one day.

The boys had arrived at St Mary's church at the same time but from different directions,

Cameron had walked up from his father's bakery in the village, and Mathew from his mother's blue 3.4 Jaguar now parked in the Red Lion car park. Mathew, dressed in a crisp black suit, a new white shirt, narrow black tie, and highly polished black shoes. Cameron looked smart in similar clothes, but when seen next to his cousin, it was apparent none of Cameron's clothes were new.

Before they entered the nave of the church, Mat said," Hi Cam, sad about our grandfather. Going to miss the old boy."

"Yes, don't know what I'm going to do without him I always thought he would be around to help me start racing in a couple of years," was Cam's sharp, uneasy reply;

but Mathew didn't appear to notice his cousin's manner.

"Suppose I'm lucky we have Hans working for us in Sussex. I'm going to get him to build me a new racing car."

"Bloody right, you don't know how lucky you are," Cam replied bitterly.
After this strained conversation, the boys parted and strolled to their respective pews.

To the left-hand side of Mary sat her brother, straight-backed Peter Cartland.
Peter's childhood had been dominated by his mother's influence, never having possessed the adventurous nature of his father or his older sister Mary. Peter was happy with a quieter life.

His grandfather, Joe Foster, became the most significant power in his life after the Doodlebug killed his mother and sister in the war.
His mother's father was the village baker, and Peter needed little encouragement to follow the Foster family tradition. His early years of regular church attendance grew in significance as he became an adult, and at the time of his father's death, Peter was churchwarden.

Peter had always been opposed to his son Cameron's interest in racing but was becoming resigned to the fact that he could no longer influence his growing son, who he realised would always have the same motoring passions as his grandfather. With regret, Peter knew Cameron would be unlikely to follow him into the bakery business. Head bowed in the family pew; his thoughts were of relief that he and his father had finally settled, or at least postponed, their conflicts just one day before Frank's death.

On Mary's right sat Lord William Marshall, her husband, his scared, angry, red scalp, the legacy of his wartime experiences. William had always had high respect for Frank Cartland and saw so much of his wife's approach to her life shaped by her father's love and influence. Mary inherited most of her stubborn determination and optimism from Frank, and William had always loved those characteristics in her.

Now, he sat, with eyes closed, and reflected on his good fortune to have met and married such a remarkable woman. But his mood was tempered by his increasing acceptance that the wartime injuries caused in his burning Hurricane were always going to haunt him. Now in his forty-sixth year, the damaged tissues on his fingers, arms and head were gradually contracting, tightening, causing him constant pain. William's smoke-damaged lungs compound his worries, on damp and cold days, each breath would signal their discomfort. The overpowering invasive smell of lilies, dominating the usual musty church fragrances, certainly didn't help.

The funeral service was sharp and short. Never being one for the limelight, Frank Cartland would have approved.

Afterwards, the plain oak coffin was transported to the bleak, rusted iron-fenced cemetery further up the hill behind the church. Its scattered, neglected gravestones are almost transparent against the low grey sky. After the short graveside dedications and tributes, the coffin of Frank Cartland was lowered into the chalk-lined six-foot black hole to rest next to his wife and daughter, and close by the graves of his long deceased, brother Joe and sister Joan.

Many of the funeral congregation then walked back down the hill to the village pub.

Reminiscing and drinking in the Red Lion continued until the early hours. Frank's old childhood best friend Fred Coles, now almost part of the Red Lion furniture, was happy to regale all with tales of Frank's many childhood adventures, which became "taller" as Green King beer consumption increased.

At the reading of Frank Cartlands there had been no surprises. Apart from the contents of his workshop, there were few material items. Objects and possessions unrelated to cars or motorbikes had never held much interest to Frank.

Ivy Cottage and the orchard willed to Peter, the workshop and all its contents, including the racing Mini, were left to Cameron. Mary had found no problem with the arrangement. Now, being Lady Marshall, she had all she needed at Sefton Lodge.

Frank had not rebuilt much of Ivy Cottage since the Doodlebug had destroyed it in the war, he had only bothered to make a few rooms habitable, preferring to spend most of his time in his workshop.

With agreement from her brother, Mary did take the little Kieft 500 racing car back to Sussex. It had been resting under an old cover at the back of the workshop for many years.

Seeing it again had remined her of how her father had lovingly prepared that car, and how with her skillful driving and his exceptional engineering, they had won races in those distant early years of the1950's.

Chapter 2.

Cameron's dilemma

His grandfather Frank's death had hit Cameron awfully hard, for mostly selfish reasons, he would admit. Of course, he had loved the old boy and admired all he had achieved, but Cameron's youth gave him little knowledge of the struggles and tragedies that had blighted his grandfather's early life.

Although the more recent successes, which he and his cousin Mathew had been a small part of, had reinforced Cameron's passion for motor racing.

Growing up, he had spent far more time in his grandfather's workshop, surrounded by racing cars and engines, than at home in his father's bakery.

Earlier in the year, his grandfather had promised he would help him begin racing when he was old enough. Now he had no-one to help him with that burning ambition. Cameron thought of his cousin Mathew down at Sefton Lodge and instinctively clenched his fists. That lucky bugger will still have plenty of help, and more than enough money to start his racing career.

The once close boys, with their mutual ambition, were rapidly growing

apart, Cameron, with a growing resentment of his more privileged cousin.
His grandfather had just started to strip down the Mini that they had used to win the European Championship. He had planned to rebuild the Mini and use it to teach Cam to drive.
'I'll take you over to my mates' airfield at Bottisham, plenty of room for you to practice driving there.' Had been some of the last words Frank had spoken to him. The farmer who owned the airfield had been an old friend of Frank's and had always let him test cars whenever Frank had new ideas to try out.

Two days after his grandfather's funeral, Cam sat in the battered leather chair in the cold, old workshop; it's flaking, plastered, once white, walls matching his sad mood. Little did he know that his grandfather had sat here repeatedly in the past in a similar mood. The almond green Mini rested forlornly on axle stands without its engine and gearbox. Their dismantled parts scattered over the ancient wooden workbench, which his grandfather had used to rebuild all his engines.

What the hell do I do now? Cam thought I can't put all these parts together by myself.

An hour later, he was still sitting feeling sorry for himself, reading one of the old Autosport magazines stacked in dusty piles around the workshop. With a sharp, mind alerting, screeching, the solid dirty green workshop doors slowly opened, allowing a shaft of weak November sunlight to fight through the workshop gloom. Standing in the doorway was a slim, tall, dark-haired figure.

"Hi Cam, I've come to find out how you are coping and see if you need some help," said Mike Coles as he walked in.

Before he had pushed open the door, Mike had been thinking of the first time he had visited Frank Cartland's workshop and how nervous he had felt. That man had transformed his life. Knowing the ambitions Frank had held for his grandsons, he wanted to repay the favour somehow. Cam and Mike had become friends during the past amazing year when Mike's driving and Frank's engineering skills had, against all the odds, won their little team the European Saloon Car Championship in their Mini Cooper.

Cam's mood lightened, as he looked up,

"Hi, Mike, really great to see you. I've just been wondering how I'm going to get this old Mini ready to practice my driving. Grandfather had promised to help me, and now he has left it in hundreds of bits".

"Well, no time like the present, we had better get going. I'll make a start by rebuilding the engine. You can begin by cleaning all the parts."

Hesitating, Cam replied, "Thanks, Mike, but I'm afraid I can't afford to pay you anything."

"Your grandfather turned me from a poor car mechanic to a works racing driver. I want to help. You owe me nothing," Mike had replied.

After his success with Frank, Mike had signed a contract and was committed to racing for the works BMC team the following year. He was going to be busy racing and testing Mini Coopers in the British Saloon Car Championship. Whenever he had time at home, he intended to spend much of it helping Cam rebuild the Mini.

"You are just as bad as your grandfather used to be, spending all your time in that old workshop." Peter Cartland had complained to his son on many occasions during the year.

By the following October, Mike and Cam had finished the rebuilding. Loading the green Mini onto Frank's old trailer, they travelled the five miles to Bottisham airfield for Cam's first drive.

Cam never forgot the sensation of freedom he got venturing out on to that old concrete runway for the first time. Over the following year, whenever Mike had free time, they would take the Mini to the former airfield for Cam to improve his driving skills.

After a year's practice, Cam had mastered all the basics of driving a racing Mini.

"Well done, you can now lap around here almost as quickly as me. You will certainly be ready to race as soon as you are seventeen," Mike had said after their last visit.

"Trouble is racing costs a lot of money. Haven't managed to save much." Cam had left Farewell Secondary School at fifteen and worked in Mike's Cambridge Garage when not at Technical College, where he had gone to study mechanics.

" Can't wait until I can race, but want to try a proper racing car," he would often say to Mike.

"This is a proper racing car. Sticking to saloon cars has done me well. You could do worse than concentrate on these and forget single seaters," was Mike's advice.

"I'm going to be Formula One World Champion, so I need to drive single seaters. Bloody Mathew Marshall will get there before me if he gets the chance."

"We all want to be World Champion when we start this dangerous game, but it's a one in a thousand chance, and there's a good chance you will kill yourself." Mike replied.

He felt uneasy about Cam's obsession, knowing it had often led to disaster for many young racing drivers desperate to succeed.

Chapter 3

Mathews racing begins

From the day of his birth, the public were interested in Mathew Marshall's life. Being only six years old at the time of his notorious Uncle David's trial and execution, he, fortunately, had no memory of the publicity and distress that event caused to the Marshall family. Although his home life was comfortable, he soon found his family's notoriousness brought him unhappiness at school.

'There goes Lord Monsters son.' Had been a taunt he had had to endure when he started Grammar School. His father's appearance did embarrass him especially as his mother and grandmother often compared his dashing good looks and blond locks to Williams younger appearance.

The young Mathew soon became tired of the usual comment.

"You've got your father's eyes."
Mathew grew up close to his mother, but more reserved and respectful around his father.

"I never know if our father is happy or angry."
He would say to his sister Florence. Mathews younger sister didn't seem to notice their fathers disfigured face and

scared body; seeing her always relaxed and happy in his presence added to Mathew's feelings of guilt.

The welcome escape during his early teenage years had been the trips to Cambridgeshire and, with his cousin Cam, helping their grandfather in that glorious, victorious, racing season.
That experience and the exciting European travel had re-enforced his desire to become a racing driver.

Impatient to start race-driving, he constantly pestered his mother.

"I have asked Hans, he said he could get the car going, but I must get your permission."

Hans had worked for the Marshall family since the early 1950s, joining to work on the racing car of David Marshall. The Crusader sports car Hans had built for David was an excellent design and had shown great potential. But after David's execution for murdering his girlfriend, it had eventually been sold to a motor museum where it had become a significant attraction, more for its association with the scandals and murder of Alice Rice than for its racing success.

Eventually, Mary gave in and allowed Mathew to drive the old 500cc Kieft; she used to race, around the lanes on the estate.

Mary stood with Hans one day watching Mathew slide the little car around, she said.

"Looks like he is getting pretty good at this."

"Yes, he is a natural driver, just like David used to be..." Hans had instinctively replied. He added quickly.

"Sorry Lady Marshall, I didn't mean Mathew is like him."

Mary smiled. "I know Hans, don't worry about it."

She turned and walked back towards Sefton Lodge.

She hadn't thought about David for some time. It was certainly not a period of their lives she wished to recall.

A little later, a hot, scratched, and dusty Mathew came into the Lodge.

"Afraid I just put the old girl through a hedge, haven't done any damage though... Think I need to get out onto a racetrack. It's stupid I can't get a racing licence until I am old enough to drive on the road," he complained to his mother.

William continued reading The Times and didn't offer any comment. Although never openly expressing it, William wished his son would take up other interests like most teenage boys, rugby, cricket, or even girls. He could see this obsession with racing leading to trouble.

The memories of his brother David's tragic, short, life often surfaced at times like this, another, unseen, layer of painful scars for William.

He knew he could not stop Mary's open encouragement of their son's ambitions. She couldn't help herself. Having been a successful racing driver herself, and growing up with a father addicted to racing, she could undoubtedly appreciate Mathew's desire to race.

"Look here, in this week's Autosport," Mary said, "there is an article on go-kart racing that looks interesting, and it says you don't have to be seventeen to start racing those."

William sighed inwardly.

"Let me see!" exclaimed Mathew.

The picture showed a simple, open frame design, with four small wheels, a seat and engine. "They do look fun, like your old Kieft, but without any bodywork. Do you think Hans could build me one of these?"

"Let's go and ask him," replied his mother.

William still didn't comment but was pleased to see the sudden liveliness in his wife. Since her father's death, Mary had become slightly withdrawn and a bit short-tempered. Although he knew his increasingly poor moods and deepening depression didn't help.

Hans was in the farm workshop feeling somewhat depressed himself. He was listlessly cleaning the engine on one of the Sefton estates Fordson diesel tractors. Hans missed the excitement of racing, often thinking back to those early days with David and more recently helping Frank Cartland with his successful Minis. He found working on the farm machinery all day, mundane and boring.

Mathews' sudden appearance in the workshop made him jump and brought him back from his reminiscences.

"Hi, Hans! Mother has had an idea. We want you to build me a go-kart," he said, his voice full of excitement.

"What is go-kart?" was Hans' bewildered response.

"Ah...not sure, but it looks like a little racing car without a body."

Mary followed her son in and showed Hans the pictures in Autosport of the racing karts.

What do you think, Hans. Could you build one of these?"

"I should think so Lady Marshall. I would certainly like to try," he said.

Anything will be better than working on these bloody tractors all day. He thought.

"I see here in Autosport they are advertising a race meeting that's being held in Kent next weekend. Shall we all go and have a look," said Mary.

"Great idea." replied to her excited son.

"I will bring my camera and take lots of pictures."

All three returned from their visit to Kent full of enthusiasm, Hans declaring to Mathew.

"I think I can build a kart for you as good as those.

"They are very noisy, like a swarm of angry bees," had been Mary's reaction. Then she smiled, remembering the similar noise a grid full of her little Formula 500's used to make.

William had decided not to go to Kent.

Ever since the Crusader sports car he had built for the late David Marshall had been sold to a museum, Hans missed working on racing cars. He had had only the Minis of Frank Cartland to work on in recent years. Even though he had enjoyed the experience of working with Frank and their success, he missed not having his project to control.

Now he had a chance to develop something himself. Mary and, slightly reluctantly, William left Hans alone to design and build the new Crusader kart. William grumbled to Mary,

"There is still a lot of farm machinery that needs servicing and repairing. We can't afford to let this new racing idea take precedence over that."

"I know darling," his wife replied. "Hans has got his son Jimmy helping him now. He is doing some simple jobs and is very keen."

"Well, I don't think we should pay him anything extra."

"Hans is just giving him pocket money. The lad is going to Agricultural College next year. He will be a real asset to the estate in the future if we look after Jimmy now."

William didn't reply. Increasingly he was becoming grumpy and withdrawn. Mary knew the constant pain from his damaged fingers and hands were causing his depression. Since he had to give up flying his beloved "Harry Hurricane" his mood swings had intensified.

Mary felt helpless; anyway, she had her own worries, her father's death reinforced her thoughts that she needed to pack more into her life, she was restless, and still needed some adventure, some excitement for herself.

On a sharp March morning in 1967, Hans and Mary pushed Mathew and his new kart until the McCulloch engine coughed, and fired into life, the wheels of the Crusader kart spun in anger for the first time as Mathew released the brake. With whoops of delight, Mathew was immediately swooping and turning the agile, little machine around the lanes of the Sefton estate.

"It' feels fantastic, you're a genius!" he shouted to Hans as he slid to a halt.

"Well, we won't know how good it is until you race it. So, don't get too excited," was the older man's simple response.

After a few meetings, Mathew had shown plenty of speed, but his lack of experience ensured he didn't win any races. Then, at his fourth meeting, everything seemed to click, and he won his first race. "Wow, that's brilliant, never enjoyed myself so much," he enthused to his mother after the race.

"There is nothing like winning is there?" she replied wistfully, recalling her victories in the Kieft before Mathew was born. It's funny, she thought, looking at her excited son and remembering her, oh-so-brief, carefree days with William at the start of the war; when you're young, you think there is nothing you can't do.

William had not attended the meeting. He found the high-pitched noise from the two-stroke engines, the dust and frantic action all rather unpleasant these days.

More wins soon followed, and people started to take notice of this confident young man and his blue Crusader kart.

"Who built this for you? I would like to try it," became a regular question from many of the other young drivers. Hans usually kept out of the way, just working on the kart, but Mat was very protective about his pride and joy.

"It's the only one. Hans has built it just for me. So, no one else is going to race it."

Mat had found it hard to mix in with most of his competitors who, he knew, resented him. After his childhood experiences making close friends had never been easy for him. At a recent meeting he had overheard two drivers he had just beaten in a race talking together:

"I'll have that cocky, bloody rich kid, off the track next time." One said to the other.

Mat didn't take much notice of the resentment. His only interest was winning races.

Unfortunately, the aggressive driving against him became worse as Mat became more successful.

"That's not a problem," he said to his worried mother after one particularly fraught race.

A rival had knocked his kart sideways at the first corner then, working with another driver, he blocked Mat's path as he tried to overtake, forcing him off the track. A broken steering-arm on Mats kart causing his retirement from the race. "It's all good experience for when I get into a proper racing car."

Mathew was counting down the days until he was old enough to fulfil that ambition.

At the end of the season, a letter arrived at Sefton Lodge for him.

"They want me to be a member of the British Kart Team next season." He excitedly exclaimed to his parents.

"That's wonderful news; you will be racing in Europe next year." His mother came over to put her arm around him to read the letter.

"Well done, Mathew," was William's lest than an enthusiastic comment. His main thoughts were about the extra cost for all the European travel.

Chapter 4

A Harsh lesson for Cameron

Cam stopped cleaning the dirty SU carburetor he had found among the mountain of old engine parts at the back of the workshop and rushed outside. He had heard the deep-throated roar of a powerful engine arrive at the garage door.

"I've got something for you," said Mike Coles as he extracted his long body from the driving seat of the red MGB.

"Wow, is this yours?" was Cam's response.

"Course not. It belongs to the BMC works, but they let me use any of the cars when an engine needs running in". Unable to hide his excitement, Mike added, "I'm down as reserve driver at the Targa Floria in an MGB later in the year."

"Brilliant Mike! Think I could come along with you, remember I helped you and grandfather."

"Not sure. I will ask the mechanics if they need an extra pair of hands."
He didn't want to disappoint Cam, but knew the answer would be no.

"What did you say you had for me?" continued Cam.

"Here," said Mike handing him a booklet. It is the latest copy of the Highway

Code. It would help if you were studying that. It's only three months until your seventeenth birthday. You had better get cracking and book your test."
"What can I use? I know my father wouldn't lend me his Hillman Minx."
"No problem, I've my old road-going Mini at the garage in Cambridge. You can use that for your test; you are already used to driving Minis. But driving around Cambridge, you will need to stick to the speed limit if you want to pass. It's not like blasting around the old airfield."

Two weeks after his seventeenth birthday at 9 am on a Monday, Cam sat nervously in Mike's slightly rusty red Mini outside the Cambridge Driving Test Centre. Mike had left him with the car and caught the bus into town for a coffee. The inspector was five minutes late, which did nothing to calm Cam's nerves.

James Berry had had a bad weekend. His mother-in-law had arrived on Friday with a huge suitcase and announced she had left her husband and planned to stay at her daughter's,

'For a while'. By Sunday evening, James felt she had already stayed long enough. Now, Monday morning, he had five bloody tests to administer. Seeing an old

Mini with a spotty faced youth at the wheel did nothing to improve his mood. Getting into the passenger seat, he looked at his notes.

"Ah, it's Mr Cartland isn't it? I hope you are not going to drive like your grandfather. He was a racing driver, wasn't he?"

"Only when he was young." Then Cam added, unfortunately," I'm going to be a racing driver as soon as I pass my test."

"Well let's see about that. Read the number plate on the car in front," replied James Berry sharply.

Cam, desperate to pass, concentrated hard and, apart from an emergency stop that almost sent the examiner through the windscreen, all went well. After the Highway Code questions, the contents of which Cam had learnt by heart. James Berry remained silent for minutes, making notes and ticking boxes on the chart he held. Eventually, Berry delivered his verdict; it was the part of the job he liked the best, especially when he was in a bad mood.

"I'm afraid you did make several small mistakes". Berry paused and watched the expected sad expression grow on Cam's face.

"But I have decided your driving is good enough to pass your test."

When Mike arrived back at the test centre and saw the grin on Cam's face, he didn't need to ask the question; he noticed the "L" plates were no longer stuck on the car.

Mike just said,

"Right, now let's get your racing licence applied for."

The first test session had not been bad, but Cam had expected more from himself and the car. Two other experienced drivers were testing their cars at Snetterton the same day and had been more than two seconds a lap quicker than Cam.

"Not sure if the car is slow or it's me," Cam said when he came in for a break. Pulling on his helmet, Mike said.

"Well, we will soon find out." After five laps Mike had lapped more than a second quicker than the quickest guys.

"Think I've got a lot to learn," Cam confessed to Mike as they trundled back along the A14 road to home.

"Don't be too depressed. The first time I tested my Mini, I was crap, much slower than you."

Mike said, trying to raise his spirits. "All you need is plenty of practice. At least you didn't crash it. A couple of more sessions and you will be ready for your first race."

Cam's racing career did not get off to a happy start. After having tested twice more at Snetterton he had become quicker, but also a bit wild, having spun the car twice.

"You're a fast driver, but you need to calm down. I know it sounds strange when you are racing, but you need to be gentle with the car. Sudden actions will startle and upset it," had been Mike's advice.
"But I think you are ready to race".

Cam entered for the first small Snetterton club meeting of March 1968.

"Bloody good effort!" Mike said as Cam climbed from the green Mini at the end of the morning practice. "I reckon you have beaten your best time around here. Let's go up to race control and get the times."

"Not bad I suppose, "said Cam with a twinge of disappointment as he picked up the practice sheet. Twelfth quickest."

"You should be pleased with yourself. Third Mini and most of those ahead are experienced drivers with works engines," replied Mike trying to encourage Cam.

Although Mike had carefully balanced and blueprinted Cam's engine, building a winning racing engine had become a job for a specialist. Never really appreciated how talented Frank had been. He thought.

Cam became extremely nervous, sitting on the narrow Snetterton start-line surrounded by twenty other excited young drivers all hungry for success. Mike's final words already forgotten:

"Good luck. Just remember you can't win the race at the first corner."

Although he knew he was a quick driver, with lightning reactions and exceptional eyesight Cam always had a small doubt in his mind that he would never be good enough to be a top-line racing driver. Seeds of doubt about his ability had been sown in his upbringing by his cautious parents.

"If you never get too ambitious Cameron, you will never get disappointed' had been his fathers' constant mantra as Cam grew up.

Despite the positive words he had always received from his grandfather, and more recently from Mike, those negative thoughts were hard to lose.

After much persuasion, Cam had his father and mother attending his first motor race. Peter had never attended his father's races.

Neither had been keen to attend. Peter, having grown up with a father obsessed with racing, was far from happy to see his son following the same path. Cam's mother Grace, naturally a nervous woman, sat in their Hillman Minx all day unwilling to watch the race.

It was fortunate she did.

The engine revs rose as the starter raised then dropped his Union Jack to start the race.

With the revs held at 4000, as Mike had instructed, Cam dropped the clutch and the front wheels of the Green Mini spun. Searching for grip on the concrete surface, they suddenly found traction, and he made an excellent start, rushing down to the first corner - the right-hand corner called Riches.

Great start! I enjoyed that. A wheel spin, the acrid tyre smoke invades my nose.

Noise is deafening, engine screaming, max revs. Change up to second gear, third gear rushing to Riches. There's a gap opening ahead; I can get through there, damn they closed! Right foot hard on the brake pedal, going to ram them. Shit! Someone hit my boot, car sideways. Turn the wheel left to hold the skid, too late; he's going to hit me! Instinctively I close my eyes and grip the wheel. A violent noise! Impact crushes door onto me, the smell of breaking fiberglass. Sudden silence, then. Pain.

All this took ten seconds, just ten seconds to destroy Cameron Cartland's racing dreams.

With the stricken Mini sideways across the track the approaching pack of cars scattered to miss him. But, unsighted, a Lotus Cortina smashed into the driver's side of Cam's poor Mini, pushing the door into Cam's right hip.

With four severely damaged saloon cars scattered across the track, the race was immediately red-flagged and stopped.

From the pits, Mike could not see which cars were involved. The anxious teams, in the pit area, were forced to wait until the cars came back into sight around Coram Curve.

"I can't see Cam's Mini," Peter said to Mike. His voice displaying no emotion.

"No, looks like he must be involved," came Mike's worried reply. "I'll run up to the first corner to find out what's happened."

When a breathless Mike reached Riches corner, he saw the track marshals and medical staff surrounding a car. His heart sank as, above the sea of bobbing heads, he noticed the Mini's, bent, almond-green top. Mike watched helplessly as Cam was carefully extracted from his bent car and transferred to a waiting ambulance. With its clanging bell, sounding like it was being rung by a demented campanologist, the ambulance rushed from the circuit along the A11 to Norwich General Hospital.

Mike got a lift back to the pits and gave the worried parents the news. Giving Mike Cole a lift, Peter chased along the A11 towards Norwich Hospital. It was a tense journey; the silence was only broken by the sobs and mumblings from Grace Cartland in the back seat.

"He's a fool, he's a fool, he's always been a fool." was Cam's mother's constant chant. Cam, conscious throughout the ordeal, felt the pain he didn't know existed. The nose of the invading car had pushed his hip entirely out of its socket. The only other injuries he

suffered were minor cuts and bruises to his right arm and leg...but this injury was enough!
Under a full anesthetic, the surgeon returned Cams hip joint to its socket.
His parents and Mike were at his bedside when he came round a few hours later.

"How's the car." his first question to Mike.
"Never mind that thing. You can forget all about it." His father's angry answer before Mike could speak.

Cam remained in Norwich hospital for a further week. Secretly his mother and father were pleased about the accident although not the injury to their son. Of course, neither would openly admit to it.

"At least now he's not going to waste his life and his money on racing cars as my father did."
Peter said to his wife after they left the hospital.

Unable to move about as his injury slowly recovered, Cam remained at the mercy of his parents, his mother fussing and happily looking after all his needs. Always she scolded him about not having gone to college to get some qualifications but, although far from stupid, like his grandfather before him Cam had dyslexia.

At the Secondary school he attended at nearby Farwell he excelled at sport and enjoyed science and math, but with his spelling problem, he hated the English lessons. The old witch of a teacher made fun of his spelling ability. He had been relieved to leave and didn't intend to return to studying.

Mike had taken the sad remains of the Mini back to Burlham and left the bent car in the workshop. As soon as he was able to Cam hobbled over to the old garage. He slumped down into the ancient, battered chair and stared at the bent green car, now wholly depressed; he had no idea what to do next. Fifty years previously his grandfather had sat in the same chair, after his crash in the Isle of Man, with his Norton motorbike lying in the same spot that the battered Mini. Frank Cartland had experienced many similar despairing thoughts as those now churning around in the head of his young grandson.

My bloody cousin Mat Marshall has got it all. Cam thought. He knew his father still wanted him to join him in the bakery, but motor racing was in his blood. And the "bad blood" between the Cartland and

Marshall families went back three generations.

He gritting his teeth against the pain.; *I'm not going to let that bugger Marshall beat me.*

In 1960, as an impressionable ten-year-old, Cameron had spent many hours in this dark, smoky workshop avidly listening to his grandfather's tales. He remembered the exploits of the famous racing driver Freddie O'Hare and how his grandfather had been his greatest rival. In the school holidays, he would arrange for his mates to call for him at the bakery with their bikes and fishing rods.

"Is it all right if I go fishing with Tom and Steve?" he would ask his mother.

When they had cycled out of sight of the Bakery, Cam would leave his friends and cycle back to his grandfather's workshop. Here he would sit on the "office" desk swinging his small legs, dreaming about being a racing driver while his grandfather, working on an old engine at his workbench, told him dramatic tales of action and adventure. Cameron always arrived home with dirty, oily hands much to the dismay of this mother.

"You haven't got in that state fishing, have you? We have told you not to spend all your time in that smelly old place. You should be here helping here in the bakery. Go and clean yourself up before your father sees you."

"Yes mother," was Cameron's standard reply, but both knew he would be back in the workshop at any opportunity.

Cam eventually found out his grandfather Frank was more mechanic than a driver. But of course, he knew he had been one of the absolute best builders of racing engines in the country. The 1950's Autosport magazines still scattered around the workshop gave evidence of that.

Remembering those earlier days, Cam felt sorry for himself. *Pity I haven't got the skills he had, I wish he were still here to teach me.* Then he had an idea, a way of making enough money to start racing again. The moment his leg was strong enough, he was going to work with oil anyway. To make money he needed, he would go and work on the offshore gas and oil rigs for a couple of years. Then he'd come back, buy a decent race car, and beat his bloody cousin. He had read about the excellent money those guys were earning out in the North Sea and seen the advertisements to recruit workers, so he determined.

I'll show my damn cousin who's the quickest driver!

Chapter 5

Mat's first car race

Mathew Marshall was looking forward to his first car race, but now he experienced a new problem for him, one always faced by his cousin; a lack of money.

The kart racing had already given him considerable experience, success, and confidence; besides, he had the benefit of the engineering skills of his full-time mechanic, Hans Kruger.

Hans skills already gave him a distinct lead over his Cambridgeshire cousin in their search for the path to Formula One glory.

Hans had been a Fighter pilot, like William Marshall in the Second World War, but for Germany, not Great Britain. After the war, with nothing to return home to, he had settled in Sussex and married an English girl. Many thought the friendship between the burnt William and Hans rather strange, but their shared wartime experiences had given them a deep respect for each other.

"Hans has designed the racing car for Mathew, but now he is going to need extra help and money to build it," Mary had explained to William during early December.

"There's no spare estate money that I'm prepared to put towards it," had been his sharp reply.

"You sound just like you and your mother did when David asked for money to go racing."

"And look what happened to him!"

"That's unfair. You know Mathew is nothing like OUR brother."

The scandals and shame surrounding David Marshall were never buried deep in William's mind.

Mary knew her last comment had hurt him, so she added quickly, "Sorry, William, you're right; we can't afford to spend more of our money on racing. Mathew will have to find something else to do with his life."

After almost thirty years of marriage to William, Mary knew her husband would take some time and think about the problem. He had always been a fair man and, despite his reservations around Mathew's racing, she knew he would never try to stop his son doing something that was his passion. Williams' youthful obsession with flying would ensure that he understood, however reluctantly, his son's ambitions.

Three weeks later, four days before Christmas, the family were sitting around a blazing log fire in Sefton Lodge. The scent of burning pine drifted through the room; the fires flames radiating orange glow highlighting the four faces. The children were reading; Mathew, sullen, becoming resigned to another year of kart racing, studying last week's Autosport, and Florence engrossed in the fashion pages of the teenage Jackie magazine. They had never known their father as a good-looking young man, the few, fading black and white photographs scattered around the house being the only evidence of his handsome youth. To them he had always been the face they could see now, fixed expression and mask-like, they had never seen the smile that used to light up his young face and had won their mother's heart.

To strangers, William's face was ugly and frightening, but to his children, it was just the face of their father.

Mary glanced across at her children's faces: Mathew with his unruly blond hair, flashing blue eyes, the image of his father as a young man, and Florence, who would soon be breaking hearts. Mary was thankful her daughter had inherited her grandmother's silky, raven-black hair and not the curly mop she had. Fifteen-year-old Florence had an innocent, angelic round face, and like her brother, beautiful blue eyes.

Mary found it ironic that their children had inherited the looks of their father as if this were compensation for his loss. William's blue eyes were all that remained of that once oh-so-handsome face.

William broke the warm silence. "I have invited mother over for Christmas." They all looked at him with a mixture of horror from Mary, interest from Mathew, and delight from Florence.

"Why?" was Mary's immediate reaction.

Silvia Marshall had been a great beauty in her younger days and a public celebrity during the heady days of the 1920s and '30s, being a socialite and one of the successful young lady racing drivers at Brooklands. In recent years she had become more eccentric, now sixty-four years old she still retains her striking appearance, despite her years of excess. Although her inky black hair now had wild streaks of white and her once porcelain-smooth face was now showing the ageing effects of recent years of sun worship.

For the past ten years, since the revelations that her son David had been the son of Frank Cartland, then David's trial, and his eventual execution for the murder of his girlfriend, Silvia had remained in France.

Rarely visiting England, she had stayed hidden away in her lavish villa in the hills above Nice.

Feeling guilty that he was losing touch with her, William and Mary had visited his mother at her home in France a few years previously. It had not been a pleasant visit; they had planned to stay for a week but had given their excuses after only three days.

Silvia had been keen to show off her Lord and Lady son and daughter-in-law to her new French friends. She had organised a large dinner party inviting ten of the local 'important' people and their partners plus two of her current young men. Silvia had not informed William of this party in advance, knowing full well what his horrified reaction would have been.

"We came to visit you, mother. Not half of Nice!" Was his expected response when she announced the party.

"But I am so proud of you and Mary. I want you to meet a few of my French friends," was his mother's tearful reply.

Mary had given William a helpless look, and he just shrugged his shoulders.

A fresh bottle of wine with each course ensured Silvia became far too drunk to notice how uncomfortable her son had become with all the unwanted attention.

Mary had to field the stream of repeated questions and comments, such as:

"était-ce d 'être brûlé?" (*what was it like getting burned?*) and "au moins vous avez survécu mon fils a été tué" (*at least you survived; my son was killed*).

On their third morning, William informed his mother: "Mary and I are returning to England today. There is some estate business that needs my urgent attention."

"Oh, that's such a shame. I hoped you would come to Monte Carlo with me tonight to play the roulette wheels," had been his mother's reply.

Since that unhappy visit they had little contact, Mary just sending her a card at Christmas and on her birthday. Silvia, to her credit, didn't forget her grandchildren. Both received generous money gifts on birthdays and Christmas.

In the obituary columns of *The Times* William read about the recent death of an old friend of his mothers.

"I think we should invite my mother over for Christmas, the children should get to know her before it's too late. She is the only grandmother they have."

"Yes, I think that would be a good idea, maybe she will have become less reckless by now." *Although I very much doubt it.*

"It sounds like she was cool when she was young. She and Grandfather Frank were lovers, weren't they? Be great to see her," had been Florence's excited response.

Mary had wanted to make sure that the experiences of that devastating time stayed in the past. Ignoring her daughter's question Mary said.

"I don't want you to talk to her about past times; it might upset her."

Of course, Mary knew it wouldn't; she expected the old girl to boast about it if Florence showed a modicum of interest.

"Grandmother raced cars at Brooklands, didn't she?" asked Mathew, becoming interested.

"She did: but it was a long time ago." William also didn't want those days dredged up.

He did, however, have another motive for inviting his mother. Silvia still had considerable wealth, mainly tied up in the property. She owned a large townhouse in Bath's Royal Crescent plus a smaller house in Kensington. Both rented out, to give her regular income. With Mathew and Florence, her only grandchildren, he knew she intended to leave everything to these two. Her daughter, William's sister, had moved to North American in the 1950s after marrying a wealthy American. William had heard the marriage ended some years ago, and Victoria was now living in a commune in Arizona. Silvia and her daughter had not spoken for fifteen years.

William planned to show some compassion for Silvia in the hope she would agree to sell one of her properties and advance the money to help fund Mathew's ambitions.

Two days later William stood nervously on the steps of Sefton Lodge as a black Mercedes taxi drew up outside.

"William it was so nice of you to invite me," Silvia said as she stepped out of the taxi.

William was relieved to see his mother appear sober.

"Welcome, Mother. It's lovely to see you."

"You to William, are Mathew and Florence here? We are going to need a hand with all the presents I have in the boot."

Christmas was a surprising success; Silvia enjoyed her drinks but not to excess for a change, and everyone enjoyed her company.

Silvia mainly had pleasure regaling her grandchildren with some of her more repeatable pre-war racing adventures. She did not refer to either of their grandfathers or the accident that had killed George. Even Mary warmed towards her mother-in-law, and William made an excellent job of sowing the seeds of his idea to his mother.

"House prices are very high at the moment, Mother; don't you think it would be a good time to sell one of yours?" William asked her as she enjoyed her second, pre-dinner gin and tonic on Boxing Day.

"Hadn't thought about it, William. But I know the Bath house is costing me a fortune, dam repair costs are more than the rent I'm getting some months. Think that bloody agent is ripping me off."

On the following day as Silvia prepared to return home to France, she announced.

"I have decided to take your advice, William, I am going to sell my house in Bath. Can I leave you to organise the estate agents? Whatever you get for it I want you to use the money for Mat and Flo". She smiled at Mary. She knew shortening their names would irritate Mary, who did not approve.

"That's very kind of you mother; the children will be delighted."
As the taxi disappeared, Mary put her arm around her husband's waist and squeezed. "Well done, William. That went well."

By the following spring, Silvia had sold the house in Bath, and half the proceeds deposited into a new account called Crusader Racing. After meeting Florence properly for the first time, Silvia had formed a real bond with her granddaughter, to the slight unease of Mary, and instructed that half the funds be invested for her. Consequently, William opened a 'university account' which would be for Florence's education.

"These twenty thousand pounds we are going to invest in your motor racing," William explained to Mathew. "It is a lot of money...I am making it your responsibility to use it wisely".

The excitement in his son's reply was evident:

"I won't let you down, father; now I'll go and give Hans the fantastic news."

After a year's solid work Hans, with considerable input from Mary, and a little encouragement from William, had built their new Crusader Formula Ford. William had needed a great deal of persuasion from Mary to agree to take on the two additional mechanics, worrying the racing funds would soon be exhausted.

The car proved to be very quick immediately, helped by the fact that they could afford to buy an engine from the leading Formula Ford engine builder, Alan Richardson.

Racing had ended at Goodwood, their local Sussex track for safety reasons, but testing was still allowed. On a bracing February morning, Mathew steered the sleek, light blue racing car along the deserted pit road, past the neglected pits and out onto the black racetrack; at last! He was driving a racing car for the first time.

The thrill of that first experience, tucked into the tight-fitting seat with his gloved hands holding the small, three-spoke, leather-covered steering wheel, never left him.

Watching the blue car disappear around Madgwick corner, William Marshall felt a moment of jealousy. He realised how much he missed flying, that feeling of being alone and in control of a powerful machine; an adrenalin-filled mix of excitement with a touch of fear—only your actions leading to success or disaster.

The vibrations from the engine inches behind my seat are increasing; I press my right foot hard down on the responsive throttle pedal. The revs rise as I move my right hand from the steering wheel to the stubby little gear-lever, depress the clutch pedal with my left foot and move the lever to engage second gear. Speeding up now I change into third gear before the first right-hand corner at Madgwick, turn the steering wheel, immediate response! I watch the front wheels just four feet in front of me, pointing into the apex of the curve. Now I'm through Madgwick, and I click the lever into top gear, speed increasing quickly onto the sweeping Fordwater bend, gliding through the fast right-hander. Fast approaching the tricky downhill left-hand St Mary's, change down to third gear. The car goes light, and the rear tyres protest as the car's weight transfer shifts. Quickly up to the tight right-hand Lavent Corner, hold third gear and feel the satisfying drift through the first apex, and second apex's then power through onto the curving Lavent straight. Revs are rising to seven thousand as I change into top gear. Flat out now, wind buffeting the car and my crash helmet as we rush down to Woodcote corner - that right-hand corner always faster than it looks. Drift through in third gear, but quickly the chicane approaches with its solid-looking walls. Braking hard and changing down to second gear, I flick the steering wheel right rapidly then immediately left, brush the grass on the right-hand side and accelerate back along the straight for another exhilarating lap.

"Well done, Mathew!" his mother said as he eased himself out of the cockpit of his sleek hot Crusader. He managed more than thirty laps of the Goodwood circuit without incident, improving his lap times gradually.

"Wow, I enjoyed that. The car handles like a dream, Hans, you have done an amazing job." Never one to show much emotion Hans just said.

"Let's see what it's like with twenty other cars around you. I think you should enter a race soon."

It was a happy Crusader team that travelled the ten miles home that evening.

Mary had taken charge of the paperwork and entered the Crusader for a small club race at Brands Hatch, which with the closure of Goodwood became their closest track, Mathew made his debut there in March 1969.
He had just turned nineteen years old when he sat on the sloping start-line cocooned in the cockpit of his Crusader Formula Ford.

His eyes were focused on the uphill stretch of black Tarmac leading to the daunting Paddock Hill Bend. Mat had been surprised to have qualified third quickest in the morning practice session.

Later the reporters from Autosport and Motoring News had descended on the tin roofed-covered area in the paddock where Mat and his small team were based.

His parents, and his beautiful young sister, had come along to support his first race.

"That is an impressive start to your racing career Mat. Think you can win your first race." asked Autosport reporter Simon Archer.

"Don't expect so, I will just be happy to finish, I need to get my five signatures and get that cross off the back." Mat replied. (All new racing drivers had to have a black cross with yellow background sticker on the back of the cars until they completed five races without incident).

Mary's past successes at Brands Hatch in her father's little Kieft had not been forgotten but unfortunately nor had Mathew's uncle David Marshall.

With the Marshall family name and past notoriety, members of the tabloid press had also descended on Brands Hatch. Not somewhere they would ordinarily frequent. The voice butting into the racing conversation was from Charlie Taylor one of the tabloid pressmen

"Are you happy with your son following in the wheel tracks of his dead uncle?"

Taylor always seemed to turn up when Lord and Lady Marshall appeared in public. Mary just gave him her absolute best scathing look and remained silent. The genuine motoring press also ignored him.

Mary and William were relieved when the rest of the attention became focused on their son's achievements in practice, although Mary had been a little disturbed when she heard Charlie Taylor tell his photographer.

"Get some shots of young Florence; she's a real stunner. Will be page three material." He added as the tabloid photographer focused his lens on the beautiful Florence.

At two o'clock, the starter raised his Union Jack flag to start the race. As the flag dropped, with spinning wheels, and a cacophony of noise, Mat Marshall's racing career began.

Fourteen Formula Ford cars snarled and swerved their way up to the first right-hand corner. As so often with those small open-wheeled cars, there was a first corner accident with wheels and bits of fiberglass bodywork flying. Fortunately, Mat had made a good start and missed the mayhem behind him. He remained third for the early laps, but on lap four his inexperience saw him leave a gap on the inside up to the hairpin at Druids Bend, and in a flash, two cars had dived inside forcing him wide around the outside of the corner.

At the end of ten laps he had settled into a rhythm, comfortable in the easy-handling car, and finally finished the race in fifth place.

Photographers again surrounded the car as Mat stopped at the pits.

"Well done, Mat", said his sister as she rushed to be the first to congratulate him after the race. Florence had enjoyed the photographer's attention earlier in the day and wanted more of it.

"Congratulations Mathew," chorused his mother and father as Mat climbed from the car.

"The car is so good to drive. Hans here deserves all the credit," replied the sweaty and happy Mat.

Never one to show much emotion, Hans added,

"The car is not going to win without a good driver. With more experience, I think you can be one."

Everyone agreed it was an excellent first effort.

Chapter 6
The North Sea Beckons

As Cam had expected, his parents were horrified when he made his announcement:

"You're mad. It's dangerous and hard work. Why would you want to do that." were his father's remarks?

"I'm going to need the money for a new race car."

"He's going to end up just like your father. Peter, it would help if you stopped him from going," a tearful Grace complained.

"You have nearly killed yourself already with this racing obsession. I thought you would have learned your lesson by now. But your mother's right, you are going to bring misery into our lives just like he did."

But then seeing his son's determined face, with his teeth clenched together and his fixed challenging eyes, he just shook his head. He knew that any attempt to stop his son would be a waste of time. He was sure his wife was right; Cameron had undoubtedly inherited his grandfather's stubbiness and his crazy addiction.

When Cam told Mike Coles of his plan, Mike's reaction was similar:

"Bloody hell Cam you're mad...I admire your guts, but you wouldn't get me out there for all the tea in China."

"Are you sure you still want to go through with this?" Mike asked when he dropped Cam off at Hull docks. It was a universally slate-grey November morning, the sky and menacing North Sea water merging, showing no horizon.

"Yes, it's the only way... I've got to try this," had been Cam's unconvincing response.

He picked up the battered, old, brown, leather bag from the Mini's back seat.

He had found the bag two weeks previously stuffed on top of the cupboard in the workshop. When he unzipped it, he could feel his grandfather standing next to him.

The mixture of smells comprised old cigarette smoke, oil, and Wright's Coal Tar soap. In fact, along with a rolled-up copy of a 1956 Autosport with the Cartland Jaguar on the front, he found a green packet of five Woodbine cigarettes and a used bar of the soap wrapped in an old flannel. It had been twelve years since Frank Cartland had left the bag, forgotten, on top of the cupboard. For eighteen-year-old Cameron, that was a lifetime ago. Now he carried the same old bag to start his adventures.

"Good luck and take care." Had been Mikes passing remark.

The boat was only five minutes out from the harbour before the heavy sea swell caused seasickness to strike him. Seasickness was another thing he had inherited from his grandfather. He soon discovered it was not wise to be sick from the side of the boat. With the first retch, the wind returned much of the contents of his stomach into his face. It attempted to re-enter by every orifice on his head.

Once he had cleaned himself up, he took up permanent residence at the stern. There he let the ice-cold salt-water spray refresh him between the regular bouts of violent sickness.

By the time the boat reached the monstrous, rust-covered, legs of the BP Sea Search oil platform, his retching now only producing thin streams of bile; Cam just wanted to stay on the boat and head back to dry land. Wretched, he thought of the horrors to come and just wanted to go home. Then from somewhere, he dredged up his stubborn, determined nature, his resolve hardened, and he followed the three other recruits into a makeshift lift lowered onto the heaving deck of the boat.

The four men were silent and white-faced, they huddled together, as swaying, cracking and grinding, the metal-sided lift slowly raised them the fifty feet to the rig platform to join the thirty other men. They had arrived at their new home.

'Why do you want to go there? It will be a nightmare.' Many had warned him of the harsh reality of rig life, the hard, physical work, and equally rough men, but the truth came as a terrible shock. The work was hard, extremely hard. The twelve-hour day shift began at 7 am with just one hour's break for a meal in the canteen.

"You won't last a fucking month here...Nancy boy," the foreman had bawled at him on the first day.

Cam had been confused by his sexuality since his early teenage years. There was a girl at school, Sally Bennett, who always followed him around wanting his attention. Cam was attracted to her but quickly realised he was also physically attracted to her older brother James. These mixed emotions were very confusing to Cam, but for the past two years, he had only room in his thoughts, for one thing, racing cars.

Being a young fit and handsome man himself, he soon attracted unwanted attention, especially from Angus Simpson, one of the large Scottish rig workers.

From that first day, he had found himself a target for Simpson. At dinner, Simpson had forced himself into a small space on the bench uncomfortably close to Cam. His mixed smell of stale sweat, and crude oil caused Cam to flinch involuntarily.

"With a name like Cameron, you must have Scottish blood flowing through your lovely young body. Treat me nice lad, and I can make life easy for you. I can keep that bastard foreman off your back for a start". Then he had whispered in Cam's ear, "So long as you let me on it," and he let out a deep, dirty laugh.

Trying not to show his panic and fear, Cam's week, nervous response was.

"Thanks for the offer... I'll think about it". Getting up quickly, he added, "Feeling sick, need to get some air."

That night in his narrow dormitory bunk Cam sobbed silently.

Cam had arrived on the Sea Search just a month before the rig was due to be moved to a new location. All his work time consisted of stacking and securing the thousands of drums, pipes, and cables securely before tugs towed the rig to its new location.

"How can they move something this big?" he had asked one of the older workers.

"They lower the legs gradually until this platform bit, you're standing on sits on the sea's surface, then they connect a couple of tugs to it and tow it to its new area. Will be the third bloody time we've done it."

Standing fifty feet in the air on this metal monster with the wind howling and the whipping sea spray constantly stinging his face, Cam couldn't imagine how that would work. The hard-physical labour, soaking clothes, and violent, loud mechanical noises ensured the end of his eight-hour shift saw Cam wholly exhausted.

Spending as little time as possible in the canteen, he would get away early, clean up in one of only three showers and get into his bunk before any other workers. Most spent the evenings in the bar and took little notice of him, but Angus Simpson was not the only rig worker interested in Cameron Cartland. Cam had noticed the tall, muscular man, tanned with long blond hair and Zapata moustache, watching him at breakfast on the second morning.

Having watched Cam's vulnerability for a few days, Australian worker Denis (Danny) Glover introduced himself to Cam. Holding his large hand out, he said, "Hi, how's it going ... your Cameron, aren't you, hi, I'm Danny."

Cam couldn't help noticing the sparkle of amusement in his brown eyes.

Cam took the offered hand and felt a tingle of excitement as Danny held it, tightly but not painfully, before replying shyly, "Hello Danny, call me Cam."

"There are some tough buggers around here. If you need any help with um, let me know."

"Thanks, Danny...I will."

The following evening Cam had rushed to the showers as usual but hadn't noticed the massive shape of Angus Simpson follow him. Cam enjoyed the sensation of the hot water and soap cleaning the oily grime from his pores, his skin, and his hair when a large, calloused hand clamped around his mouth, and another clutched his groin.

"Don't make a sound, you pretty boy and just enjoy what I'm goanna give you," came the harsh, foul-smelling whisper in Cam's ear. Shivering with fear, despite the hot flowing water, Cam closed his eyes tight and waited.

Violently both were thrown to the floor as the massive fist of Denis Groves smashed into the side of Angus Simpson's head.

"Get yourself away from here and get some clothes on," Danny said as he pulled Cam up and out from under the big man.

"What about him?" Cam sobbed in panic.

"I'll sort him, don't you worry."

It was 3 am and dark as pitch. Cam lay awake, shivering in his bunk, alert to every unusual sound. He had grown used to the constant noises on the rig. The night-time silence of his home village, where only the hoots of barn owls disturbed his sleep, was already a distant...longed for memory. Here there was a constant, metallic ringing from the platform as the night shift worked and a ghostly groaning from the rig's ten hollow legs as the continuous sea-swell swirled around them. He let out an involuntary yelp when he felt a gentle hand on his shoulder:

"Suh It's only me, Danny. I just wanted to make sure you are ok."

Cam instinctively reached out and pulled Danny towards him. He made no resistance as the big Australian pulled back the bed covers and snuggled onto the narrow bed. Cam relaxed into Danny's arms and enjoyed the feeling of security and warmth radiating from the body hard against him. Cam was woken by the alarm bell rung every morning to get workers up before their eight-o clock shift.

A wave of disappointment came over him as he realised, he was alone. He didn't see Danny again until two hours after their shift had started; Cam had been given a job in the stores, much to his relief, instructed to give out requested parts to the rig workers.

Danny had turned up with another member of his work-gang. He gave Cam a list of the hydraulic parts they needed to repair a sticking ram on one of the rig's legs.

"Give us two sets of those ram seals lad. Bloody things are always failing; this one's pissing out oil all over the place," complained the older man Cam knew as Harry.

Danny had remained quiet, but as they were leaving, he said,

"See you later," and gave Cam a wink.

"Haven't seen Angus Simpson today," Cam said casually later to one of the crane operators who called at the stores.

"He's in sickbay. He fell down some steps last night and smashed his head on the platform. He got a concussion. Drunk most likely," the crane driver said. Cam allowed himself to smile.

Over the following two weeks of work, it became bearable, although far from enjoyable, for Cam. He had the evenings to look forward to and Danny's strong arms.

They snatched their private pleasures whenever they could, and if any of the other workers thought the relationship unnatural, they didn't show it. All were wary around Danny Glover after he had dealt with Angus Simpson who, although back on duty, was always complaining of headaches, and hardly acknowledged Cam's existence.

Danny Glover had been born in 1934 in Perth, Western Australia. His father had died in the Second World War, Danny, being the eldest of four children, needed to leave school early to earn money to help his mother feed their family. At seventeen, he had found work at the Kalgoorlie Gold Mines five hundred miles east of his home. Cam knew no more about his friend. The reason he had given up the forty-degree heat of Australia for the freezing conditions of the North Sea, Cam had not, so far, found out.

A biting north wind chilled Cam to his core as he struggled with the hard-physical job; he was helping dismantle parts of the drilling rig. The rusted steel painfully cold, even though his thick gloves. At 11am, an alarm signalled the start of the lowering of the rig's legs, and all work stopped. Any men not directly involved in the operation stood to wait for the platform's expected shift as it began its slow descent to sea level.

Danny had moved from his work at the far end of the platform to stand next to Cam.

"Its bloody cold, isn't it?" Cam said, shivering as the sharp wind sent a snow flurry sweeping across the exposed deck. With a grin, Danny replied.

"Yer it is, let's go inside. It's going to take hours to lower this bloody thing…we can warm each other up."

Just as they reached the door to the cabins, a shuddering, shrieking, metallic scream preceded the whole rig platform lurching downward at one corner. In seconds, the platform pitched to a fifteen-degree angle. Machinery and men were tumbling down the metal floor towards the icy grey waves of the North Sea.

Instinctively Cam grabbed the door frame of the cabin and hung on desperately. He watched incredulously as, with arms flailing, Danny tried to find something to hold on to as he began to slide down the rig, away from him, towards the immense angry sea.

Chapter 7

Peter Cartland's demons

While their son was facing the horrors of the North Sea, Peter and Grace Cartland were sitting quietly, enjoying afternoon tea and freshly baked scones in the front room of Bakery Cottage.

Peter Cartland had been only sixteen years old when his son Cameron had been born. His first sexual experience had led to, after just six months, his marriage, and an instant family.

'Don't worry son, the same thing happened to me.' His father had told him at the time. That information had been no comfort for Peter.

His wife Alice had wanted more children, but after three miscarriages, Peter had lost interest in sex, afraid his weaknesses were the cause of all their disappointments.

"It is God's will that we have only been blessed with one child." he would often repeat to his wife.

He knew he had not met the expectations of his father, who had never made any secret of his wish for Peter to follow his motoring passions. Now, still a young man of only thirty-four, he had realised that he had been trying to suppress his true nature.

Peter had spent his whole childhood surrounded by, and influenced, by women. With his overprotective mother, three older sisters and his Aunt Joan, always fussing around him, he had found he could relate to women far more naturally than to men. Always more comfortable in their company, and he often wished he had been born one.

Gradually his urges had become so powerful that he had recently secretly begun dressing in his wife's clothes.

Guilt always followed these private sessions, and he found his salvation in the church. The walk along the narrow gravel path up to St Mary's had become a frequent trip. A pilgrimage for him.

Peter had never been able to understand or share his father's dreams, and now sadly, the same was true of his son. He knew he couldn't stand in the lad's way, but neither, would he encourage nor give him any support in the madness, this addiction to racing cars.

Chapter 8

Henry Sutcliffe

Henry Sutcliffe's birth came just an hour before the murder of his father.

The East End of London in the 1930s was a violent place. Freddie Sutcliffe ran a small gambling club and brothel but made the mistake of standing up to a big-time crook who demanded protection money.

Freddie had been shot in Petticoat Lane, without ever seeing his latest son.

Henry had a harsh childhood, he quickly learnt to fend for himself, and by the time the war arrived, he was already streetwise. His war years were spent in London with his mother. With no husband to support her Iris Sutcliffe had turned back to the profession she had pursued when Freddie married her.

Iris Sutcliffe was a tough woman, still, only twenty-two when she had her fourth son Henry. Even in wartime, she found plenty of customers. The business was excellent as most of the younger prostitutes left the capital when the bombs started falling.

The intense heighten dangers of death increasing the sexual needs of many.

Iris would not leave their Whitechapel mid-terrace house when most of her neighbours moved out.

"These are my business premises; I'm not leaving." She also refused to allow Henry's evacuation to safer areas.

By 1940, with his oldest brother Ronald in prison, and his other two brothers in the army, Henry had no male role models.

That rough, war-time education, would shape his future life. After uncomfortable nights spent in the grimy underground air-raid shelter at Whitechapel, Henry would rush out at first light, excited to check out the latest devastation. Henry and his young gang spent their days scrabbling about on the smoking ruins, robbing the bombed-out homes of any valuables they could find. With his mother's help, he always kept one step ahead of the law.

"Don't worry son anything you find you bring to me, we can store it in the cellar under the coal, bloody coppers won't find it there, and I'll find plenty of customers for any of the shiny stuff."

With his mother an able ally, by war-end, they had amassed an extensive collection of jewelry and cash which, true to her boast, Iris had managed to keep securely hidden. Both her army sons had been killed during the evacuation of Dunkirk.

Henry had no memory of his mother mourning her sons; with her oldest still in jail, Iris devoted herself to Henry's clandestine operations.

Henry, in turn, was dedicated to his formidable mother, her dominating presence would remain a significant influence into his adult life.

By the early 1950s Henry, the scruffy thin boy of the war years had grown into a thickset but handsome young man. Although only five feet seven tall, he had the money to dress with style and always made sure his shoes had at least two-inch heels. 'Flash'was what many of his associates called him. But only when he was out of earshot.

Also growing was his business operation, mainly dealing in black market goods. His mother's support, and his sharp brain saw him build an extensive network of underworld contacts around him in his London' manor.'

"It's high time you found yourself a wife; you need a few kids before you get too old. I know you love the ladies, but you're going to want a son, or two, to carry on the family business." His mother said as they sat drinking gin around the swimming pool, he had had built in the garden of their new West End home. This a far cry from their East-End, Whitechapel roots.

"What about that blond girl with the big tits working in Charlie's club?" she added.

Despite his success, Henry had unease about his impoverished upbringing, he had taken elocution lessons, but as soon as he became angry, which was often, his East End roots were evident.

Worn out by her nagging and resenting her interference, but afraid to argue, he replied.

"Yer, spose she'll do mother."

Henry Sutcliffe married Barbra (Babs) White at Islington registers office in 1952, their son Wilfred being born nine months later. The name had been insisted on by Iris; it had been her father's name. The marriage turned out to be short and very unhappy, Babs had been flattered by the attentions of the flash mate of her boss and been delighted to accept Henry's offer of marriage.

Babs suffered severe depression after Wilfred's birth, unable to cope with the demands of motherhood and the constant interference of Iris Sutcliffe. After six months she gave up caring, leaving Iris to look after the baby boy, gin became her constant companion until she disappeared from a fog-bound Tower Bridge on a grey November evening.

"She's no loss. We didn't need her, not going to miss the bitch, I can bring up little Will for you," had been the reaction of Iris to the news.

One week later the body of Barbra Sutcliffe was discovered at low tide on the banks of the Thames at Shoreditch.

Pushed, fell, or jumped? The police half-heartedly investigated that question. They did interview Henry and his mother.

"What were your movements the night your wife died Mr Sutcliffe."

"I was at my Club all evening." Looking smug, he added. "You can ask your Chief Superintendent; he was there all night and seemed to be enjoying himself."

"She was a little slut, expect she was pissed and fell in; good riddance, I say." Was his mother's less than sympathetic response to police enquires.

Eventually, an open verdict was given as to cause of death of Babs Sutcliffe.

It only took a few months for Henry to move a nineteen-year-old dancer from his new night club into the family home.

"Why have you brought another little slut back here. You don't need another woman in this house," was his mother's immediate reaction.

With Iris's dominating influences and open hostility, the poor girl had fled back to Wales after just one month.

"Good riddance to that little slapper. What you need is a classy woman. We got plenty of money now; I'll find you a new wife."

"Yer alright mother."

For all his tough ways, Henry always had one fear...his mother.

Chapter 9

Victory Celebrations

The season racing had been hugely successful for Mathew Marshall. His first taste of victory came at Silverstone in May in a typically hard, and fraught slipstreaming battle on the Silverstone Club circuit.

Mathew managed to lead into the last corner and take the chequered flag inches ahead of the pack, with the first six cars were finishing within two seconds of each other.

He enjoyed four more winning races, and six-second place finishes to make him the leading novice Formula Ford driver of the season. Two big crashes did little to dent his confidence.

“You have to expect that in Formula Ford, everyone crashes. Your photos keep me in business!” Autosport photographer Geoff Hunter said to Mat after his sorry looking Crusader came back behind the breakdown truck after one Mallory Park accident.

"Thank goodness you have Hans to rebuild the car." Mary had told her son after the second crash.

"Don't know where we would be without his hard work and skill."

"It's been a great season, hasn't it?" Mat said as the family who, along with Hans and his wife Frances, had gathered for his father's birthday dinner.

"Yes, well done, Mathew," his mother replied. Adding, "and thank you, Hans, for building such a great racing car."

"And rebuilding it when Mat destroyed it...twice," his father added. It was hard to say, but Mathew thought his father was joking.

"Thank you...father! Next year I'm going to make sure we win the British championship."

"You will need a backup car to do that or miss some races if you crash. I can't rebuild a car in a few days", said Hans.

"You had better ring your grandmother and beg her for some more money." William said to his son.

Mary had been quiet for most of the evening, with William's birthday reminding her time was moving by so fast, her mood was melancholy.

Lady Mary Marshall never had part of the smart, rich set of Sussex ladies who would spend their lives shopping, partying, and doing the odd bit of charity work to ease their consciences.

Her role as the wife of Lord William Marshall did mean that she attended the grand functions in the county and cut the ribbons to open village fates. These duties had never been enjoyable for her, but she had always felt being William's wife made the effort worthwhile.

With William's increasing mood swings and silences, she felt there must be more to her life than this. Of course, she now had Mathews racing to focus on, but even this, at times, made her long for the days she had felt that excitement and adrenaline rush that racing provided.

With Mathew's successes in that first season of racing, the whole family attended the end of season BARC (British Automobile Racing Club) awards dinner at the Grosvenor House Hotel in London.

Even William, who hated the attention he received at these events, was determined to celebrate his son's season. All were looking forward to seeing Mathew presented with the 'Young Driver of the Year' award at the dinner.

Having Lord Marshall attend the function was an honour for the organisers, and they put the Marshall party on one of the top tables. The round tables seated twelve people. Those attending were William and Mary, Mathew, Florence, Hans, and his wife. Mathew, who had brought along Isobel Bennett, the daughter of the largest landowners in Sussex. Mathew and Isobel had been friends since childhood, and both families expected them to marry one day.

That left five seats to fill on the Marshall table, and it seems the highest bidder for those seats was London nightclub owner Henry Sutcliffe.

Henry Sutcliffe's son Will had started racing in Formula Ford this year, often in races against Mathew.

Although his father had spared no expense on his racing efforts, Will had not been successful so far; his best result being a third place at Snetterton.

No one seemed quite sure how Henry Sutcliffe had made his money, but now he owned two top-class night clubs and had a share in the Playboy Club, which all the stars of films and music regularly attended.

The well-known motto of his clubs bodily displayed on the racing car of his son. They showed a drunken cat laying in a giant champagne glass sipping from another glass of champagne.

Insuring, his party shared a table with Lord, and Lady Marshall had cost Henry ten times the standard rate for this dinner.

"Send the money left over to the motor racing marshals fund, if you get me on that table." He had told the club secretary.

Sutcliffe intended to make sure the press knew he was now a friend of Lord Marshall.

Although not apparent by his mask-like face, William's feelings were made clear in a whispered comment to Mary when he first saw his table guests.

"Oh my god. Anyone but Sutcliffe".

Henry Sutcliffe had arrived in style. With him in his gold chauffeur-driven, Rolls Royce Silver Cloud were two of his business associates, Florence had commented to Mathew when she saw them.

"They look like American gangsters to me."

Accompanying Sutcliffe was his long-suffering third wife, ex-model, Louise, and son Will with a beautiful young hostess from one of his father's clubs on his arm. He made a play with his greetings.

"Good evening Lord Marshall so good of you to invite me to your table this evening." He said this loud enough for all the surrounding guests to hear.

William gritted his teeth and just replied.

"Good evening Mr Sutcliffe."

"Please call me Henry, William." He replied.
Turning his attention to Mary, he said, taking her hand and kissing it.

"Lady Marshall, may I say how beautiful you look tonight."
There was then silence as no one knew how to respond.
Sutcliffe broke it by shouting to the waiter

"Bring the first bottle of Bollinger champagne I have ordered for this table."
He soon became the 'life and soul' of the party as the third bottle emptied.

Sutcliffe then embarrassed Mathew and his son Will by shouting, when Mathew went to collect his prize.

"Look at this young Lord, he's going to be world champion...if he can beat my son."

As soon as politeness allowed after the dinner, the Marshall party made their excuses and left, but not before Henry Sutcliffe had insisted on a dance with Mary.

Holding her closer than she was comfortable with, he said.

"I have been admiring you at the race tracks all season. You are a remarkable woman, would love to get to know you better,", he whispered.

Pulling away from him the moment the music died, Mary replied sharply.

"I'm sorry, Mr Sutcliffe, I don't think that's a good idea. If you will excuse me, I need to go back to my husband."
Giving her a broad smile, he just replied.

"Please call me Henry. Can I call you Mary?"
Giving him a cold stare, Mary turned on her heel and walked swiftly back to their table.

"We have a long drive back to Sussex. Your father is tired, so I think we should go home."

Abruptly she said to Mathew and Florence who were starting to enjoy themselves.
Taking William's arm, she led the family as they left the ballroom.

"What did you say to upset Mats' mother," Will asked his father as they watched the Marshall party leave the room.

"She's a feisty woman, I'm sure she fancies me but is afraid to show it," his father replied, smiling.

"Now, let's get on with the party."

In bed that night, William repeated that question.

"What did Sutcliffe say to upset you. I've not seen you so angry since the day I first met you."

"It was nothing; he's just a flash playboy who thinks a lot of himself. It was quite different when I first met you. I thought you were the enemy that day." She snuggled up to him and added.

"But even then, I knew I loved you."

William turned and gave his wife an awkward cuddle.

Later that night, Mary lay awake, but it was not her husband's rasping loud breathing, preventing her sleeping; it was thoughts of Henry Sutcliffe. Parts of her which had laid dormant for years were stirring, longing for some more excitement and adventure.

She had almost forgotten the night of the dinner when, two months later, she received a phone call from Henry Sutcliffe.

Mary had been keeping herself busy at Sefton Lodge helping William with estate business, since the evening of the Grosvenor dinner.

"I just wanted to offer my apologies for my behavior at the Dorchester Lady Mary. I had had too much champagne that night".

Surprised by the call, after a pause, Mary just said.

"Thank you, let us forget about it... Mr Sutcliffe. We needed to get home early that night".

"Well, to make up for it, I would like to invite Lord Marshall and yourself to my box at Ascot races next summer. Any day that suits you."

Not wanting to appear too keen, she replied.

"That's good of you. I am not sure when we are free but will confirm with William, and let you know," she replied.

Putting the phone back on its receiver before he had a chance to reply, Mary had felt an unexpected tingle run down her spine.

The 1969 motor racing season for Mathew had been all planned out; he would take part in the two major Formula Ford championships, which would mean twenty-five races at seven different race circuits between March and October.

When Silvia had picked up the phone and discovered it was Mathew calling her, she smiled and waited for his greeting.

"Hello, grandmother, just called to see how things were in the South of France."

"Hello, Mathew...I know you haven't phoned me to find out how I am. Your father tells me you did well racing last season, so I don't suppose you need any more money from me." she teased.

"Aah... well, actually we could do with building a second car so that some extra funds would be wonderful." To fill the silence, he added.

"When I win the Championship this year, we will be able to sell both cars for a profit." Another pause. "So, I will be able to pay some of the money back." These words came out slightly less convincing than he had hoped. Mathew had been rehearsing this pitch for extracting more money from his grandmother for the previous two hours.

"I am not bothered about getting some money back... I don't need it, but there will be one condition before I send you any more money."

"What's that grandmother?" asked Mathew nervously.

"That you stop calling me bloody grandmother, I feel old enough without that. My name is Silvia."

"Ok, it's a deal...Silvia."

With the extra funds, Mathew had been able to instruct Hans to build a second Crusader car. The following Formula Ford season was fast and furious, but Mathew managed a string of six victories despite two significant accidents. True to his boast to his grandmother, he did win the championship, which led to a test session in a March Formula 3 car at the end of the year, and the promise of a drive for the following year if he could bring extra funds. The amount needed being £10,000 pounds. Mathew knew that even by selling the successful

Crusader Formula Fords; he would need another £6,000.

He could not ask his grandmother for that sort of money.

It was a beautiful June day when the Marshall family attended the Goodwood race meeting at the invitation of Henry Sutcliffe. Since his first phone call to Mary, he had continuously requested they join him at a race meeting. Sutcliffe owned boxes at both Ascot and Goodwood racecourses. And finally, he managed they ran out of excuses.

"If we go this once, maybe he will stop asking us." Mary had replied to William's protests.

"Very well as it's just down the road this time we will go." had been Williams resigned response.

It was a hot, sun-drenched day, for the 'Glorious Goodwood' Ladies day meeting.

Mary and Florence confessed their excitement, both buying new dresses for the occasion. William and Mathew felt far less comfortable in their formal top hat and tails.

"You both look beautiful...you could be sisters!" Had been the greeting from Henry Sutcliffe when they arrived at his lavish box. It was a magnificent setting high in the Sussex Downs, the view from the box looked down on the lush, luxurious green

Goodwood turf and miles of snaking strips of startling white running rails.
They were only three boxes away from the Royal box,

Florence immediately attracted all the men, with her Christian Dior emerald green dress, a striking contrast to her long jet-black hair and startling blue eyes. Especially smitten was Henry's son Will.

Much to William's increasing discomfort Henry Sutcliffe focused his attentions on Mary.

William hated horse racing, knowing full well what its hold had had on many of his family in the past.

His grandfather primarily had managed to lose much of the Marshall family wealth with his racehorse ownership and gambling addictions. With all the glamorous and healthy, happy people surrounding him, William soon felt uncomfortably hot and depressed.

Being introduced to new people always meant he had to endure their unmistakable fascination when they first looked at his face—usually a mix of pity and horror.
Typically, Mary would have sensed this, and noticing his unhappiness, protected him from the growing issues. Now he could see she was enjoying the attention being

lavished on her by Sutcliffe and his wealthy cronies.

The first race had just finished when she rushed to his side.

"William, we have won ten pounds!" Mary was beaming and looking happier than he had seen her for an exceptionally long time.

"That's good, darling," he said without much enthusiasm.

An hour later, after agreeing to watch the horses and their small jockeys, in their beautiful multi-colored silks, milling around the Parade Ring, he said to her.

"Mary, I am not feeling very well, so I would like us to leave shortly."

"But there have only been three races so far, and Florence is enjoying herself." Mary's disappointment was palpable.

Standing next to his father, Mathew overheard the conversation.

"It's alright, mother; I'll go home with father. You stay and enjoy the rest of the races with Florence."

Mathew was happy for an excuse to leave; he much preferred racing cars to racehorses.

"Henry has invited us all back to the house he has rented in Chichester after the racing has finished, for drinks. It would be rude not to go. "Mary added.

Sensing the expectation in his wife's voice as he turned to leave, William said.

"You go and enjoy yourself then. Come on, Mathew, let us go home." He could not keep the trace of bitterness from his voice.

"See you later," a happy Florence shouted to the receding backs of her father and brother.
Then pulling at her mother's sleeve, said, "Come on, Mum, we need to place our bets; the next race is about to start."

It was 1am when a taxi dropped Mary and her daughter back to Sefton Lodge.
They had had a great time but on the drive home, for Mary at least, with the effects of champagne wearing off, guilt was setting in.

Both had spent most of the evening fending off the attentions of the male members of the Sutcliffe family.

"Haven't ever seen you this happy, Mum." Florence had commented as they giggled together in the back seat of the taxi on the way home.

"Your Dad and I used to have some fun...before."

"I know, I've seen those few old black and white photos, you looked so happy back then."

"We were...and still are." Mary had snapped back, sharper than she intended. Unaware of her mother's discomfort Florence snuggled up to her and quickly fell asleep as Mary stared out at the black night and recalled a day in late Spring of 1940.

She and William had managed a rare day's leave together and had ridden the Brough Superior to the South Downs. They had found a secluded silent spot high on the ridge under some young beech trees, the trees winter; depressive brown leaves were gradually evolving into a vibrant, bright, optimistic green. Their lovemaking had been slow and satisfying as they moved in rhythm with gentle swaying branches of the overhanging trees. Afterwards, they had lain side by side in perfect peace.

"I wish this day could last forever." She had whispered.

William had not replied; his gentle breathing signaling his light sleep.

Mary watched him for minutes and now remembered the sunlight as it shone through the blond locks of his unruly hair, forming long dark shadows across his young, soft, smooth face.

The taxi tyres crunching on the gravel drive of Sefton Lodge washed away the sweet old

memories and brought her back to the present.
"Wake up, Flo. We are home," she said to her beautiful young daughter.

Chapter 10

Florence Marshall

William did not acknowledge her when she crept into the bedroom, but Mary could sense he was awake. Both lay silently, unsleeping until the farmyard cock crowed to signal the arrival of morning.

"I am going out early to walk around the estate, so don't wait for me at breakfast," William said as he got out of bed.

Mary had finally dozed off, and from her hazy sleep managed to say.

"I'll come with you if you wait for a few minutes."

"No, you get some sleep, I'm sure you need it after getting home so late." He said as he quickly dressed and left their bedroom.

Concerns about the drifting relationship with her husband were compounded for Mary by her daughter Florence.

The pre-teenage years for Florence Marshall were as comfortable as one would expect for any young girl from a privileged, wealthy background. Although Mary had attempted to keep her daughter away from the lavish lifestyles of many of her school friends, Florence's main influences soon became the pages of Country Life and Lady magazines.

It had not taken long before she realised that the constant remarks about her beauty were an actual reflection of her stunning looks.

"You are the image of your grandmother at your age; she was a real beauty."

These became common comments from the remaining friends of Silva living in Sussex as Florence turned into a beautiful teenager, her raven black hair, startling blue eyes, and endless legs the envy her school friends.

As the daughter of Lord and Lady Marshall, her every move soon became scrutinized by the tabloid newspapers, and Florence enjoyed all the attention.

"Please don't encourage them," was the constant mantra from both her parents.

Once Mathew began to experience racing success, the newspapers' attention heaped upon him had given Florence the chance to get in front of the photographers.

At that first Brands Hatch race meeting, their interest had opened her eyes to the new opportunities her appearance might give her.

The trip to Goodwood horse races had only increased her awareness of her attractions, where she had been the centre of attention for the gathered press.

"What did that horrible little Daily Mirror photographer give you?" Her mother had asked as they were being driven back to Sutcliffe's house after the meeting.

"Just his card. He said if I want some professional pictures taken, he would be please to do them for me."

"Why would you want pictures taken by him."

"It's grandmother's idea; she thinks I could be a famous model. She still has some contacts in the modelling industry and said I should send them my pictures."

Mary, angry, turned on her daughter.

"That woman has no business interfering in your life! You are far too young; your father and I will not allow you to start modelling.

"Twiggy was sixteen when she started, and I'm going to be a model whether you like it or not"

Florence's pout pronounced. It looks like she has been practicing that in front of a mirror. Mary thought.

Mary could not think of intelligent response to her daughter. She could see the same stubbornness in Florence that she still possessed and was surprised to feel a pang of jealousy.

Mary remembered how following her heart as a young girl, had caused her to defy her parents. Who was she to disapprove; Mary decided she wouldn't burden William with their daughter's ambitions.

It was six months later that William picked up the hall phone. It had rung three times, previously and he had ignored it, the rest of his family and their housekeeper were out; otherwise, he would never have answered it.

"Hello, can I help you?" asked William.

A plummy female voice said, "This is the Arch Modelling agency I would like to speak with Miss Florence Marshall."

"She is not here at the moment can I take a message."

"Could you ask your mistress to phone the Agency. We would like here to attend an interview here in London next week."

"She is not my mistress. I am her father." William slammed the phone down, slightly harder than he had intended.

When Mary and Florence returned home after their trip into Chichester, Mary walked straight to William's study. Unusually the door was closed. She knocked and turned the handle, but the door was locked.

"I'm very busy with the estate accounts, haven't got time for small talk." He said abruptly from the other side of the door. Surprised by his harsh words, Mary could only reply.

"Oh, I will leave you in peace then." Mary had learned to sense when her husband was angry. This time the signals were powerful.

William's anger had not subsided since the phone call. What is wrong with this family, he thought, none of them are prepared to have a simple, comfortable life. Then realisation made him smile what right did he have to criticize anyone. His flying passion had altered the lives of everyone he loved; for sure, the war had caused his injuries, but he knew he would have flown regardless of any danger.

Unlocking his study door, he called to his daughter to give her the news from the Agency.

Within six months of starting her modelling career, Florence had become 'The new young face of fashion.' Of course, being a member of a famous old family did not hinder her progress. The already infamous Marshall family was always in the news with handsome dashing Mathew's racing exploits. Plus, his beautiful sister and her modelling assignments to exotic places were the tabloids, dream family.

When William had decided he had no right to stand in his daughter's way and unlocked his study door to speak to Florence, he had accepted this action would soon be bringing more unwanted attention and aggravation for the Marshall family.

"Dam... looks like there are more pressmen at the gates." He said to Mary one September morning.

His experience had taught him that trouble must be brewing for the family when the press arrived at the gates of Sefton Lodge. Their daughter had just skidded her Triumph sports car to a halt outside the front door of the Lodge.

"Aah, I meant to tell you. Florence phone yesterday, I should think the press are here because Lord Latchford has asked Florence to be in next year's Pirelli calendar." His wife replied.

When Florence had first told her the news, she had been apprehensive.

"Do you think it's a good idea, it's going to be different from your normal modelling jobs...you will have to take your clothes off for a start." Mary said to her daughter when she called.

Laughing her daughter replied. "It's all very tasteful; they wouldn't be showing my tits in the calendar."

Mary and William were no longer shocked by their daughter's colourful language.

"All the same, I'm worried about you. There are some nasty old men in that industry."

"Well, don't worry, Silvia...I mean granny, has given me some good advice.

William shook his head, not expecting to like what was coming next; his mother's advice had always been unusual.

"Granny says you just grab them by the balls and squeeze. Like that trick at Christmas when you press two walnuts together and break their shells. If that does not work, you tell them your boyfriend and his mates will be round to cut off their little willy."

"Oh...I hope you don't take her advice." A shocked Mary had replied.

"Haven't had to ...yet." Her daughter said, still laughing.

Later, as Florence left for a night out with old friends, William said.

"Wouldn't it be nice to be a normal family and not have this constant press attention? Sometimes I wish we could have a life like your brother."

It was Mary's turn to laugh.

"Like Peter! Don't think either of us could ever have had a simple life like his." She walked over to the window next to William and squeezed tight as she put her arm around his waist.

Watching their daughter slide into the sleek silver sports car, she remembered some of the good things their collective sense of adventure had given them.

The irritating press shuffling around outside the gate, she became introspective.

With a father like mine, I will always need the adrenaline rush that being close to danger brings. With a growing regret, she realised she would forever have this restless need deep inside her. William still has his escape with Harry Hurricane, for the moment, and Mathew and Victoria are following their adventurous paths. But what do I have now; I still need some excitement in my life? It is in my blood.

Chapter 11

Mary's dilemmas

Mary's affair with Henry Sutcliffe began three weeks later in the Bell Hotel, Farnham, near Brands Hatch.

Mathew was racing in the Formula 3 race, supporting the Guards Trophy race for sports cars. Sutcliffe's son Will was running in the Formula Ford race.

It was a two-day meeting with the Formula 3 cars having races on Saturday and Sunday. Mary had booked herself and William into the Bell Hotel, attending to support their son. On the day before the meeting, William had walked into the workshop were Mathew and Hans were making final preparations to the racing car.

"Sorry, Mathew, don't think I will be able to come to Brands Hatch this weekend. I have some important estate business to attend to tomorrow."

"Never mind, I will bring back the winner's trophy for you." His confident son had replied.

They walked back to the Lodge together, where William gave Mary the news.

She had half expected her husband's excuse. He had shown little enthusiasm for racing despite his sons' continuing success.

"Alright, darling, I will cancel the hotel and stay here with you."

"No... I do not want you to miss the race, Mathew needs your support. I'll be fine here".

Mary had not protested his decision.

When Henry Sutcliffe realised William had not arrived at Brands Hatch, he saw his chance.

"I am also staying at the Bell tonight, why don't we have dinner together?" He had said to Mary as they stood in the Brands Hatch pits watching their son's practice sessions.

"Not sure, I will probably have a light meal in my room. Anyway, I'm sure your wife will not want me tagging along".

"Oh, she's not here, gone away with her friends at Champneys on a girls' beauty weekend. So, I would like some company for dinner". He replied, giving her a shy smile.

Before she had a chance to reply, the noise from Mathew's Formula 3 car invaded the pits.

Mathew removed his helmet and fireproof balaclava.

"I'm going to sleep here in the caravan tonight, Mum, and help Hans with the car; we need to change the gear ratios and the setup. The car is going to need some extra work; not quick enough today, I'm only fifth fastest."

As she entered the Bell Hotel reception area that evening, Henry Sutcliffe was waiting for her.

"I'm not taking no for an answer." He said. "We are both on our own, so what's the harm in having dinner together?"

Mary only hesitated for a couple of seconds.

"Very well, Henry. I'll be down at 7.30."

A flutter of excitement made her legs weak as she said it.

After a shower and careful makeup preparation, she put on her favorite blue, figure-hugging dress. Although now forty-seven years old, Mary had managed to keep a trim figure and had to admit admiring herself in the long mirror. Then she studied the face looking back at her. What was she doing, she loved William, grateful, and happy to have him, and their two lovely children, but recently her family had gradually swamped her own identity.

Tonight, was just for her; at that moment she felt twenty again. She had given up twenty-seven years to look after William, sure she had some fun, and a far to brief time driving her Dad's racing car before Mathew was born. I deserve a bit more excitement before it is too late.

She convinced herself.

Turning away from the mirror, Mary walked to the door, opened it, and with just a slight hesitation, pulled it closed behind her.

"You look stunning, I've ordered you a Martini," Henry said, meeting her in the bar.

"I have reserved us a table. The food here is simple but delicious".

Smiling, Mary replied. "I like simple things, get fed up with all the airs and graces of some of the people I normally have to mix with."

"I just knew I would be able to relax with you. Most women I met are just after my money".

They settled down to a dinner of steak and kidney pudding and a vintage bottle of Nuits St George wine.

Mary was surprised to learn that Henry Sutcliffe was ten years younger than her.

He was not handsome in a conventional way, his sunburnt face lined, his mousy brown hair already receding, but he had an air of confidence and steady brown eyes which exuded danger. In a conversation, he could lock his eyes into yours as if reading all your wildest thoughts.

Starting the second bottle of the heady red wine, Mary had become relaxed in his company. Laughing together at the many strange events of their younger lives.

Both had come from poor backgrounds, utterly alien to the worlds they now both inhabited.

Henry told Mary he had been born in the East End of London in 1930, the youngest of four children.

He told her he had spent the war years in London.

"Dodging bombs." Two of his older brothers had joined the army, and both were killed one, Tommy, at Dunkirk and the other Harold by a flying bomb when home on leave.

"That's amazing...my mother and sister were killed by a flying bomb". Mary had butted in.

Mary explained her village background and how she met William, his love of flying, and her war-time dispatch riding and how William received his burns when his Hurricane crashed.

"So, while I was digging in rubble on a bombsite, you were racing around on a motorbike. You've had an exciting life."

"Not exciting... William's accident changed everything." Her almost wistful reply.

"How did you cope with that. A beautiful young girl suddenly stuck with a monster."

Mary put down her knife and fork and just stared at him in silence.

"Sorry didn't mean it to come out like that," Henry added quickly.

"Well, it bloody did. I loved...still love him. His looks don't matter to me. Now I'm leaving."

Henry grabbed her hand as she rose from the table.

"But now you need more, don't you, why else be here with me?" He said his large brown eyes were boring into her.

"Sorry...this is a mistake. Thank you for dinner, Mr Sutcliffe. I'm going to my room."

She pushed her chair away from the table, got up quickly, knocking over a half-full glass of wine. It is rich red stain spreading, corrupting the pure white tablecloth. Mary had hurried towards the stairs before Henry had a chance to stop her.

But Henry Sutcliffe had not made his money by giving up.

Mary had changed into her nightdress when a soft knock came on her door.

"Just wanted to make sure you are alright. I am deeply sorry I upset you." came the whispered voice through the door.

The moment she decided to open the door, all her resistance dissolved.

Mary soon realised what she had missed most, it was not the actual psychical sex but having someone hold her in his strong arms and the feel of warmth and closeness, the sensation of fingers exploring, the soft kisses all these things she had lost in the Autumn of 1940 from the man she loved.

That was twenty-eight long years ago, but her thoughts were always there, not here with Henry Sutcliffe. She may have given him use of her body, but her heart would always be Williams.

All of Mary's previous sexual experiences had been with William; now, a worldly younger man had wanted her, she knew it was wrong, but she thought after years of selflessness, surely I deserved to be selfish just this once.

Chapter 12

The Sea Search disaster

Initially a 5,600-ton steel barge; in 1964, British Petroleum had converted the Sea Search to function as an oil rig.

The oil rig consisted of 10 steel hydraulic legs, which made it possible to raise its floor fifty feet above the water's surface and lower it again to move to other sites. The steel floor contained a helipad, living quarters for the crew of 34, the drilling derrick, and a mixed assortment of cranes.

When the two legs had crumpled, it triggered a further collapse of adjacent legs, causing direct tipping of the platform; within seconds, the angle had reached forty-five degrees.

Cam still clung to the frame of the living quarters, with horror he watched as the tonnes of screaming metal that made up the rig broke free and slid into the sea; at the very point, Danny had disappeared seconds earlier.

Survival was Cam's only thought, his senses swamped by the chaos that had erupted around him. With a sharp crack he heard the retaining bolts for the cabins snap. Collected by the collapsing cabins Cam fell inside one of the rooms, as the crumbling mass slid into the raging sea. A sea now turned black and slick by leaking oil.

The cabins, made up of aluminium panels, folded like a pack of cards and, chaotically, crashed into the waves. Cam had been lucky. He tumbled into the sea along with the wreckage of the cabins and managed to haul himself up on some floating debris. It was impossible to see, or know, what was happening, luck determined if he lived or died.

Desperately, covered in a thin film of oil mixed with blood flowing from the cut on his head, caused when a broken aluminium panel sliced into his scalp, he attempted to paddle his ‘life raft’ away from the rig. The monstrous shape, now almost at a forty-five-degree angle, towering and swaying above him. He could hear men shouting and some screaming in pain, their sounds were blown distant by the strong winds and the waves' swell.

Gradually the rig settled, partly submerged, with one twisted pathetic leg shaking as it pointed skyward like a nervous schoolboy asking to be excused.

Some small amount of calm began to return; Cam, with senses returning, looked around him. Among the mass of wreckage, three men close to him were clinging to debris just as he was, two others were floating passed him unmoving faced down on in the black heaving sea.

Exhausted, those that had so far survived began to feel the bitter cold creep through their bodies as their adrenaline settled, and their misery and pains set in. They drifted helplessly away from the disaster scene shouting to each other to engender some optimism.

With his whole body hurting, eyes forced shut by stinging saltwater, throat sliced by razor blades each time he tried to swallow, Cam started to lose hope of rescue.

With the light fading fast, his stupor was broken by shouts, as nearby someone heard the first welcome sounds of helicopter rotors blades.

The rescue from the sea and flight back to land, later seemed like they had been a dream to Cam when he awoke in a room of Hull General Hospital. Only his bandaged head and parched throat confirmed the reality of the experience. The sedation and the impact of the shocking events ensured he had slept for ten hours.

"Where am I?" His first whispered words to the nurse at his bedside.

"You are in hospital, one of the lucky ones." The nurse replied.

"How many are here ...is Danny." He hesitated, unable to remember Danny's last name.

"There are twelve of you here but not sure of everyone's names yet."

"Is that all. There were more than thirty of us."

"Don't worry, some went to the other Hull hospital, and they have sent the helicopters out again this morning to continue searching."

Recovering, he tried to get out of bed.

"I need to let my family know where I am. How can I reach them."?

"Stay where you are; there's no need to worry.

We found your wallet in your trousers and could just read your name on your driving licence. The police are contacting your family this morning."

Peter and Grace Cartland found out about the oil rig disaster from the radio news. They were already desperately worried when, an hour later, local policeman Sargent Collins knocked at the bakery door.

"What's h... happened to him." Grace blurted out before the policeman could say anything.

The information they heard on the radio news was that there had been some loss of life in the accident. Peter and Grace convinced themselves that their son would have been one of those killed.

So, it was with considerable relief when the Sargent told them Cameron was in a Hull hospital and although injured his life was not in danger.

While they were preparing to leave on the trip north, Mike Coles arrived at their door.

"Just heard there'd been an accident on the rig Mr Cartland; have you heard from Cam?"

"He's in a Hull hospital. We are just about to drive up there".

"I'll take you," said Mike immediately.

For the second time, Mike Coles drove the elder Cartland's to a hospital to see their son.

Cam felt sudden relief when he noticed Mike walk into the ward behind his parents. His mother's face was full of worry, his father's stern but devoid of emotion, and then the open, smiling face of Mike.

"What have you done to yourself this time" was his father's welcome. Grace had no words just tears when she saw his cream bandaged head and chalk-white face.

Cameron Cartland had been one of the lucky ones.
The accident killed thirteen crewmen in the disaster, and three were still missing, including Danny Glover.

One-week later Mike returned to transport a recovered but despondent Cam back home.

Over the following three weeks, a constant stream of officials arrived at the bakery to interview Cam.

Burlham newsworthy once again, the landlord of the Red Lion pub enjoyed the increased takings, swelled by the growing pressman's alcohol consumption.

"Don't know what it is about that bloody Cartland family, but they always manage to bring more reporters here than dogs around a bitch on heat." Old local Billy Prentice had complained when a London pressman commandeered his regular seat at the bar.

Cam explained the events just as he remembered them to the police before the disaster struck. He then had to repeat his memories of the catastrophe to accident investigators and finally insurance assessors.

"One minute, I was standing with Danny at the entrance to the restrooms, and then there were loud cracking sounds. Next second the whole floor tilted down at one corner, Danny slid straight down the metal floor into the sea and disappeared. I managed to grab the door frame until the building collapsed, and I slid into the sea with all the others."

He had repeated these words at least six times.

"Do you know what has happened to Danny?" He asked each of his inquisitors as they were leaving.

"He is still missing, I'm afraid," had been the standard answer.

Once the visits had stopped, his father had asked him.

"Who is Danny?"

"Just one of the workers I got friendly with," replied Cam as depression set in for the young man.

Two weeks later, a more exciting visitor arrived. Growing increasingly depressed, he had been reading in the previous weeks Autosport a glowing report of Mat Marshalls latest Formula Ford victory when his mother knocked on his bedroom door.

"There's someone downstairs to see you, Cameron." She said through the door.

In the living room, Cam met a tall, stick-like, bespectacled, middle-aged man.

"Good morning Mr Cartland. My name is Ronald Green. I am an insurance agent representing your claim against British Petroleum. By signing on to the Sea Seach crew, you automatically qualified for the insurance offered to all the rig workers. I need you to fill in these forms; it is just a formality. After the inquest, all the claims will be settled, and there is every expectation that yours and the other surviving rig works will receive a substantial sum."

"How much will I get?" asked Cam showing the first signs of any enthusiasm since the accident.

"We would expect the settlement to be around one thousand pounds for each of you." The smile was the first Cam had managed for a long while.

"What did he want?" His mother asked the moment Cameron had shut the door on Ronald Green.

"At least that's something." His mother had said when he told her that he should be entitled to a pay-out of about one thousand pounds from the BP insurance scheme.

Peter Cartland walked into the house from the bakery, hearing the news he said, more in hope than expectation.

"You could afford to go back to college and get some qualifications with that sort of money."

Cam wanted to answer but knew what his father's reaction would have been if he had. This morning he had converted a new Titan Formula Ford racing car current advertised for sale in Autosport magazine.

One week before the inquest into the disaster, a body washed up on the Norfolk coast near Hunstanton. Although badly decomposed, with dental records and distinctive tattoos still visible, it was identified as the body of Angus Simpson. Cam felt no regrets when he heard who it was. There had been no sign of the two other missing rig workers, one being Danny Glover.

The enquires and inquest recorded a verdict of accidental death for the thirteen men killed in the disaster. Structural failure of two of the hydraulic rams supporting the platform's ten legs blamed for causing the accident. No personal responsibility was attributed, and BP's insurers made compensating payments to the families of the men killed, and lesser amounts to those that had survived.

Nine months, almost to the day of the accident, Cam received a cheque in the post for one thousand five hundred and twenty pounds.

Chapter 13

A Return to Racing

The Titan Mk4 was Cam's Formula Ford racing car of choice for the following season. It was 1969, he was already nineteen and concerned that if he ever wanted to become a Formula One driver, he needed to make a name for himself, and quick. His cousin had a year's start on him and was already known as a promising young racing driver. Cam had decided to paint the Titan in the same green and yellow colour scheme that had been successful on his grandfather's famous sports cars of the 1950s.

"Going to enter the car under the Cartland Racing name. It worked well for grandfather."

"Good idea, old Frank would be delighted," replied Mike when he called to inspect the new car.

With Mike Coles away racing himself most weekends, Cam knew he would need extra help running the Titan at race meetings. He certainly didn't expect any help from his father.

Many of the local village lads were often hanging around the old workshop, just like he had done in his grandfather's day.

Two of the keenest were sixteen-year-old twins Gary and Steve Sheldrake.

On a cold February morning the twins had turned up to watch Cam unload his new Formula Ford car. He had just picked up the car from the Titan works.

The boys were, to all appearances, identical with wild, flame red, wavy hair, a mass of freckles on their faces, and continually chattering. They were tall for their age, but their skinny bodies had not yet caught up with their long arms and legs, giving them a gangly appearance.

They grew up in their farmworkers' cottage, surrounded by pictures of the Cartland Jaguars. Their father had been a keen supporter of Frank Cartland's racing exploits.

"Want some help, Mr Cartland?" One of the boys asked nervously. His brother gave him a dig in the ribs.
That made Cam smile: it was the first time anyone had called him Mr.

Turning to look at the fidgeting boys, Cam asked.

"How does anyone tell you to apart?"

"Our Mum can, but even our Dad gets it wrong quite often, which is useful." Replied Steve.

"You can tell us apart anyway at the moment, Mr Cartland, look Steve has that large spot on his nose!"
Gary said, then he ducked as Steve took a swipe at his head.

"Are you boys interested in motor racing."

"Of course!" They both shouted.
"Dad took us to Snetterton a couple of years ago to watch Mike Cole drive your granddads Mini," said Steve.

"I got Mike Coles autograph," added Gary excitedly.

"Well, let's push this beautiful machine into the workshop. I am going to need some help this season. Would you boys like to come along?"

"Yes, please!" was the immediate chorused reply.
The power of their enthusiastic, positive response almost knocked Cam over.

Laughing for the first time since the rig disaster, he said.

"Well lads, if your parents approve, you are hired! Think I will just call you Tweddle Dum and Tweddle Dee.

Who wants to be Dum?"

“He does.” They both replied.

With his cousin Mathew and many of the other successful drivers from the previous season moving up to race in Formula 3, Cam enjoyed a phenomenally successful year.

He had managed to get Mike to help his early-season practice sessions. Mike had been surprised by Cam's speed.

"You're a natural for single-seaters. You wouldn't get me in one of those things." Mike had said after the final pre-season test at Snetterton. Cam had lapped the Norfolk track in 1.40 seconds, just outside the Formula Ford lap record.

By midseason, he was usually one of the quickest drivers, and by the time of the last race at Silverstone, he had won four races and finished second six times. He was going into that final round, needing to finish third to gain enough points to win the Esso Formula Ford Championship.

"Just keep out of trouble, and it's yours." Mike Cole had advised Cam as he sat on the Silverstone starting grid.

Cam had qualified second quickest, fastest in practice had been his chief rival for the Championship Will Sutcliffe, who had raced against Mathew Marshall the previous year. Henry Sutcliffe had turned up at Silverstone to watch his son and brought with him a large entourage. Mainly sycophants and hangers-on.

Just as Will was pulling on his fireproof balaclava and crash helmet before the race, his father had said.

"Go out there and win the bloody race. I have spent a fortune on you this season. Remember, Sutcliffe's don't come second."

When the flag dropped, Cam made a solid start, Will Sutcliffe and Andy Harrison, the other young driver who started on the front row of the grid, charged neck and neck into the first corner with neither driver prepared to give way. Cam felt himself smile as they locked wheels in front of him and spun into the bank on the outside of Copse corner.

Left in the lead Cam relaxed, he led the race for the following ten laps and duly won the Championship. The celebrations of the Sheldrake twins were a joy to watch.

There had been a few bad days during the season as the twins learned their trade. A couple of mistakes early in the season did cause some tension in the team.

An angry Cam had been towed back into the paddock after breaking down in one race at Brands Hatch.

"I've run out of bloody petrol. I asked you to fill the tank up before the race," Cam said to the twins. He was never sure which of them he had asked; the large spot on Steve's nose had cleared up.

"I had a look in the tank, and it was full," volunteered Steve.

"Look in here. Its empty - bone dry now," said Cam.

With his face going as red as his hair, Steve replied.

"Ah...I thought this was the petrol tank," he said, pointing at the engine bay's tank.

"That's the sodding oil tank! You are Dum." an exasperated Cam said as he stomped away to change out of his race suit.

Another early race saw Cam finish well down in the field.

"Can't understand it. The handling was crap, could hardly keep the car on the track. It was fine in practice."

Sheepishly one of the lads owned up.

"Sorry, Cam. I think that was my fault. I asked one of Andy Harrison's mechanics what tyre pressures they were using because he was quickest in practice, and he told me 25psi, so that's what I put in your tyres."

"Idiot! You know we run 14psi. He was just winding you up."

There were also happy days that season.

The first race victory for the Cartland Racing team had come on a sweltering June day at Mallory Park. The Mallory Park track surrounds a large lake, and this proved too much of a magnet for the twins.
Jumping up and down after Cam arrived back in the paddock with his winner's garland around his neck, Steve said.

"Gary bet me I wouldn't jump in the lake if you won!"

"Well, go on then!" The joyful reply from Cam.
With that, Steve wiped off his shirt and jeans, ran towards the lake in just his white underpants,

"Think I'll join him'" said his excited brother stripping and running after him.
They looked like two startling white matchstick men from a Lowey painting as

they reach the lake and with shrinks of "bloody cold," they waded in.

"Mad buggers," shouted Cam, then shrugged his shoulders and continued to enjoy the congratulations of all the other competitors. "I intend this is the first of many" was the comment he gave in his interview with the Autosport reporter Simon Close.

After the Mallory Park meeting, the twins grew in confidence and ability, and they became an increasing asset to Cam's young team.

The end of season BRSCC dinner saw both Cameron Cartland and Mathew Marshall crowned champions.

Cam's parents had declined the offer to attend, but Mike Cole and the twins attended to share his success. Unfortunately, the fact that his cousin had won the far more prestigious BP Formula 3 championship did dilute Cam's sense of achievement.

A little drunk on champagne, Mathew couldn't resist a joke at his cousin's expense.

"Look," he said, holding up his sparkling silver trophy, "BP has given me this. They tried to drown poor old Cam in the North Sea."

Especially frustrating for Cam was the certainty that he would not be able to afford to progress into Formula 3 next season unless he could find an excellent sponsor. His bloody cousin looked sure to be moving up to Formula 2. Just one step below their shared dream of racing Grand Prix cars.

He sat at the table, sipping his beer while the rest of his party was on the dance floor.

Watching the Sheldrake twins, happy, leaping around like demented puppets, he wished he could share their straightforward, pure joy.

"Why do you look so unhappy when you have just won the Championship, you should be dancing with the other youngsters, enjoying yourself." his Aunt Mary asked, noticing him sitting alone.

He could not tell her what he was thinking about her son.

"I am pleased, of course, Aunt, but I don't know how I'm ever going to be able to afford to move up to Formula 3 next year."

Mary had had no immediate answer.

Chapter 14

Mary's Regrets

Her family soon noticed the personality change in Mary, but of course, did not know the reason was her night with Henry Sutcliffe. William could see and hear the change in his wife's manner; she was far less snappy than she had become in recent months.

You look radiant this morning, Mum." Florence had commented at lunch on the Monday following the Brands Hatch weekend.

After a short pause, her mother replied.

"Y... yes it was a good weekend, it's a shame Mathew didn't win, but it was a good meeting.

William said nothing, Mary glanced at her husband, but it was impossible, even for her, to read his thoughts through his mask-like face, which was just as well.

He had encouraged her to go out more often without him, and enjoy herself, but now he was in torment as he felt sure he knew the reason for her change of mood.

Deep in his unhappiness, he knew his increasing depression and long silences had driven her away from him.

That one night with Henry Sutcliffe had been enough for Mary. A mistake, a moment of madness, but she hadn't anticipated the persistence of her new lover. At every opportunity, he invited her, always including William, to his multitude of social events.

Mary consistently made their excuses.

"You go, we can't keep turning him down." William had said, as an invitation to the opening of a new Art Gallery Henry Sutcliffe was sponsoring, dropped through the Sefton Lodge letterbox.

"I'll only go if you come with me," replied Mary

"No, if I turn up, his other guests will spend more time looking at me than the paintings," replied William giving her what she had come to know as a forced smile.

At ten o'clock on the evening of the event, Mary phoned William from the gallery.

"I've had a bit too much champagne, dear. Think I'll stay up in London tonight with two of the girls if that's ok with you."

"That's fine, Mary; I am off to bed now anyway, have to be up early, so see you tomorrow," had been Williams terse reply.

That second night of passion spent after the Art gallery opening soon became three and more as a sporadic affair began between Lady Mary Marshall and Henry Sutcliffe.

"I'm expecting we will be on more equal terms, socially, soon. Been spreading lumps of my money around worthwhile charities, and I am expecting a knighthood will be on the cards." Henry boasted as they lay in the large oval bed in his penthouse flat in Knightsbridge.

Mary was preoccupied. She desperately wanted to end this crazy affair. William had accepted her lies that her nights had been spent in London with girlfriends without question. But increasingly, she was desperate to stop these lies, and the deceit. The initial intense feelings of excitement and adventure had gone, now replaced by growing guilt.

With Sutcliffe in an unusually mellow mood, she sensed an opportunity to gain something positive from the affair.

"As you are in a generous mood Henry, would you do me a favour?"

"Of course, my dear Lady." His constant emphasis on calling her his dear Lady always brought bile to her throat.

"What is the favour?"

"Would you have any work for my nephew Cameron. You know he is racing, like our two boys, and is an excellent driver, but unfortunately, he has no money to progress passed Formula Ford, and he needs a job."

"Why do you want to help him. He's not your responsibility."

"Well, his father, my brother Peter, will not lift a figure to help him, and since my father died, Cameron has struggled to race, you know he was on that oil rig that sank."

"I remember that, the poor sod. And I remember your brother; he's the one that looks like he's got a pole suck up his arse."

Mary didn't comment. After a while Henry added.

"Tell you what I'll do. I will give Cartland a job driving my Ferraris and Maserati's back from Italy to my dealerships in England.

And just because he is your nephew, and as my son, Will is going to be racing in Formula 3. I'll buy two cars, March or Lotus will give me a bloody good discount for cash, but Cartland will have to find the money to run the car. And it runs in my colours and remains my property.

I will sell it if he doesn't perform in the first five races. I've told Will the same thing. If he's not going to cut it as a Formula One driver, I'm not going to waste any more money on him."

Despite herself doubt, Mary put her arms around Henry and, for once, instigated their lovemaking.

Shortly after, Henry said.

"But now I'm going to want something from you in return. I want you and Lord William to support my applications for a knighthood. Put in good words for me around your upper-class chinless mates at all those expensive functions you attend. Bastards never send me an invitation."

Suddenly it hit her...like a punch in the face.

This arrogant man was not here because he had any feelings for her, and why should he, he had a free reign to sleep with any of the fresh, young women that chose to work in his clubs. She had been flattered by his attentions, but how could she have been so stupid, so blind.

He was using her for his ambitions, but she could play that game for a while. If Henry Sutcliffe helped Cam, she would go along with the pretense. Was he foolish enough to think William could influence any of those self-important lackies surrounding the Royal family, sure they had been to

Garden Parties, and a few state dinners, but William had only spoken to the Queen twice in his life.

She smiled at the smug, arrogant man lying next to her.

"Not sure how much help we can be…but of course we will try."

Mary certainly did not look forward to broaching any subject involving Sutcliffe with William.

Chapter 15

__Breakthrough for Cam.

They were sitting having breakfast in the bakery kitchen when the postman arrived.

"There is a letter for you, Cameron." His mother said, as she brought through the post.

"Looks like I've got a car to race next season," Cam exclaimed excitedly to his father when he had read the letter.

"The letter is from Aunt Mary, she says Henry Sutcliffe has offered me a drive in his Formula 3 team."

"Well, don't get your hopes up yet, Cameron," said his father without any enthusiasm.

"I've met his sort before; he is a boastful, arrogant man from what I've seen of him."

"I'm sure Aunt Mary would not have sent me the letter if it wasn't true." Wanting to share his excitement with someone, Cam added.

"I'm going to see Mike to give him the good news. Aunt Mary says in the letter that Mr Sutcliffe wants to see me next week at his Richmond car showrooms. He sells

Ferraris and Maserati's, you know, would love to get to drive one of those."

When Cameron had rushed off to give Mike Cole the news, Peter Cartland shook his head and said to his wife.

"Just listen to him. I had hoped he would get this madness out of his system. My sister is to blame; she is as bad as our father was; I am going to ring her and tell her not to interfere in our family's lives."

Grace did not reply.

When he turned up at Sutcliffe's Richmond showrooms, Cam decided to park his battered Mini on the road, around the corner from the entrance. He had slowly driven passed and seen the row of gleaming sports cars parked on the forecourt. The deep rich reds and sparkling chrome were dazzling even in the weak winter sunshine.

Not one for formalities Henry Sutcliffe said the moment a nervous Cam opened the showroom door.

"Come in, Cartland; I hope you don't make me regret taking you into our team. Of course, my son will be the lead driver, and I will expect you to support him."

Cam didn't have an answer; he knew he would take anything offered to him. He certainly couldn't tell Henry Sutcliffe that he knew he was a much better driver than his son Will would ever be.

"That's fine, Mr Sutcliffe, Will is a good race driver. I'm sure we will make a successful team."

"Another thing accepting this drive means you work full time for me when we are not racing. You can start by cleaning and polishing those two Ferraris on the forecourt. Later in the week, I want you to drive a car like these back from Italy."

With an expansive hand, he indicated the gleaming cars sitting proudly in the showroom.

“That's wonderful. I would love that job." Cam had blurted out in reply.

"Good, you need to go on Thursday, there's a Ferrari that needs picking up from Modena. Hope you've got a bloody passport."

"Could I ask what Formula 3 car we will be driving." Cam nervously asked.

The choice of a Formula3 car had been made for him by Sutcliffe. He had a deal with Ken Champion, the head of the Lotus team, and purchased two Lotus 69 Formula 3 cars.

"I've brought two Lotus 69's. With that number, I couldn't buy anything else, and Champion was happy to take a wad of cash." Sutcliffe boasted.

"Would have liked to have gone with a March, but I'm sure the Lotus will be a competitive car," Cam said to Mike Coles in the Red Lion that evening.

"Anyway, I'm sure to be quicker than Will Sutcliffe."

"Just be careful, you do want to do anything to upset that bloody man, he will not think twice about getting rid of you," Mike said.

Those words would be recalled by Cam many times in the future.

Early in January, Cam had visitors to the workshop.

"Why it's "Dee and Dum. Good to see you, boys."

He had been putting off calling on the two boys, worried that they would be upset when he told them he didn't need their help for the following season. Sutcliffe had his team of mechanics to work on the Formula 3 cars. He certainly would not want these two scruffy lads hanging around.

"We've come to give you some news, Cam." said one of them...Steve, Cam thought.

"Sorry to let you down, but we can't help with your racing this year." Added Gary. They then took it in turns to add to their story.

"We're off to Australia."

"Our dads got a ten-pound ticket; they want people to go over to work there, so the whole family is going."

And Gary needs to get away from Ruthy." When Steve added this, he got a punch on the arm from his brother.

"Hang on." Said Cam. He knew they would soon be fighting if he kept quiet.

"Where in Australia are you going to live, and who is Ruthy?"

"Dunno where, it's a boy's name, Sid something."

"That will be Sydney; it's one of the big towns." Cam volunteered.

Steve continued. "Ruthy was Gary's girlfriend. She's got herself in the family way."

"It's not mine." Gary protested. "I was always careful; I used a French letter. Expect maybe one time in the cricket Pavilion when we had had a sinful in the Railway Arms. Anyway, she's got a new Yank boyfriend."

"They met at a dance in Newmarket. He's on the base at Lakenheath. She reckons he's her ticket to America."

"His tour ends in a couple of months; she's going back the States with him."

"Like to see his face when a screaming, red top comes out."

It was Gary's turn to punch Steve.

"Ruthy's not stupid. She's going to say she fancied lots of carrots when she got pregnant.

"Well, I'm going to miss you both." Laughed Cam when they paused from breath. "It certainly not going to be the same around here without you two. Those poor Australian girls don't know what they are in for."

They all shook hands, and the boys left. The last Cam heard of two gangly boys, their wild red hair blowing in the wind like flames in a fire, was their continued arguing as they walked away from him.

The following week saw Cam on a train heading southwest to Italy. His previous experiences with this grandfather's European adventures ensured he had become quite used to travelling abroad. But he was excited to be going to the Ferrari factory. He had to pinch himself to believe his luck.

He smiled as he thought, I am driving Supercars in the week and racing cars at the weekend, what could be better.

"Thank you, Aunt Mary, don't know how I can ever repay you for this chance." He had phoned his aunt the day after his interview with Henry Sutcliffe to tell her he had got the job and the Formula 3 drive. She had been surprised to hear that Cam was to drive Sutcliffe's cars back from Europe so soon.

"Don't know why he wants you to do that for him. He's got plenty of other older men that can do that."

"Don't know, but this is a dream come true for me—driving Supercars in the week and racing cars at weekends. I'm so grateful to you. I'll never forget it."

Mary put the phone down and felt a wave of sadness wash over her. Knowing Sutcliffe as she did, she felt uneasy that she had gotten her nephew involved with this man.

Her unhappiness had increased, and regret compounded, only half an hour later when her brother phoned. The call had been abrupt.

"I'm only ringing to tell you to keep your nose out of my family's business. You may think you are helping Cam with this racing madness, but he doesn't need your kind of help." Peter hung up the phone before she could reply.

Mary let out a deep sigh; she couldn't tell William about her growing worries, and there was no one else she could confide in. She longed to be back as a little girl, snuggled into that smelly, old, oily blanket in the back of her father's van next to his Norton motorbike waiting for him to go racing. Then she remembered how he had found her, lifted her in his strong arms, and carried her back to her little bed in Ivy Cottage.

He had said, *"Don't cry; I'll take you next time." He turned back as he went to the door and said, "I love you, speedy."*

Now she was all alone with her tears.

Cameron's trip down to Italy had been by train to Milan. At the station, a driver had been waiting to take him to Modena.

It was a slight disappointment to Cam when he arrived at Modena. He had heard tails of the fabled Ferrari factory, but unfortunately, he was not allowed anywhere near the Ferrari racing department.

Instead, the driver transported him to a compound, half a mile from the main factory. The ten-foot-high metal fence of the sealed plot, topped by razor type, barbed wire, clearly showing warnings that it was an electrified fence. Inside it held a mouth-watering line of Ferrari's, Maserati's, and Lamborghini's.

Two huge muscled, and tattooed men guarded the narrow gateway. A shiver went through Cam as he remembered Angus Simpson, the foreman on the North Sea oil rig.

The driver dropped him outside the compound.

"I've come for a car for Mr Sutcliffe." Nervously he handed one of the guards all the paperwork Sutcliffe had given him.

"Yea, you've gota take the red 308 at the end."

Cam was surprised that the guy had an English, East End accent.

He handed Cam a large envelope.

"Your instructions, you need to head for Antwerp, the address and maps are in the envelope."

"No one told me that." Replied a confused Cam.

"I expected just to drive back to Calais."

The guard gave him a long intimidating stare.

"Just follow the route and do as yea fucking told."

The threatening tone stopped Cam's questions.

The envelope contained maps, instructions and money, Italian lira, plus French and Belgium francs.

When he started the V12 engine of the Ferrari, the throaty roar made him smile despite his nervousness. I can put up with this beautiful noise in my head, he thought.

Cam carefully drove the Ferrari out of the compound onto the autoroute heading north towards Switzerland.

Once away, he started to relax, the effortless response of the Ferrari engine and the racing pedigree handling made it a joy to drive. Although this was the first time he had driven on the right-hand side of the road, his experiences watching his grandfather and Mike Coles driving the old bus years earlier meant he knew to be careful.

Mike had a couple of times forgotten he was no longer in England, after stopping for fuel, and the hair raising near misses in the old bus was etched onto Cam's brain.

Crossing the boarders into Switzerland then back out into France went without incident. Just the admiring scrutiny of the border guards slowing his progress.

His instructions had told him to stop for the night in Reims and travel north into Belgium and onto Antwerp.

He delivered the car to the garage of George Pieters and left it there until the following morning. He was to spend the second night in an Antwerp hotel and drive back down though France onto Calais and catch the lunchtime ferry. Once he returned to England, he was to take the car directly to Sutcliffe's Surrey Ferrari Dealership.

The trip went without any real incidents, and Cam was pleased to get a couple of days rest before repeating the operation.

By the time Cam drove his Lotus 69 out onto the Silverstone circuit for his first test session before the start of the season, he had made four trips to Italy. All followed the same pattern with the diversion to Antwerp on the return leg.

Each trip went well and he had safely delivered a gleaming Ferrari back to 'Sutcliffe Automobiles of Distinction.'

The racing season also started exceptionally well for Cam, he was third at the first race at Thruxton, became involved in an accident in the second, not his fault, and then won the third race at his home circuit Snetterton. The lap times from all the testing showed, even to Henry Sutcliffe, that his son Will would not be able match Cam's pace.

"I want you to put Will in Cartland's car this afternoon." Sutcliffe had said during a test session at Silverstone.

"I've spent all morning sorting the handling of my car, and its perfect now." an annoyed Cam had protested.

"Well, now you can spend the afternoon setting my son's bloody car up perfectly." had been the angry reply from Henry Sutcliffe.

With Mikes warning he his head Cam remained quiet. The change of car had made no difference; Cam was always quicker than Will Sutcliffe.

Halfway through the season with Cam in second place in the Championship, just two points behind the works March driver James Humphries, and with his son down in tenth place, Sutcliffe was beginning to lose interest in motor racing.

"I need you to pick up another car from Italy on Wednesday, Cartland." He said to Cam after the Brands Hatch race. Cam had finished second and Will Sutcliffe last, after a hair-raising spin at Paddock Hill Bend halfway through the race.

"But we are due at Oulton Park next Friday for testing," Cam's shocked reply.

"You will do as your bloody well told. Will can have the full attention of all the mechanics, without you around, it might make him go a bit fucking quicker."

It was a despondent Cam that relayed the story to Mike Coles when Mike called around the bakery to find out how he had got on at Brands Hatch. Mike had just returned from a successful weekend race in France.

"What can I do?... Even if I get back for practice on Saturday, all the other drivers will have had much more experience than me, and if I miss this race, I've no chance of winning the Championship."

"I'm not racing next weekend, so I could meet you in Surrey when you get back Friday evening and drive you up to Oulton overnight." Said Mike.

"Thanks, Mike, that's something I suppose. Lets' hope this trip goes without a hitch."

Cams' pick up at Modena this time was a deep blue Maserati. Desperate to gain time, and despite the previous warnings not to drive the cars fast, he arrived back at Antwerp much earlier than usual. Unfortunately, it didn't help him.

"Why are you back here so quickly. We are not ready for you. You still have to wait for tomorrow," had been George Peeters angry reaction to his early arrival.

"Why can't I just go straight onto Calais, you don't do much to the cars when I stop here."

The threatening looks he received from the garage mechanics caused Cam to shut up.

When he finally left Antwerp on Friday morning he was in a terrible mood, now desperate to get home, Cam thought it would be possible to catch an earlier ferry if he put his foot down. He was thinking of all his rivals at that moment out on the circuit practicing up in Cheshire at Oulton Park.

Usually sympathetic to the engines of these powerful cars, Cam used full revs in each gear. The Maserati was running extremely hot by the time they reached

Calais catching the earlier ferry with just five minutes to spare.

Feeling pleased with himself, Cam drove the car up the ramp onto the boat. Then panic set in as he could hear strange tinkling sounds coming from underneath the Maserati.

Three hours later he carefully drove off the boat at Dover, with the strange noise still apparent, he found a phone box and rang Mike Cole.

"There's a weird noise coming from under the car when the engine is running Mike. Think I've wreaked the bloody thing, Sutcliffe will kill me."

"Don't go straight to Sutcliffe's garage, meet me at Brands Hatch, my mates got a lock-up there, I can check it over," Mike said.

It was double relief for Cam when he reached the Brands Hatch entrance. Relief that the car had not blown up and seeing Mike waiting at the gate for him.

With the blue Maserati on one of the garage ramps, Mike stood underneath and said.

"Fire her up, Cam."

A metallic jangling noise accompanied the deep throaty roar from the engine.

"OK, turn it off. I can see where the problem is. It looks like one of the exhaust silencers has blown. I'll take it off; then, we can pull it apart and repack the asbestos packing. Think the high revs you have been using must have loosened it."

"Thank god it's nothing too serious." said a relieved Cam.

With the silencer removed from the car and on the workbench, Mike shook it. Sure enough, it rattled.

"Going to have to get this end cover off. It looks like it's been recently re-welded, so I'll have to re-heat it." Mike said.

"Bloody hell. Wasn't expecting that." Cam exclaimed when the end panel came loose, and a trail of bright white gemstones fell onto the dirty dark workbench.

He was looking down at the startling sparkling array.

"Christ." was all Mike could say.

"There must have been a hundred stones packed in there," whispered Cam. Fortunately, they were alone in the workshop.

Once they recovered from the shock, Mike said.

"At least we now know how Sutcliffe makes his money. The bastard is a diamond smuggler! Let's pack this lot back in, and I'll re-weld it. Don't think we should get involved with these crooks."

Unfortunately, they were now deeply involved. Not helped when Cam, on the spur of the moment, managed to pocket one of the stones without Mike's knowledge. Some insurance, he thought.

Cam delivered the Maserati back to Sutcliffe's garage by 7 pm without further incident. The manager Terry Thatcher took the keys from him.

"Any problems," the question was blunt, and he stared at Cam as he asked it.

"No, all went fine… as usual." Cam managed to keep a tremor from his voice.

"Ah, here is my lift," he said, and before Thatcher could ask more Cam turn and walked quickly to the door.

Mike had waited around the corner and then drove in a few minutes after Cam.

They were quiet as Mike started the long, four hours, drive north in his red MGB, both thinking about the days' experiences.

It was 2.30 am when they parked in the Oulton Park paddock, they reclined the MGs' leather seats and attempted to get some sleep.

"Didn't expect you to be here today, Cartland." Henry Sutcliffe said when he stepped out of his white Rolls Royce with a surprised look on his red-faced on seeing Cam dressed in his racing overalls.

"Had a good, fast trip. No problems, " was Cam's short reply.

The two young men then did their best to ignore him. They were trying not to indicate any sign of what they had discovered.

The Sutcliffe racing team mechanics had been relieved to find Mike and Cam in the paddock when they turned up on Saturday morning.

"Thank God you're here, Cam. The practice session yesterday was crap, Will Sutcliffe couldn't set up a bloody pushchair." His chief mechanic Alf Giddings had said when he saw them.

"Going to be tough to do much in this half-hour session this morning." Replied a worried Cam.

A light rain had begun just before the 11 am practice session was due to start. The weather had been remained dry for the previous two weeks, now a thin film of water covered the layer of rubber and oil around the whole circuit. Very quickly, the track became more like a skid pan than a racetrack, from the first lap of practice, with the rain falling heavier, cars were spinning off the road at every corner.

Cam had pulled into the pits after only two laps.

"It's bloody impossible out there." He shouted to Alf from the cockpit.

"Detached the roll-bars and soften the shocks." Just then, considering the conditions too dangerous, the Clerk of the Course ordered the session to be red flagged until the rain eased off. It was a relief to all, including Cam.

"Thank god for that, it's slippery as hell out there." Cam said to Mike as they watched Will Sutcliffe's Lotus delivered back to the paddock after he had slid off the road at Lodge corner.

For the following three hours, everyone waited, but the rain persisted and became much heavier.

By 2 pm over a foot of water had accumulated in the bottom of the bend called Deer Leap, and the Clerk of the Course abandoned the meeting
Driving back south that evening, Cam said.

"Think that's turned out for the best, I'm sure I wouldn't have been able to concentrate fully after what we have found out about Sutcliffe and his operation."

"You're not kidding...but what the hell are we going to do about it?" Replied Mike.

Chapter 16

Lord William Marshall

By the time of the funeral of Frank Cartland, the available movement in the fingers of William's hands had decreased markedly as the constant pains gradually increased. Each morning, he held his locked fingers in bowls of water, water close to boiling point, to release the joints tightened during the night.

Mary had become accustomed to the morning ritual; she usually had water boiling on the kitchen Aga by the time William came downstairs.

"You don't have to do this every morning. I can do it myself."

"It's no bother to me William. I want to help you."

"Bloody funny actually, too much heat got me in this state, now I need even more of it to get out of it." He said, adding an involuntary "Ah" as he placed his hands into the hot liquid and felt the joints begin to release their claw-like shape.

Mary smiled; she had become used to Williams jokes; they were always a defense against his pain.

William knew he was gradually being worn out by the constant pain and the isolation he was forcing on himself. He loved his family but was aware that his increasing melancholy moods and sudden anger were causing both his children to feel uncomfortable when they were around him.

Mary, of course, was different. Ah, Mary, what a life I have given her, he thought, she has wasted thirty years, her best years, looking after me.

His annual assessment to retain his pilot's licence was due on October 1st, and William had become convinced that this year he would fail the strength test.

The power of his grip had been marginal the previous year, and now his hands had grown much worse.

He had only taken Harry up three times in the preceding year, and each time the effort he needed to control the old girl had become harder.

"I am going to put Harry up for sale." He had said to Mary when he came back from the medical.

"Oh, William, I'm so sorry," had been his wife's response. Inside she felt a measure of relief. With William's increasing depressive episodes, she had been nervous each time he took the Hurricane into the skies.

"Going to miss the old girl, but I've been lucky to have had these extra years of flying her."

"I'm sure you will find plenty of things to do." She said, then regretted it. She knew, for William, there would be nothing that could replace what he had just lost.

She was full of remorse for her weakness in putting her pleasure before her husband, now determined to dedicate her time to his happiness in the future.

But she did not realise it could already be too late to help her husband.

William had always been determined to show no weaknesses in front of his family. He was desperate not to become a source of pity as he knew his father had become towards the end of his life.

He was worn out by the constant, nagging pains from his wartime injuries. In a state of acute depression, he decided to take his own life.

But I cannot even use Harry to kill myself now that I'm unable to fly.

Then has an idea about the next best thing began to form, I will find a tall building and jump off. At least I will be flying again for a short while.

The black humor still surfaced occasionally.

"Going to take a trip up to London tomorrow to see an old friend from the war," William announced to Mary at dinner.

"Oh, that's good, think I'll come with you; it would be good to meet one of the old pilots."

"No," he replied a little too sharply.

"It's not anyone you knew. Someone I trained with at Brooklands before the war started.

Anyway, I will probably stay up in town overnight at the RAF Club."

Mary looked directly at her husband's face trying to find some sign of the true feelings hidden behind the ridged mask.

She knew she had no right to question him, those times she had deceived him, staying overnight in London 'with her friends.'

"All right, William, that's fine. I'm sure you need a break from all the daily trials and tribulations we get here on the estate. I can look after the place for a couple of days."

William caught the 10.30am train from Chichester. Mary had insisted on driving him to the station.

They had not talked during the 10-mile journey, but as Mary pulled into a parking bay in the station car park, William leaned across the Jaguar's front seat and put his large arm around her. In a horse whisper, he said.

"I love you, Mary."

"I love you to William and always will." She had replied, although automatic, it was heartfelt.

"I'll come and wait with you on the platform."

"No... you get off, I will be fine from here." He had replied.

William stood in the car park and watched as the blue Jaguar's tail disappeared around the corner at the exit.

The RAF Club in Piccadilly was the natural "home from home" for all the commissioned RAF servicemen and women retired from the service and still serving. It had been more than ten years since William had last visited the club.

Charlie Barker had been a young mechanic during the war, based at Duxford. Group Captain William Marshall had been one of the pilots he most admired. He was now steward at the club and was delighted to see William.

"Lovely to see you again, Lord Marshall, it's been a long time."

"Thank you...Mr. Barker." William had immediately noticed the name badge pinned to Charlie's jacket lapel.

"Please call me Charlie, Sir. If there is anything, I can get for you while you are here, please let me know. Are your bags at the reception? I will take them up to your room."

"Only got this one leather bag, not staying long, so I can manage it thank you, Charlie." Replied William.

William's room was on the third floor of the six-story building.

He sat on the edge of the double bed for an hour, reflecting on his life and the many events that led him to this moment.

Life will go on when I am gone. Mary can find freedom and marry a real man; she will be better off without me. Mathew does not need me to help with his racing now, and Florence would not have to have my ugly face interfering with her modelling career.

Only the previous week, the Mirror had printed a picture of him next to his daughter with a caption that said, 'how could this beautiful girl be his daughter.' His children both had exciting futures in front of them.

His thoughts had taken him to his darkest places.
Suddenly, coming to a decision, he got up and left the hotel room. The door, with its stiff return springs, slammed heavily behind him. He didn't take his room key, or the lift.

It is only three flights of stairs, and William climbed to the sixth: the top floor.

He had recalled there was a roof terrace, remembering a party he had attended at the club just before the outbreak of the war.

It is 2.30pm as Lord William Marshall steps towards the edge. The surrounding wall is just four feet high; he can hear the familiar traffic noises far below. A light breeze has sprung up, catching the flaps of his blue RAF dress jacket. He had carefully dressed in his best uniform before leaving his room. It had been the only clothing in his leather bag.

Six floors should be enough, he thought, looking down, but it wouldn't be much of a flight.

Committed, he closed his eyes.

A worried voice came from close behind him. "Everything all right, Lord Marshall."

The sudden voice startles William, instinct causes him to take one step back. Without turning, William replied.

"Y... yes just admiring the view. Did you know you can see right across Green Park from here?" Charlie Barker stood still behind him. Uncertain.

"I've been looking for you, Sir. I just noticed you on the stairs when I reached your room. Lady Marshall has called. She would like you to phone her back as soon as possible.

" For five long seconds, William stood unmoving equally balanced between life and death.

Then, slowly, he took another step back from the edge, turned and walked away from death, and passed Charlie without looking at him.

"I will come down to reception now and ring her." He had said as he went past—the words coming out sharper than he intends.

"Very well, Sir." said the concerned Charlie to William's back as he watched him slowly descend the stairs.

Poor old bugger having to spend his whole life looking like that were Charlie's private thoughts.

"Are you alright, William?" were Mary's first words when she picked up the phone. It had only rung once. "I have been worried about you. I had hoped you would ring to let me know you had arrived safely."

"Yes, I am fine... is there a problem with the estate?" He tried to appear calm, but he was fighting to control his emotions; all he wanted was to collapse into Mary's arms and cry forever. He desperately needed to release the many years of pent up constant pain and misery.

"There is no problem here; I just wanted to hear your voice. I love you, William."

"I love you too, Mary." He managed to say, before gently replacing the receiver.

"I am afraid I have locked my keys in my room, just going out for some fresh air." He said to the receptionist.

"That is alright, Lord Marshall we will have the keys here for you when you return."

William walked outside, his senses immediately invaded by the hustle and bustle of the busy, noisy, traffic-filled, Park Lane.

By early afternoon William found himself along the embankment outside the Knights Templar Chapel.

He walked into the silent, grey, and gloomy space and stood before the tomb of his ancient ancestor, the crusader Lord William Marshall. He studied the likeness of the man whose actions had shaped the lives of many generations of his offspring. *Helped get many of them killed,* thinking of his father.

This thought gave William a new resolve; he had come so awfully close to the same self-destruction his father had achieved.

Although pleased, the ancient tradition of male bloodletting on his ancestor's tomb had ended with his generation; this visit had given him a strength that ceremony had failed to achieve. Standing over the cold marble figure, he became determined to return home and become a better husband and father.

William returned to the RAF club and rang Mary.

"I've decided not to stay tonight, thought I might take the train to Weybridge on the way home. Going to call in at Brooklands and look at the old place."

"Wonderful. I will drive up and meet you there. Then we can come home together." Came the relieved and excited reply from Mary.

"Where shall we meet?"

"There is only one place, isn't there? The top of the old test hill where we kissed for the first time." He could sense her smiling at the other end of the line.

"Yes, of course." Replied William. When he replaced the receiver this time, he had what Mary would have known as a smile on his face.

When the taxi dropped him in front of the old clubhouse, his first sight of Brooklands came as a massive shock to William. Since his last visit when Frank Cartland still had his workshop in one of the Brooklands sheds, back in the early 1950s, the whole place had become a neglected crumbling ruin. There remained a tiny hint of the past glories the track had enjoyed.

Roger Wainwright and Frederick Butler were attempting to repair some wooden railings that had fallen off the old clubhouse. They stopped their labours as they noticed William approaching.

"Good afternoon gentlemen is it alright if I walk up to the old test hill," William asked.

The two men recognised their visitor immediately.

"Good afternoon Lord Marshall; of course, you can go wherever you like." Said Roger.

They introduced themselves and explained they had both recently retired from work in the city.

"Very nice to meet you both, it has been a while since I've been here what's happened to the old place?" William replied.

"That bloody war, old age, and more recently, industrial vandalism." Replied Frederick with undisguised disgust.

"We are trying to get people interested in saving what's left of Brooklands before the bastards obliterate it." Frederick continued.

Looking around at the ravaged buildings and the flaking paint on the once proud and famous names emblazoned on the neglected sheds, William suddenly knew where his future lay.

"Well, I would like to help with that; you can count me in."

Both men excitedly shook his hand.

"That would be wonderful, Lord Marshall; your support will make people want to join us."

Just then, a familiar blue Jaguar came swiftly into view halting the men's conversation.

Mary stopped the car next to her husband. With a nod to the two men, William got into the Jaguar.

Mary drove the car slowly up the narrow, steep, neglected test hill. An easy climb for a modern 3.8 Jaguar, it used to be a real test for some of the pre-war machines. At the top, they were delighted to see the pines they had first sat underway back in 1939 had survived—their sturdy, full, dark brown trunks, displaying a defiant permanence.

"I've brought a blanket, some sandwiches and a thermos of coffee. I thought it would be nice to sit out here once again." Mary said.

"Yes, I would like that," William replied, his voice just a whisper.

Gazing out from their vantage point on inside the members' banking, both remembered far off, happier, past times.

"Oh, I would give anything to transported back to the time we sat here in 1939 with the cars roaring around the banking behind us," Mary said.

William did not reply but wrapped his arm around her shoulder and pulled her tight against him.

They huddled together, finding warmth in each other's bodies to dissipate the cool October breeze. Silently, they watched the last rays from the weak sun disappear behind the distance Byfleet banking.

With her head nestled into William's shoulder, Mary asked

"Who are those men you were talking to down at the old clubhouse?"

"They are attempting to clean up this poor old place. Roger and Fredrick are planning to get a team together to save the remains of Brooklands from further destruction. I've said I would help if I can."

Suddenly alert and excited, Mary said.

"That's wonderful; I will help as well...From the look of its sad state, Brooklands is going to need plenty of work. We can do this together...if you want to."

Also, now alert William replied.

"There's nothing I would like more."

They made love that night for the first time in three years. It was slow, silent, and loving, and afterwards, with William's coarse breathing in her ear,

Mary lay in her husband's scared arms, determined to devote the rest of her life to her family's happiness.

The mutual interest in the Brooklands project began to heal the rift that had grown up between the couple.

The Brooklands Society was formed, with William and Mary's as patrons and quickly grew with their enthusiastic support; its purpose was to save and repair the historic site's remaining track and infrastructure.

Their weekly trips to Brooklands and fundraising efforts had given William a new interest and enthusiasm for life. It also helped take his mind away from his constant physical and mental pain.

Chapter 17

Closing in on Henry Sutcliffe

Cam and Mike arrived back to their Cambridgeshire homes after their aborted trip to Oulton Park, around 8 pm. When Mike dropped him off outside the bakery, Cam looked forward to a hot bath and his bed.

Unfortunately, that would have to wait; a visitor was waiting for him.

"Ah Cameron, at last, you are back. This friend of yours has been here since five o'clock. Danny tells me that he had worked on the oil rig with you in the North Sea."

His father gave him this relieved welcome the moment Cam walked in. As usual, he didn't ask how well the racing had gone.

All the colour drained from Cam's face when he saw Danny Glover sitting in his father's armchair.

The face of the man that turned to look at Cam was undoubtedly that of Danny Glover, missing thought dead, from the Sea Search rig disaster. He appeared to have aged more like ten years than the actual three years since the accident. Danny's face carried deep lines, his eyes were sunken, and he had a full, untrimmed, beard. From his appearance, it was apparent Danny's clothes had not been changed for some time. He is a tramp, Cam's first thought.

"Hello Cam." said the scruffy, disheveled man as he got up from the chair.

Seeing the look of surprise and shock on his son's face, Peter Cartland quickly said.

"I will leave you two alone to catch up." He hurried to the door and, with considerable relief, left the room.

The two men looked at each other in silence for many seconds. As he gathered his thoughts, Cam managed to say.

"What the hell are you doing here, you're supposed to be dead."

"Well, that's a nice welcome. I at least thought you might give me hug." Replied the gruff voice of Danny. Cam realised the old familiar twinkle in Danny's bright brown eyes still affected him. Ignoring the remark, Cam said.

"Where have you been... it's over three years since that bloody rig disaster."

"Can't talk about it here. Do not think your old man approves of me. Where can we go?"

Having Danny Glover suddenly appear was the last thing Cam wanted. He was exhausted after all the events of the recent days, Henry Sutcliffe's diamonds were never far from his thoughts.

"We had better go down to the Railway Arms...too many gossips in the Red Lion." He said without any enthusiasm.

They walked the quarter of a mile down to the pub without talking. Once there, they ordered their drinks, paid for by Cam as Danny informed him he had no money, they tucked themselves into a corner of the smoky old pub, Cradling his pint of bitter in his large calloused hands, Danny began his tale.

He remembered sliding away from Cam down into the sea with crashing metal all around him. He had dived down to avoid being hit and eventually surfaced close to one of the still-standing rig legs. He struggled to it, wrapped his arms around one of the steel girders, and held on for hours. The bitter cold had invaded his whole body, he said, he was about to release his grip and let the North Seas take him as he felt himself slipping into unconsciousness. Then he heard shouts from a small boat searching for survivors; he was fortunate they had seen him and managed to drag him on board.

When they asked him his name, he told them it was Gary Young. He had seen Gary's burnt and lifeless body float passed him as he clung to the leg of the rig.

"Why didn't you give your own name?" Cam had interrupted.

"Because I didn't want the authorities to find out who I was. I'm still wanted for murder in Australia."

This new revelation causes an involuntary,

"What." from Cam. Loud enough that the three other drinkers in the pub turned around and stared at him.

Danny continued his story.

"I was about the same age as you were when you turned up on the rig when I went to work in the West Australian gold mines. I got onto a fight with the sadistic foreman. He was just like that barsted that gave you trouble. Even then, I could handle myself, punched him once, and he fell down a pit.
Bugger broke his bloody neck. The law arrested me and sent me to Freemantle prison near Perth."

"How long for."

"A minimum of twelve years."

"Bloody hell."

"Three of us managed to dig a way out, and I stowed-away on a boat headed for England.

"Got a forged passport and the job on the rig. The rest, you know."

"So where have you been for the last three years," Cam asked.

"The boat hauled two other guys out of the sea; one was dead; the other had broken both his legs. The poor bastard didn't stop screaming until we got back to Hull. An ambulance was waiting, and that took us to the hospital. They checked me over and put me in a bed for the night. The next morning, I nicked some clothes, walked out, and caught a train to Scotland. I have been there until this week."

"So why come back now?"

Danny gave Cam a sheepish grin.

"Had a bit of trouble, so decided it was time to come back South."

"I've got enough trouble of my own, don't need any of yours," Cam added sharply.

"Haven't come to cause you any sweat mate, just wanted to look you up. Been thinking a lot about the short time we had together." Danny added with a smile. Rather too quickly, Cam replied.

"That's all in the past. I've got a girlfriend now."

"Good for you, lad. I just need a bed for the night; then I'll move on.

"You can't stay at the bakery; my Dad certainly wouldn't allow that, even if he had the room. You can kip in my workshop, but just for tonight."

When Cam had left Danny with his old camp bed in the workshop, he went home.

His father was still up, waiting for him.

"Who is that scruffy person. You have never mentioned him, but he said you were terrific friends on the oil rig before it sank."

"It's Danny Glover; I thought he was one of the men killed in the accident. Danny helped show me the ropes when we were on the rig. I've let him stay in the workshop tonight; he is moving on tomorrow." Without giving his father time for a response, Cam said.

"I am exhausted. Goodnight "and went quickly to his bedroom.

Sleep wouldn't come for Cam. With the Henry Sutcliffe problem and now Danny Glover turning up, he knew he needed some good advice. By 3 am, he had resolved to ring his aunt Mary in the morning.

At 7 am Cam quickly dressed and walked to the workshop, to his relief, it was empty. There was no sign of Danny. Also missing was the battered Mini Cam used as a runabout. Worried, he went to his old office desk and discovered the fifty pounds he had in a tin box hidden at the back of a draw had also gone. There was a note left which in capital letters read

SORRY CAM. I WILL PAY YOU BACK IN FULL.

That's a small price to pay if I never see him again, Cam thought as he walked to the phone box to ring his aunt.

Cam asked her if he could call down to Sefton Lodge later today to see her. Although surprised by Cams' request, Mary had agreed.

"Your Uncle has just left, he is on his way to do some work at Brooklands, and Mathew is testing at Silverstone." She told him.

"That's alright; it's you I need to talk to." Cam had replied.

Cam had been buying and selling second-hand sports cars from the workshop when he had the time and had recently taken in a well-used 3.8 red E Type Jaguar in part exchange. The Jaguar was a car he had always dreamed of owning. The trip would be the perfect opportunity to give it a good run.

Good job Danny didn't nick this, he thought, as he started his drive south.

It had been a pleasant, uneventful drive, the rich pulse of the powerful Jaguar engine allowing him to forget his problems for a short while.

He was sitting in the drawing-room of Sefton Lodge with his aunt Mary. They had steaming mugs of coffee in their hands before Cam began his tale.

"I'm in a spot of bother Aunt Mary. You know I will always be grateful for you getting me the sponsorship and the work from Henry Sutcliffe, but I've discovered something and don't know what I should do about it."

With the mention of the Sutcliffe name, Mary immediately felt uncomfortable.

"What has happened?" Her voice was little more than a whisper.

Cam then explained what he knew about the diamond smuggling operation he and Mike had accidentally discovered.

"You need to go to the police straightaway. If you don't, the police will arrest you and Sutcliffe when it all comes out." Mary had replied without hesitation.

"Are you sure no one else knows what you have found?"

"Mike, of course, he re-welded the silencer, but one else. Thanks to Mike, the silencer looked just the same as it did before we found the diamonds, and I delivered the Maserati back to Sutcliffe's showroom without any trouble."

Getting up and going to the phone in the hall Mary said.

"I'm ringing Scotland Yard, the Chief Superintendent knows us, he served with William in the RAF."

Thirty-year-old Detective Richard Hurst had sore eyes and a headache, not his usual sort, the legacy of a few too many whiskeys. This one was the result of six hours spent in his car outside the Astor Club watching Henry Sutcliffe's movements. It had been another a wasted evening.

He was becoming desperate to find real evidence of this man's criminal activities. It had become Richard Hurst's' life's work. Sutcliffe and his close associates had long been of interest to the metropolitan police. So far, there had never been enough evidence to connect Sutcliffe to any of the serious crimes committed in London.

Richard was irritated, he just wanted to go home, have a long drink and some sleep, but now he had been summoned to the office of Chief Superintendent Bernard Oliver. What the hell does he want with me, it was his first thought as he replaced the phone receiver.

Do not think I've done anything lately to upset that old bastard.

"Enter Hurst." Came the deep crisp voice when Richard knocked on his Chief's door.

Richard was surprised to find two other people sitting in his boss's office.

"This is Lady Mary Marshall and Cameron Cartland; they have some news that will interest you." Chief Inspector Oliver said.

After hearing the story of the diamonds from Cam, Richard Hurst felt his headache and tiredness suddenly fade away.

"This is bloody ... please excuse me, Lady Marshall, great news, could be just the breakthrough we have needed. Thought we were going to have to just nail him for prostitution and extortion, but this sounds much better. I'm convinced he was involved with the train robbery last year, but we haven't found any evidence yet." Then he added, looking thoughtfully at Cam.

"But it is the same old problem; we are going to need concrete evidence, got to catch him with the stuff before we can arrest him.

He always makes sure he is not directly involved; it's his underling's that do the dirty work."

After a pause, he added.

"When are you due your next trip to Italy, Cameron?"

Mary had been quiet until this point.

"Just a minute, you can't expect Cam to carry on with this, it's far too dangerous."

"One more run should do it, and we can track him all the way, then when he delivers the car back to Sutcliffe's showroom, we can catch the whole operation red-handed.

Mary started to protest again, but Cam butted in.

"It's ok, Aunt Mary. It will be quite safe, and they have no idea that I've found the diamonds."

He said this with his right hand in his jacket pocket, feeling the hard stone laying deep in the lining.

"I'm due to pick up another car next Thursday," he said to detective Hurst.

"What do you mean someone has tampered with the bloody car "An angry Henry Sutcliffe shouted at Terry Thatcher in the secret and soundproof room of his Richmond garage. Sutcliffe had the place built below the legitimate operation; it was only accessible through a hidden ramp.

"They have re-welded one of the silencers, did a good job as it happens, only noticed it when we found out one of the stones was missing. There are always twenty in each silencer, only nineteen in this one.

They never make a mistake in Antwerp. It was from the Maserati Cartland brought back."

The nervous Terry showed Sutcliffe the silencer. Sutcliffe knocked it out of his hands, it crashed to the ground and spun wildly across the workshop floor.

"Bloody greedy little bastard. I didn't think Cartland had got enough guts to try something like this. He's a liability; we need to get rid of him now; he knows too much of the operation. No one steals from Henry Sutcliffe."

With his anger subsiding, he coldly added.

"Take him to the usual place, Gallows Wood. I'I leave it to you, Terry."

He turned and stomped towards the ramp, then turned and said.

"Just had a better idea, turns out there's been a lot of depression in his family, a couple of his old relations hung um selves. Do the same for him, make sure it looks like suicide, I'll tell the press I had just sacked him because he had stolen money from me, and his driving was crap. I'll say last time I saw him; he was depressed."

Terry Thatcher had worked for Henry Sutcliffe since the brutal early days of the 1950s when they had both done their fair share of killing. He was used to getting rid of his bosses' unwanted problems, but recently had become increasingly concerned over Sutcliffe's growing reckless behaviour. Forcing his son to drive one of the getaway cars in the train robbery had been stupid, and this instruction from Sutcliffe would be risky.

Chapter 18

Mathew gains a sponsor.

Success always seemed to come easy for Mathew Marshall. He had excelled at school sports, and his early racing years had already proved successful. Now having won the BP Formula 3 Championship against some of the best young drivers in the country, his path towards his goal of racing in Formula One grew ever closer.
But the next step into Formula 2 would take much more money. So far, talent and family money had been enough, but now he needed to find the backing of a wealthy sponsor or support from a works Formula One team.

Much to his disappointment, the latter now seemed unlikely for the following year. Unusually there had been no driver fatalities in Formula One during the past two seasons, and the current crop of drivers were staying with their existing teams.

"Don't know what I'm going to do next year, mother," Mathew complained to Mary towards the end of 1970. Christmas had finished, and it was in the waiting period before the new year. A time which tends to put many in a melancholy mood.

"Don't want to spend another year racing in Formula 3, I've already won that.

I've nothing to prove there; if a quick guy comes along and beats me, I'll be finished."

"Well, unfortunately, darling, there is not enough money in our racing budget. Even selling the Formula 3 car will only buy drives for a race or two in Formula 2, as you know. "

"Looks like I'll have to take a chance. It's a big gamble, but if I'm quick, one of the teams might sign me up for the season."

Mathew's successful exploits in Formula 3 had been followed closely by another young wealthy Sussex man Reginald Alexander Montague. Or RAM as he encouraged all his friends to call him.

"Well done Mathew, You really are bloody good at this game." Reginald had said as he slapped a surprised Mat on the back after a Silverstone victory.

"Thanks, Reginald, great to have your support." Mat replied.

"Call me RAM. All my friends do."

Whenever he attended race meetings, it was impossible not to miss his entourage of colourful and noisy friends. Supporting the progress of his fellow Sussex resident Reginald had become passionate about motor racing. He loved the good life he had been born into, and the glamour, colour, and excitement of motor racing soon became his obsession.

On the day that Mathew was bemoaning his situation to his mother, Reginald Alexander Montague's life had changed forever.

Twenty-five-year-old Reginald hated anything to do with horses, especially hunting. As in many other wealthy, old Sussex families, Fox Hunting had been a tradition for generations.

That cold December morning, a low light mist hung over the valley, part of the Montague family estate, as the hunting party gathered in front of Montague House. Reginald had dutifully taken his place on his chestnut cob at his father's side.

The strong smell of sweating from the snorting horses and the constant yapping of the hounds did nothing to ease Reggie's pounding hangover headache.

The 'Tally Ho' rang out, and the hunting began; the

great and the good of the Sussex hunting scene followed the baying hounds and cantered their horses to start their chase of the fox.

Reginald had always been a disappointment to his father, who could never understand his son's disinterest in hunting and polo, his great passions.

"Keep up, boy." Had been the last words Reggie had heard his father utter. The older man spurred his horse and charged off across the fields on his great black stallion, sods of turf flying up behind him. Reggie continued at a sedate trot. He smiled, and thought; you stupid old fool, as he watched the rapidly receding red jacket of his father bouncing around high above his horse.

Reggie had been back at Montague House for more than an hour and was already enjoying his second whiskey when his older sister burst into the library.

"Reggie, our father, has had an accident, the old boy is dead, broken his bloody neck, I think. You are now Lord Montague, my little brother."

"Jolly good show sis," Reggie said, then taking a large gulp of whiskey added.

"Now, I can start to really enjoy myself."

While leading the chase, Lord Montague's stallion had galloped into a rabbit hole. The poor horse had screamed as he fell with a broken fetlock, the fall catapulted his helpless rider violently headfirst into a large oak tree. Lord Montague felt no pain, his snapped neck and crushed skull ensuring death was instant.

"Are you going to the Racing Car Show at Olympia next week, Mathew?" Had been the question Reginald asked Mathew Marshall the moment they met at the New Year's Eve ball hosted by the Montague family each year in the Ritz.

It had surprised Mathew when he received the invitation from Reggie Montague. He had, of course, heard about the accident to Lord Montague only three days earlier. It had been the talk of the county, most had expected the ball to be cancelled.

"Sorry to hear about your father, Reggie."

"Remember, call me RAM old bean all my friends do... Oh, yes, thanks. The old boy had a good inning. Has left the whole pile to me. Think the death duties are going to be a bit of a bugger though."

Mathew had been a little bit surprised by Reggie's uncaring attitude; he knew Lord Montague had been younger than his father.

"...yes, I'll be going to the show to talk to the race teams, I need to get an F2 drive for next season somehow."

"Good show. We can meet up there; I have an idea you might be interested in." before Mathew had a chance to carry on the conversation, Reggie was whisked away by some of his drinking pals.

Reggie certainly had no plans to become a racing driver, he didn't have the shape to squeeze himself into a single-seater racing car.

His plan was to be a top team owner. He especially looked forward to enjoying the Monaco Grand Prix's glamour, glory, and excitement from the new boat he planned to have in Monte Carlo harbour in May.

"Greetings Mat, What car do you want to race this year." Had been Reggie's first words when they met at the show.

"Ideally, I would like to test a March and a Lotus before deciding, but I can't afford to buy either."

"No problemmo my boy." If you sign for my new team, I'll buy either for you."

Unable to believe what he was hearing; a smiling Mat had said." Where do I sign."

Reggie wasted little time assembling his new racing team. He was basing it at his home in the extensive Montague House stables.

"We are still going to have lots of horsepower, but without all the horseshit," had been Reggie's boast to the motoring press.

With his best friend, Charles Holland, a fellow hedonist, acting as the team manager, and a large bag of money persuading the chief mechanic of a rival team to join them, Montague Racing was established.

From the moment Reggie had announced the team and his grandiose ambitions to the motoring press, at a launch in the Playboy club, the motoring world buzzed with excitement.

"Bloody cocky toffs, haven't got a fucking clue how to run a race team." Had been the reaction of the elderly chief reporter of Motor Sport magazine Julian Jakes, who always hankered back to the 'good old days' of the 1950s.

The new Montague Racing Team received a mixed reception when they turned up at Hockenheim for the first round of the 1971 Formula 2 Championship with its flash new transporter, and purple March.

"Why pick purple for your team colours." Motoring News reporter Simon Close had asked Reggie.

"It's to remind me of my old man. He always used to go purple with rage when he was telling me off. Which was often by the way."

Mathew Marshall had embraced his new position as star driver with enthusiasm. He enjoyed the praise, and wild parties at Montague House, but was intelligent enough to always kept a part of himself in reserve. His only focus would be on race driving and becoming World Champion.

On a late January night, Mary had lain wake listening for her son to come home. The florescent hands on her bedside clock showed ten past two when she heard the flying gravel thrown around from the spinning wheels of Mathews three-litre Ford Capri.

The next morning at breakfast, she said to him.

"You need to keep yourself fit for this racing season. All your new friends are only interested in partying and drinking, so don't get carried away with all."

Mathew just smiled and said." Don't worry, mother. I can handle it; I can race and still have fun, going out for a long run now."

But she did worry. Her son was starting to show a little of the same arrogance her half- brother David had done fifteen years ago.

Chapter 19

Danger at every turn.

It was with great apprehension that Cam drove his E type Jaguar on to the forecourt of Sutcliffe motors at 8 am on Thursday. The day was already warm and muggy, the forecast for oppressive heat and heavy thunderstorms.

"Drive your car round to the workshop at the back," Terry Thatcher told Cam as he came out of the car showroom to meet him.

"Then come into the office workshop and have a cup of coffee before your trip."

Cam was surprised by thc friendliness of the big man. He had never shown any interest in Cam before.

The coffee was strong and bitter, but Cam, not wanting to appear ungrateful, quickly drank it all.

"I had better get going otherwise I'll miss my train," Cam said as he got up from his chair. But that action caused him to sway and with his head spinning his legs folded and he collapsed onto the concrete floor.

Vomit filled Cam's mouth as he awoke. It took seconds before he stopped choking and panic began to kick in.

He tried to move, but it seemed impossible. His hands and feet were bound tightly with tank tape.

How did I end up here, bound and bleeding in a car boot? he soon realised he lay stuffed into the boot of his own speeding Jaguar. There's not enough room for a set of golf clubs in here he thought let alone my body.

Body. That word sobered him up; he knew his body would soon be naked and cold on some neon-lighted mortuary slab ready to be sliced open.

Collecting his muddled thoughts, Cam realised what a fool he had been to think Henry Sutcliffe wouldn't have found out he had discovered the diamonds.

He felt the car turn onto a bumpy gravel road the rough surface causing his head, arms and legs to be smashed continuously into the boot lid. Cam felt sudden relief when, after another minute, the car braked heavily and stopped. Then fear really set in.

He screwed up his eyes when the boot opened, as the sudden sunlight blinded him. The two men said nothing as they roughly hauled him out of the boot and dropped him face-first on the floor.

Cam could see they were at the edge of wooded area, pine needles were painfully pricking his face squashed into the ground. He managed to pathetic shout of "HELP" before he received a kick in the ribs and a dirty rag was stuffed into his mouth to silence him.

"Careful." He heard one of the men say. "This has got to look like a suicide."

Detective Hurst's forehead creased in worry. They had watched Cameron Cartland's green Jaguar leave the Sutcliffe garage twenty minutes earlier, without Cam in it, the tracker they had sealed into his shoe showed on their monitor that Cam was still in the workshop.

"He should be well on his way to the channel by now. Something has gone wrong."

The Detective said to the Constable sitting next to him as they watched the blinking blue light stubbornly stationary on the screen.

"We had better raid the place now."

Police moved in quickly, but the surprised garage mechanics gave them no trouble. The workshop at the back of the building contained two gleaming Ferraris, but there was no sign of Cam.

"Over here," shouted one of the police officers.

Richard Hurst rushed over, in the five-gallon oil drum, with the top cut off, in the corner of the workshop they looked down on a pair of black scruffy, slip-on, shoes. His first reaction was a relief; he had half expected to see the body of Cameron. Then Richard Hurst recognised the footwear and his heart sank.; in one of these shoes he had inserted the tracker.

For confirmation he held the blipping monitor over the barrel, it's continued agitation confirming the shoes belonged to Cameron Cartland.

"Shit they must have him in the car. They could be anywhere by now; send out the alert to look for the green Jaguar. Radius from here thirty miles, they couldn't have got further than that." The Detective swung a hard kick at the metal bin.

Danny Glover had not arrived in Burlham intending to ask Cam for anything, Danny was tired of hiding and had just wanted to see a friendly smile.

Unfortunately, on the face of Cam, he had found surprise and anger which was soon replaced by worry.
He had not seriously expected a warm welcome, but he could see in his young friends eyes the same panic and venerability he had noticed when they first met on the oil

rig three years earlier. Danny still felt a need to protect him, but this time he was unsure what from.

Once Cam had left him alone in the workshop that night, he had looked on the old desk and noticed Cam's desk diary. Opening it he noticed on the date for the following Thursday circled in black ink 6 am and the name SUTCLIFFE written in bold letters, also in bold letters, on Friday was written ITALY.

For the past year, Danny had been calling at newsagents and skimming through copies of Autosport on the shelves to follow Cam's racing. He had seen the name Sutcliffe mentioned as the entrant of Cam's car.

During the three days since he had taken the Mini and the money, Danny Glover had not moved far away from the village. He had booked into a small Bed and Breakfast in Cambridge, shaved, and smartened himself up a little, he spent his days mooching around the collages of the town. Determined to stay around, to keep an eye on Cam and find out whatever or whoever was causing him such concern.

6.30am Thursday found him travelling along the A11 just south of Royston, ahead in the distance he could see the rear of Cameron's green E Type Jaguar.

Fortunately, he found the engine in the old Mini extremely responsive, making it easy to keep the Jaguar in his sight. Remaining a safe distance behind, Danny followed until the Jaguar turned into the swish Ferrari dealership. He parked, hidden from view, but within sight of the entrance.

Fifteen minutes later the E type had turned left out of Sutcliffe's garage. Danny could see two people in it, but the car was too far away to recognise who they were.

He decided to follow the Jaguar, expecting Cam to have been one of the men.

Keeping just far enough back to make sure he wasn't noticed by the car ahead, Danny missed seeing it turn off the main road, and carried on for another mile before he realised, he had lost contact.

Sod it, I've lost them. He turned the car around and returned in the direction he had just come. It was sheer luck that Danny noticed the dirt road on his right, a small amount of sandy dust hanging in the air indicating that the dirt had recently been disturbed.

Following the rough road for about half a mile, he braked suddenly. Four hundred yards ahead, the Jaguar was parked on the edge of a wood.

He watched in horror as two men carried a struggling body into the woods. The boot of the Jaguar remained open. Abandoning the Mini, Danny ran to the Jaguar, and grabbed a metal jack handle he saw laying in the boot, then ran to the place where the men had disappeared into the woods. Hearing muffled voices direct ahead of him he stopped, desperately trying not to make a sound.

"Stop fucking struggling or I'll finish yer now." came a harsh voice.

"Careful Les, you know Mr Sutcliffe wants this to look like a suicide." The other voice much calmer.

Cam continued struggling and by rubbing his face into the dirt floor managed to loosen the rag in his mouth. At the same moment Danny took a chance and looked around the pine tree he was hiding behind.

With a wave of bubbling anger, just twenty yards ahead, two men stood with Cam writhing about on the floor between them. His hands and feet were tied, and a dirty cloth gag covered his mouth. Danny could also see a thick rope with a noose on one end hanging over the large branch of a sturdy pine tree.

That sight was the trigger for his anger to explode. Danny rushed out from his hiding place with the heavy metal bar in his hand, surprise on his side; reaching the first man before either had time to react, he swung the bar with all his considerable might into the man's shin. The snapping of the bone was like a gunshot, instantly followed by a high -pitched scream as Terry Thatcher collapsed in agony.

Danny charged on leaping at the other man who just had time to draw a revolver from his belt before both men fell to the ground and a real gunshot rang out. Neither man moved.

With Thatcher still writhing in agony, Cam, bewildered, struggled to his feet, and hopped towards the two prostrate bodies.

His hysterical cries of "Danny, Danny," were partly lost behind the half-removed gag as he managed to push the two bodies apart with his shoulder.

As Danny flopped off the still form of Les, there was much for Cam to take in. The body of Les lay with its head against a large boulder; blood tricked slowly down the rock turning the grey stone to a dirty dark red.

A smoking gun was in his hand, his sightless open eyes staring up at the pine canopy. Cam was relieved to hear a moan from the lips of his friend, but then noticed a sizeable growing patch of red oozing from Danny's chest.

"Danny, please speak to me." he tried to say.

Looking into Cam's eyes and coughing blood Danny spluttered "S...Sorry, Cam, think you are on your own now," these were his final words as Danny's, once sparkling, laughing brown eyes closed for the last time.

Struggling to stand, Cam wildly looked around, Terry appeared to have passed out, and the other two were dead. He knew he had to get help, but bound and still partly gagged, he didn't know how.

By the time he had managed to hop, fall and roll back to the Jaguar half an hour had passed, bleeding from numerous scratches, he was utterly exhausted.

After many attempts he managed to release the driver's door to open it, leaning in he pressed his bleeding head onto the horn button in the centre of the steering wheel and left it there allowing the loud alarm to blast out across the sandy heathland.

Walking a footpath half-mile from the edge of the wood, a doctor and his wife, annoyed at the harsh sound corrupting the peace of their walk, marched to the car.

The doctor managed to lift Cam away from the steering wheel, thankful to stop the noise.

They released his bound arms and legs and tried to make him comfortable. Noticing the key was still in the ignition of the Jaguar, the doctor said.

"I'll go and get some help."

"No! we all need to get away; there's been a murder in the woods." Came Cam's panicked, hoarse reply.

That was enough for the doctor to bundle his wife into the small back seat, and helped Cam into the passenger seat, he started the engine, and with a lurch and spinning wheels rushed away from the wood.

It was a hair-raising ride; the poor man had only driven the family Rover before, the "E" Type was a whole new experience. A mile along the main road he had been relieved to find a red phone box. He rushed in and dialled 999.

"We need help quick, police and ambulance...where? Oh, It's on the B145 near Gallows Wood."

Back in the car, he said.

"Police are on their way, told them we are near Gallows Wood," he said with relief when he got back to the car.

Why's it called Gallows Wood." Cam had managed to ask him.

"Used to be some gallows up there until the 1800s. Locals don't go near the place; they think it's haunted." Cam didn't reply, but thought, *it certainly will be now.*

They waited what seemed like an age until just over fifteen minutes later a convoy of siren whaling police cars and an ambulance arrived. Detective Richard Hurst was in the first car to reach the site. Relieved to see the battered but alive Cam, he asked.

"What the hell has happened?"

"Sutcliffe's men tried to kill me, and they have killed Danny, they shot him, they had a gun." It was all Cam could manage to say, he just sat still and stared ahead, the shock setting in.

"We had better get you straight to the hospital." The Detective said, and immediately got on his car phone to request urgent armed back-up.

When Terry Thatcher came round, he saw the two bodies close by, and dragged himself across to them, involuntary cries of pain accompanied every movement.

He took the gun from the dead hand of Les. *There's no sign of bloody Cartland; he's sure to have gone for help.*

Then he decided his best chance of escape would be to make his way down to the river.

Gallows Wood covers an area of about three acres; it is boarder by the B145 on its north side and slopes down to the River Cherwell at its southern end. Using a large branch as a crutch, Thatcher eased his way down the steep hill, every move causing him to wimpier as intense pain from his shattered right leg shot to his brain.

Half an hour later armed police arrived. Cautiously entering the wood; they soon discover the dead bodies of Danny and Les.

The sharp sound of a long scream alerted them to focus their attention towards the sloping area of the wood.

The old branch Thatcher had been using had snapped sending him tumbling quickly down the slope until a large Willow tree stopped his progress at the edge of the river. This time his left leg took the impact.

In no condition to offer resistance, he had lost the gun in his fall; police soon surrounded him. Considering he now had two broken legs, the handcuffs seemed a little unnecessary.

It was two days after the events in Gallows Wood. During that time police had raided the Ferrari dealership, discovering the secret underground workshop, and had raided both night clubs belonging to Henry Sutcliffe.

They had also managed to interview Terry Thatcher under arrest in Surrey General Hospital who to no one's surprise protected his boss.

"Thought the morphine might loosen his tongue, but the basted knows Sutcliffe has ways to snuff him out if he squeals." Richard Hurst had commented.

The evidence against Henry Sutcliffe for his involvement in the kidnap of Cameron Cartland and murder of Danny Glover was now overwhelming, and they had Cam's confirmation that he had heard Terry say.

'You know Mr Sutcliffe wants this to look like a suicide.' as they were about to murder him.

As a bonus after three hours of 'interview' Harry Sutcliffe's son, Will, was formally arrested when he admitted driving a getaway car in the train robbery. But, he insisted, knew nothing about the diamond smuggling business or attempted murder of Cameron Cartland. In a combined operation the Antwerp police had raided the garage in their town, and Italian police arrested Sutcliffe's two men in Modena.

His whole diamond smuggling operation had collapsed.

"You bastards are not coming in here without a warrant." Had been the greeting from Iris Sutcliffe when police, led by Detective Hurst hammered on the door of the west London home she shared with her son.

"If it's my son you want, he's not here, so fuck off. Oh...why don't you ask high and mighty Lady Mary Marshall where he is. He boasted to me he'd been sleeping with her." she added slamming the door.

Richard Hurst had not expected that revelation. He phoned Mary Marshall to let her know what Iris had said.

“Thank you letting me know Inspector Hurst.” Was all Mary said before she put the phone down.

The following day he returned to Sutcliffe’s house with a warrant, but despite turning the place upside down, there was no sign of the man himself or any further incriminating evidence of his many criminal activities.

Henry Sutcliffe was already relaxing in his villa in "The Costa del Crime" in Spain. By lunchtime, on the day of the kidnap, one of his police contacts had warned him that police were raiding his Surry showrooms, and all hell was breaking loose at a place called Gallows Wood.

He knew what all this meant. It meant he had to get away from England, and quickly. Fortunately, he had put plans in place for just this situation which he always knew could arise someday. With no extradition treaty in place, Spain was a home from home for all the criminals fleeing the English police. As he said to one of his fellow crooks in Harry's Bar.

"Knew I'd retire here one day, that bastard Cartland has just brought it forward a few years."

For the third time in his short, eventful life, Cameron Cartland found himself in a hospital bed. This time it was Surrey General.

The visit from his mother and father had as usual been stressful. They had had to fight their way through the press gathered at the hospital entrance and the moment she saw her bruised and battered son Grace Cartland burst into streams of tears. His father just shook his head and said

"I hope this is finally a lesson for you. That is three lucky escapes you have had God will not be on your side forever. When you come home, you can settle down to a proper job and live like a normal person."

"I have phoned your Aunt and told her she is responsible for all that has happened to you. I've also said we want nothing more to do with her or her family."

Cam's physical recovery from his kidnap ordeal had been quick; despite his cuts and bruises, he had been fortunate to have no broken bones. However, mental recovery would take much longer. Even before his grandfather’s day, mental illness had caused distress in the Cartland family.

The fact that he had no racing car to finish the Formula 3 season compounded his depressed mood. The Sutcliffe owned Lotus 69 he had raced had confiscated together with all Henry Sutcliffe's other assets.

"I'm right back where I started. Going to have to write off this season now." He complained to Mike Coles when Mike had come to visit him in hospital.

"You should thank your lucky stars you are still alive. Without that guy saving you, it would be you dead, not him. Who the hell was he, and why was did he turn up there?" Mike had asked.

Quiet for a minute, Cam replied: "Sorry Mike...yes I know, the police asked the same questions, he was someone I made friends with on the oil rig, still haven't worked out why Danny bothered to get involved."

"He must have thought a lot of you."

Cam remained silent. He didn't want anyone to know what had happened between Danny Glover and himself.

Then his depression lifted a little as he allowed himself a slight smile, he remembered there was a diamond still sealed in the lining of his jacket at home.

Chapter 20

Love for Mathew

The publicity interest over another scandal involving the Cartland and Marshall families was immense.

For three generations, the activities of both families had filled the news pages of the tabloid papers, and this story was turning out to be one of the best.

Before long, the association between Mary Marshall and Henry Sutcliffe became headline news, much to the distress of everyone, but to Lord William Marshall in particular.

Although he knew Mary's affair with Sutcliffe had been over long before these disastrous events, the press attention brought the raw pain of it back.

Mary's father, Frank, had practically lived at Brooklands during her younger years. So, it came as no surprise when William said.

"I'm going to stay up at Brooklands with Rodger Wainwright for a few days."

Staying at Brooklands would become regular for him during this challenging period. Just as it had been for her father, Brooklands became a place for William to escape too.

His growing band of loyal friends there giving small change to any pressman that attempted to annoy him.

The only person not to be severely affected by the publicity from these events, in either family, was Mathew Marshall. He was far too busy enjoying life, balancing embracing all the pleasures that his association with Reggie Montague brought, and being a successful racing driver.

Much to the surprise of all the motoring press, they had become the team to beat with Mathew driving confidently and very quickly in his Formula 2 March.

"Wine, women and song seem to be doing you good old boy," Reggie said slapping Mat on the back after he finished third in his first Formula 2 race at Silverstone.

Once the press had tried of the sensations surrounding Cam and his aunt Lady Mary the celebrity pages focused their attentions on the Montague racing team. The beautiful girls, wild parties and outrageous antics surrounding the race team, providing them with plenty of copy. There were two opposing camps:

'We don't need this sort in motor racing; it's a serious business.' Or 'What a breather of fresh air, more glamour and fun, it's just what motor racing needs.'

Most racing fans were in one camp or the other; there was no 'in-between' when it came to Reggie Montague.

"Isn't that Linda Young" Mat asked Reggie. He was looking across the room at a stunning blond woman talking to an older, tall man with dark hair greying at the sides. They were attending a party at the Playboy Club, the owner Gino Polios, a friend of Reggie's, had organised.

The teams Formula 2 March sat outside the club; the party was to announce Gino's agreement to add his sponsorship to the teams' racing operations.

"Yes, that is the famous actress Linda Young, she is over here promoting that new film she has just made in Hollywood, you know, Deception. She is standing with Omar Gallio her love interest in the film. They say he has had more lovers than Rudolph Valentino, lucky sod."

"Will you introduce me to her." was Mat's response, not taking his eyes off the stunning woman.

Reggie, with Mat close behind, interrupted the actors.

"Good evening Miss Young, jolly good to meet you again."

"Can I introduce you to Mathew Marshall he is my star racing driver."

"So, you are a racing driver Mr Marshall. Are you any good."?

Linda said when they were introduced by Reggie, as their eyes met. the mutual attraction between the couple was immediate. Being reluctant to let go of Linda's soft, warm hand or be the first to break eye contact Mat's response was.

"Yes, I am a racing driver, and I'm an excellent one. I hear you are an actress, are you any good."

He was nervous and knew it was a stupid response.

Reggie rolled his eyes and walked away.

Linda smiled and studied the young man standing in front of her, as Gallio also moved away, his eyes on other prey.

Linda had been an actress since she was nine years old, her angelic round face, golden curly hair and startling light blue eyes made her a natural for the big screen. As a child, she had stared in many of the English romantic films of the 1950s, but her mother had higher ambitions for her daughter, a failed actress herself before the war Lilly Young was a formidable woman.

When Linda was just fourteen, Lilly moved them both to America and signed her up with MGM studios. It was a harsh contract, Linda committed to making a minimum of four films a year. Her mother controlled the money, but soon became embroiled in the Hollywood drugs and drink scene.

Linda had been just nineteen when she had found her mother dead in a bath.

Now aged twenty-six, she had made more films than she could count, and had become disillusioned with the whole social scene surrounding the film industry.

She was also tired and fed up with constant harassment from the press. Their intrusion into her life had been made much worse as she had recently divorced her husband, of three years, fellow actor James Taylor.

His blatant public affairs with young actresses had embarrassed and upset her, she had vowed to give up men, and was seriously considering giving up acting.

'Men are all a waste of space darling, so just get used to it.' Had been the less than helpful advice from her three times married mother before she died.

Linda had not wanted to attend this party but attending functions to promote her latest films was a large part of her contract.

Now, this handsome young man had brightened her evening, like sudden sunshine on a grey day.

"Sorry...of course, I know who you are, and you are even more beautiful in the skin than on film."
Mat's face was now turning pink. You fool, he thought.
To save his blushes, Linda removed her hand from his. Reluctantly, and said.
"Why thank you, Mr Marshall, it's been lovely to meet you; now if you will excuse me, I have to retire early, I am flying back to American tomorrow morning."
Impulsively Mat replied.
" Please call me Mat, can I drive you home."
"That's very kind of you, but no need, I am staying with friends just down the road tonight." She hesitated for a moment, then added.
"But we could have dinner next time I'm in London, Mat...if you like, and please call me Linda."
"Yes, please." Was his almost shouted reply.
She smiled and said.
"Good, I will look forward to it. Now I really must go."
He watched the shapely rear in the figure-hugging red dress glide away from him across the room, with the heads of every man turning to follow her progress.

"Well done old boy you have certainly made a good impression on the lovely Linda; would have thought she was well out of your league."

"So would I." Was all Mat could think to reply, then he added. "Bloody hell I didn't get her number."

With Linda back in America, Mat focused on his racing. His meeting with the stunning young women had had a profound effect on him.

"Come on, superstar; I'm having a party tonight, it would have been my old man's birthday. There's a couple of smashers I've got lined up for us."

Reggie had said the week after the Playboy Club party.

"No thanks Reggie, think I'll get an early night want to be fighting fit for Zandvoort next weekend."

This new approach paid off as Mat won the following two races.

When he was home at Sefton Lodge, his mother noticed the change in her son.

"What's happened Mathew, you have seemed different the past two months; whatever it is it's certainly helping the race driving, you were brilliant at Thruxton last week."

"It's nothing, just not interested in partying or going out much anymore." Mat had been wanting to tell someone about his newfound love. *But is my mother the right person.*

With her own experience, when she had first met William, Mary could sense the reasons for her son's change of attitude.

"You know, when I first met your father, I felt like that. Have you met someone special?"

Then Mat couldn't help himself.

"Yes, I have, she is wonderful, but I don't know what to do about it, Linda is a famous actress and is living and filming in America...expect she has forgotten about me by now." He was breathless once he had finished.

His mother smiled.

"Is that the actress Linda Young, I've just been reading an interview with her in The Lady."

The whole family had stopped reading tabloid newspapers, all the lies and exaggerations about the Marshall and Cartland families insured their complete distrust of the press.

Excited, Mat picked up his mother's magazine and found the article.

His heart rate increased when he saw the beautiful women looking back at him.

In the interview, Linda had said that she intended to move back permanently to England after she finished her latest film. She planned to take a long break from filming, she missed the English countryside, and new friends she had recently made over there.

Mat's hand was shaking when he asked his mother.

"Do you think she is talking about me?"

"How would I know, but why don't you contact her and find out." Mary laughed, thinking of her early days of infatuation with William.

Five times in the following two days Mat phoned MGM studios trying to talk to Linda. Each time he was told that Miss Young was terribly busy and didn't take calls from strangers.

"But she knows me and will want to speak to me." He protested.

'We get hundreds of calls every day from young fans like you, and they all say that.'

"Mathew all these calls to America are costing me a fortune." His father had protested.

Disappointed, and frustrated Mat was relieved he had the following weekends race to focus his attention,

The Formula 2 Championship reached its penultimate round at the Brands Hatch late August Bank Holiday meeting, and a large crowd had gathered in glorious sunshine to watch the action. Mat sat in the Montague team caravan after practice studying his lap times, slightly disappointed he had only managed third quickest. There was always noise and laughter around the team, Reggie, the centre of attention, but Mat was suddenly surprised when the level outside the caravan door increased dramatically. One of Reggie's celebrity friends has probably turned up, he thought.

The caravan door opened and as he looked up, a voice said.

"Hello Mat, can I come in." For the second time, their eyes met and locked onto each other. The surprise and confused warmth radiating from Mats face made Linda smile.

"I... I thought you were still in America. Of course, you can come in." Mat stood up suddenly and hit his head on the caravan roof.

Linda laughed and moved towards him.

"Did that hurt," she said, lifting her hand to touch his head.

Mat took that hand in his, and they moved close together, almost magnetically their lips met, and he kissed her gently.

"I've wanted to do that from the moment I saw you." Whispered Mat.

"Me too." Linda's laughing reply.
A loud bang on the door interpreted their intimate moment.

"Come on Mat, get your gear on, the race starts in 20 minutes."

Still holding him, Linda said.

"I'm looking forward to seeing you race."

"Having you here. Now I don't care if I win or lose."

He didn't win, but after a close battle managed to finish third and keep his chances of winning the Championship alive.

However, after the race, with Linda at his side Mat received far more attention than the winner.

As he climbed out of the hot racing car, she came close and put her arms around him. This photograph of the sweaty handsome racing driver in his dirty race suit and beautiful actress in stunning red dress was front-page news in all the tabloid press on Monday morning.

After a shower and change of clothes, Mat rescued Linda from the clutches of Reggie, who was telling her about his plans to build a Formula one car.

"Ah," he said. "Here comes my superstar driver. Come on, Mat; we are all off to the Astor Club to celebrate another good race." Reggie was already into his second glass of champagne.

Mat moved to stand by his car with Linda by his side.

"I've promised to take Linda to dinner, so you go on ahead. We may catch up with you later." Looking at the beautiful happy women next to him, he knew they would not be in the Astor Club tonight.

The couple watched the eclectic mix of Ferraris, Porsches and Maserati's follow the Rolls Royce of Reggie up the steep hill and disappear out of the Brands Hatch Paddock.

Mat opened the passenger door of the old blue 3.8 Jaguar saloon to let Linda enter.

The pleasant rich smell of old leather invaded her senses.

"I thought you would have a flash car, like all your friends," Linda said as she elegantly slid her slim body into the worn, soft brown seat, her red dress barely covering the top of her tanned thigh.

"No, I prefer a British car with character, anyway, they are Reggie's friends, not mine. This Jag is my mother's car, her pride and joy," he said, trying not to stare at the shapely exposed leg.

There is a lot more to this young man than I expected. She thought.

Before they left Brands Hatch Mat had phoned The George Hotel in Sevenoaks to book dinner.

They said little on the fifteen-minute drive, Linda watching the gentle way Mat treated the driving of the Jaguar, all his actions were smooth and natural. She realised it was as if he were making love to the car, Linda shivered as she realised, she wanted those hands caressing her breasts, not this wooden steering wheel. As his hand moved to change gear, she felt an immense urge to grab it and plunge his long, slender figures into her groin...her whole body ached for him.

"Am I driving too fast for you." A concerned Mat asked, noticing her looking uncomfortable.

"No, I love your driving...just excited to be here with you." Linda reached over and gave his thigh a gentle squeeze.

Mat gave a slightly nervous giggle and thought. I am in a dream; generally, after a meeting, all I want to do is think about the race and work on my mistakes. Now, nothing in the world matters except being here with this beautiful woman.

It was a long simple dinner of steak and chips followed by Crepe Suzette, during the dinner Mathew Marshall and Linda Young told each other their life stories, both being honest about their past romantic attachments.

None of that was important to either of them, here and now all that counted. Often their fingertips were touching across the table as if charging the building passion between them. Their infatuation with each other was evident for all the other dinners to see.

"Shall I try to get us a room?" He nervously asks her once the waiter had taken away their dessert plates and the empty bottle of Mateus Rose.

"Of course, if you want to." Linda looked deep into his eyes as she replied.

When the hotel room door clicked shut behind them, and they were alone, panic suddenly seized Mat, what if I'm no good, she has far more experience than me.

Linda quickly quelled his doubts, holding his hand and pulling him towards the old four-poster bed, she removed his jacket, shirt, shoes and socks and pushed him back onto the bed as she unbuckled his belt and pulled off his trousers. Stepping away from him, he watched as she slid out of the blood-red dress and stood before him in black bra and matching pants.

"You look magnificent. God, how I want you." He managed to whisper.

"I can see that", she said laughing. " I want you to."

Linda moved to the bed and laid down beside him. He wrapped his arms around her and released the clasp on her bra freeing her firm smooth breasts, the breasts she had ached for him to caress.

With all clothes removed, they lay together, skin pressed hard against skin, the wonder of the moment reflected in their eyes. The heat between them rising and turning to sweat as their bodies moulded together. Linda let out an involuntary sigh as Mat's gentle fingers first found her left breast. Their lips parted, and tongues greedily sort each corner of their mouths. His fingers moved slowly down her smooth flat stomach, reaching her warm, pulsing mound, he cupped it in his hand and gently parted her wet lower lips, Linda could no longer control the loud moan now released from deep inside her.

Despite their aching desire for each other, their lovemaking was initially slow. Then the couples sudden urgency was loudly announced by their passionate actions, the protesting squeaking, and creaking from the ancient bed promoting banging on the walls from the room next door, and causing the loving couple to giggle like naughty school children.

His father had looked back on his first night with the women he loved and remembered it as the best night of his life. Later Mathew Marshall would do the same.

For once, the publicity surrounding the Marshall family was mostly positive.

With a famous film star and an aristocratic racing driver becoming a glamorous couple, the press was delighted, following Mathew and Linda whenever the public saw them together. There were, as always, a few negative headlines in the cheaper red tops. **Famous Actress and a racing driver-sounds like a car crash.**

Mathew's parents initially also had reservations.

"She's older than you, and is used to a glamorous life; anyway, she will soon want to go back to her Hollywood friends. Please don't get yourself too involved son."

These had been Williams reactions when he had first found out about his sons' new love.

"No Linda is staying here, she has had enough of all that life, and is moving back the England... permanently." Mat had replied defensively.

Mary was also worried that this beautiful woman would break her son's heart.

Their first meeting with Linda caused Lord and Lady Marshall to relax their reservations a little. They were both impressed with her natural open personality, her lack of pretensions and her evident love for their son.

"Mat has told me so much about you both; it is lovely to meet you. I am so lucky to have met your wonderful son." Had been her first greeting on meeting Mary and William. Completely relaxed in their company, she showed no reaction to Williams appearance.

They were sitting in the lounge at Sefton Lodge having afternoon tea when Mary asked.

"England must seem very quiet and dull after the life you have been used to Linda."

Taking hold of Mats hand, she had said.

"It has been the only life I've known since I was a girl, until the moment Mathew and I met I hadn't believed in love at first sight, but that meeting changed my life," She looked at the smiling handsome young man siting close beside her, and added.

"I realise how superficial and unimportant my life has been until now, whatever happens between us I will be staying in England from now on."

Mary looked at her husband and smiled; her experience all those years ago had been the same.

Chapter 21

The Inquest

"TIPPED FOR THE TOP" This had been the headline in an October edition of Autosport reviewing the 1971 Formula 2 season. In angry frustration, Cameron Cartland ripped the page from his copy and threw in into the dirty old topless oil drum that had acted as a waste bin since his grandfather's day.

The article referred to his cousin Mathew Marshall who had just finished second in the season's Formula 2 Championship. Cam couldn't bear to read any of it.

He has everything; now he even has a beautiful famous girlfriend. As usual, the article contained a photograph of Mat with Linda on his arm. How can I get anywhere near him? He will be world champion before I've even got passed Formula 3. These were his dark thoughts as he sat alone in the old workshop.

It had been a frustrating few months for Cam, the fallout from the Sutcliffe disaster taking up most of his time.

"Remember you may be able to lie to us about that strange man, but you have to tell the truth to a court." Had been his father's remarks as Cam, uncomfortable in his black suit, prepared to leave for the inquest.

The inquest of Danny had been exceedingly difficult; no one had any explanation as to why he had been at Gallows Wood that day. It was a nervous, and hesitant Cam as he swore on the bible when called to give his evidence. He said he could not explain his presence, other than the fact they had both survived the Sea Search Oil rig disaster.

Until Danny had turned up on the bakery doorstep a few days earlier, he had been sure Danny had died in the North Sea accident. He had no idea Danny had followed his car to the wood, or why.

But he had added, he was thankful that he had otherwise this inquest would have been for him, not Danny.

Cam had also been thankful that neither his father nor mother had attended the inquest.

The court case of Terry Thatcher for kidnapping and attempted murder would take place on November 17th, with the date fast approaching Cam was becoming extremely nervous, not looking forward to reliving that experience.

He still had the diamond but was not sure what to do with it. He had no idea how to sell it without prompting more trouble.

The Marshall family were desperately hoping that the fact Henry Sutcliffe had so far escaped British justice would mean Mary did not have to appear in court as she had no direct connection with the case against Thatcher. Terry Thatcher had remained faithful to his boss throughout his interrogation by not implicating him in the kidnapping and murder.

"He is a bloody fool, but he is so afraid of Sutcliffe, he knows if he spills his guts, Sutcliffe will find a way to have him killed." Inspector Hurst had confided to Mary Marshall when she had asked him if he thought she would have to give evidence.

"You weren't involved, and we can't get to Sutcliffe at the moment, so unless Cameron wants you to back up his story, it's unlikely you will have to appear in court Lady Marshall."

For the previous two months, Cam had been trying to re-start his car sales business; he had room for just two cars on the forecourt of the workshop where his grandfather's Shell petrol pumps had once proudly stood.

Cam was determined not to fall into the trap of helping his father in the bakery. He knew that once he did that, his parents would put pressure on him to keep working there, as his mother said so many times.

"You should give up all this foolishness with cars now; it's only brought you trouble. You can be safe and have a secure future working with your father."

He knew she was right, and on low days he came very close to giving in, but there was still a restlessness he could never deny. Although he knew the envy of his cousin was part of it, something inside would always kept his racing dreams alive.

He had arrived home at the bakery at 6 pm after a depressing day. A buyer he had lined up to purchase the Vauxhall Victor, 'only two lady owners Sir, and extremely low mileage.' Had turned up and offered Cam just £100 for it. Cam refused the offer as it was less, he had paid for it.

"Your friend Mike Coles has just phoned to talk to you. I hope he's not getting you mixed up in racing again," had been his father's comments.

Cam waited for his parents to leave the room before he phoned Mike back.

"Hi, Mike, what's up?"

"Hi Cam, I've had an idea about getting you back into racing if you are still interested."
Unable to keep the sudden excitement from his voice Cam said.

"You bet I am... but can't talk here; let's meet down the Railway Arms later."

Getting them, both half a bitter Mike said.

"Why don't we get you an entry for the Formula Ford Festival."

"What...that's only three weeks away and going back to Formula Ford won't do my career any good. Besides there are two other problems, I've no money and no car."

"The winner of this year's Festival is getting a test and sponsored race in a Formula 3 car for next season, so it's worth a shot. As for the car, I'm going to buy you a drive, just for this race meeting.

Cam was silent, unable to take in what he had just heard.

"I've had a great year with BMC, I've earned more money than I need, and I promised your grandfather I would try to look out for you."

Cam couldn't prevent his eyes watering as he said.

"Don't know what to say...but thank you, Mike. I haven't driven a Formula Ford all year, and there are some good young hot shoes out there this year."

"I know, but we can get a test in at Snetterton next week if you are up for it. I've already got a car organised for you."

Cam jumped up from his seat and threw himself into Mike's arms, much to the consternation of the locals in the pub.

Although as one old wag said.

"That bloody Cartland family has never been normal."

Cam zipped up his anorak to shut out the cold wind blowing towards him down the pits straight at Snetterton. He walked towards a small party gathered in front of the concrete pits, the pit walls flaking white paint, giving them a neglected feel on this grey Autumn morning.

Mike greeted him.

"Cam this is Ralph, and the car he has for you to drive."

Cam recognised the man as they shook hands, he was, short, around five foot five inches, not fat but chunky with a bald head and thick black beard.

Shaking hands, Cam said. "Hello Ralph, don't you work here at the racing school?"

"Good morning Cam, I did but Just started up on my own, looking forward to seeing what you think of my car. "

Noticing the Formula Ford for the first time Cam had a shock.

"That looks a bit like my cousins old Crusader."

"That's because it was... once, it's now the Apollo. I brought all the Crusader project, drawings, spares and one complete car, from the Marshals, I've been improving the design and changing the bodywork." Ralph replied.

"Hans Kruger has been a great help with the re-design of some of the suspension, think the car should be even quicker now. When Mike said you were looking for a Festival drive, I agreed to you giving it a try. All the quick drivers this year already have cars, so it will be good to see what you think of it."

Cam removed his coat and slid down into the cockpit of the Apollo. Immediately he felt at home, all the controls, steering wheel, and gear lever just the right distance and the brake and throttle pedals correctly aligned for his 'heel and toe' movements.

"Feels right." His only comment.

After three steady laps, he called back to the pits to get the tyre pressures checked.

Ralph leant over the side of the cockpit.

"How's it feels?"

"Good so far, but I've not tried extremely hard yet. Now I need to have a bit of a go."

Ten laps later he switched the engine off, and the silent red machine rolled back into the pit area.

The egger faces of Mike and Ralph appeared on either side of the cockpit.

"Well, what do you think of it now?" Mike asked. Ralph said nothing just looked worried.

"It's damp and slippery at the hairpin and through the Bomb hole, but it handles well. Most revs I have seen on a Formula Ford coming out of Riches. All I can say is I'm not surprised my bloody cousin won the Championship; this car is brilliant."

Ralph allowed himself a smile.

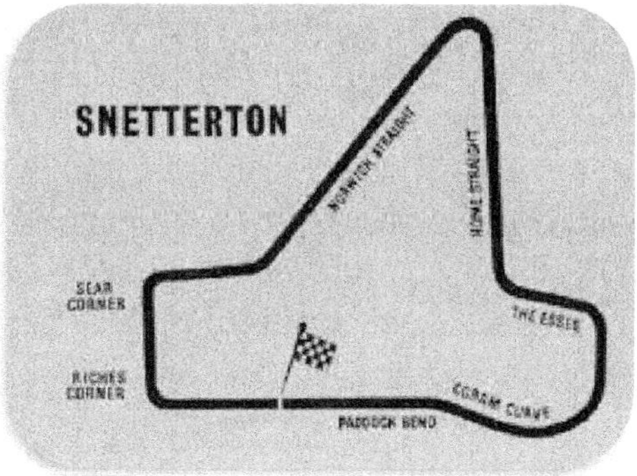

Race day brought a typical, for Norfolk, late October Snetterton day. The cold wind that blew directly down the home straight carried a misty drizzle that soaked everything it contacted.

The one hundred and five hopeful racing drivers huddled with their cars, close together on the rough concrete and grass that made up the Snetterton paddock. From a distance, they looked like a large group of Antarctic penguins huddling together for warmth.

The news that Cameron Cartland was returning to race in the Formula Ford Festival after his kidnapping ordeal created a great deal of interest in the motoring press. The fact that he would be driving a version of his cousin Mathew Marshall's old car added spice to the story.

"You ready for this?" Ralph asked him as they pushed the red Apollo into the collecting area before the start of the Festival Final.

Cam had driven carefully and very well all day, finishing second in his heat then third in his semi-final. He would take the fifth place on the grid for this all-important final race.

"Yes, of course, I am. I appreciate this chance you have given me Ralph; I'm not going to let you down.

The thirty drivers that had qualified for the final were some of the best Formula Ford drivers of the season, most young and desperate. Already two of the expected potential winners had crashed out in the semi-finals.

The Union Jack dropped, and thirty drivers released the clutch and floored the throttle pedal. In a crescendo of noise, with smoke and spinning wheels, the cars disappeared in a massive misty cloud of spray as they hurtled towards Riches Corner. You cannot win the race at the first corner...this had been Cam's mantra ever since his first race here in the fated Mini.

He had made a good start, but as he approached Riches, he braked fractionally earlier than usual. Two cars on a kamikaze mission hurtled passed him the drivers missed their braking points and charged into the two Formula Ford cars in front of Cam. Instinct took him through the carnage, and he emerged from the corner in second place, glancing in the mirrors he smiled, noticing the accident had delayed most of the field. Fortunately, by the time they reached Riches on the second lap, the marshals had done a magnificent job of moving the wrecked cars off the track. Cam breathed a sigh of relief when he saw there were no yellow flags to slow the cars down.

For the following ten laps he and his fellow leading competitor Australian Larry Hopkins exchanged places at the head of the field, by slipstreaming each other down the long Norwich Straight they drew well clear of the third-place driver. It was apparent that with only two laps to go the winner would be Cam or Larry.

In the car Cam felt utterly relaxed, he had realised early in the race that he could drive quicker than Larry through the long Coram Curve which leads onto the finish line. On the final lap, Cam hung back slightly as they came out of the Esses, allowing him to enter Coram much faster than Larry.

On the outside of the corner, he pulled alongside and with his car carrying more speed the red Apollo flashed across the finish line one car length ahead. Cam Cartland had won the Formula Ford Festival, and more importantly, a sponsored Formula 3 drive for the following season.

Chapter 22

The world changes for Mat.

Life for Mathew Marshall could not get better. Linda had quickly moved in with him to his cottage on the Sefton estate, and apart from the usual press intrusions, the couple remained idyllically happy.
They had spent a wonderful Christmas and New Year with his parents, sister Florence and Silvia who had become mellow in recent years.

"Your mother is like a different person these days." A delighted Mary said to William.

"Do we have to go to Reggie's party tonight? I'm feeling exhausted now."
Linda had said as they arrived back at their cottage after a long walk with their dogs around the woods of the Sussex Downs overlooking Sefton Manor.

Linda had always wanted a dog, but until moving to Sussex, her lifestyle hadn't made owning one possible. Now she embraced the country life and loved her two dark brown Springer Spaniels. She had never been happier.

"I'm afraid we do darling, I need to show my face, and everyone always wants to be introduced to

'The famous Linda Young'. We will just stay a short while, I promise, and can catch the 10 pm train back here to Sussex."

Tomorrow we can lay in bed all day if you like." Mat added as he wrapped his arms around her soft, smooth shoulders.

"Sounds like a fair deal." She replied, turning in his arms, and snuggling into his chest.

Reggie had organised the party to attract potential sponsors for his ambitious plans to run Mat in Formula One the following season. It was a big expensive, jump from Formula 2 to Formula 1.

"Having you as part of the team is our best asset. Every one of our potential future sponsors wants to meet you."

"Don't think I want to be called an asset...and besides, I may be busy time with more important things."

"What could be more important than me racing in Formula One." said an indignant Mat, rather more sharply than he had intended.

Linda gave him one of her 'little girls lost' smiles, usually reserved for the camera. Suddenly the penny dropped.

"You're pregnant! Mat exclaimed.

"Yes...well I think so, I intended to wait until I went to the doctors next week before I told you, but I'm so excited, and thought you would like to know."

Mat wrapped his arms tighter around her. He had tears in his eyes when he said.

"You know that saying, my heart is bursting with happiness." Mat whispered. "Well I now understand why someone would say that."

Then added.

"Your right darling this is far more important than bloody motor racing."
She gave him a long gentle kiss, and they giggled as joyful tears ran down to their lips. Linda broke the moment.

"Well, of course, I think it is important... but so is your dream to be World Champion. We will go to Reggie's party tonight, and I'll charm the socks off anyone we meet."

"I'd rather have their wallets."

The evening had gone perfectly, Linda, the usual centre of attention, effortlessly charmed all around her.

"You are the luckiest sod in the world," Reggie said to Mat as they both stood and watched the happy, stunning women.

"I know, I have to pinch myself every day." Then looking at his Tag watch said.

"Dam. We are too late to catch the 10 pm train now. I promised Linda we would catch it."

"Don't worry, old boy; you can take my Aston." Reggie was in an expansive mood. With his arm around his star driver, he added.

"Look after the beautiful old girl and look after Linda as well." He laughed at his joke.

The car, Reggie's pride and joy, was a burgundy 1968 Aston Martin DB6. The number plates
REG18, Reggie had removed two parts of figure eight to spell his name.

"Are you ok to drive?" A concerned Linda asked Mat. "I'm sure Reggie would let us stay here tonight."

"Yes, I'm fine, I've only had two glasses of champagne all evening, and I promised to give you a day in bed tomorrow so let's go."

The happy couple set off, waving their goodbyes,

"Thank you, darling; you knocked them all out tonight." Mat said as he guided the Aston south onto the A3 road.

There was no reply
With the six-cylinder engine purring Linda had fallen asleep before they had left London.

Cruising down the A3 at a steady, effortless, 60mph Mat glanced across at the sleeping girl next to him and smiled, soft lights from the Aston's instrument panel illuminating her natural beauty.

Eric Evans had passed his motorcycle licence test one week earlier, that evening he had been doing a shift in the bar at the Rose and Crown pub in Woking to earn extra money. During the day he worked as a motorcycle mechanic in his father's village garage. Eric was enjoying the ride home on this dry moonlit night, as his 250 Honda reacted to his every move, filling him with confidence.

The two fast bends he approached now had become his favorites on this familiar ride home; he banked the Honda to the right feeling pleasure as he powered through the curve, now for the left-hand sweeper taken fast just like his hero Mike Hailwood. He leant the bike to the left into the corner, but this time one inch too far, the Honda's footrest caught on the black Tarmac and instantly unbalanced the motorcycle. Eric's automatic steering correction turned the front wheel of the bike to the right and onto the crown of the road.

Relaxed, but perfectly alert, Mat eased the elegant Aston into the fast-right-hand bend. His cat-like reactions were no help when the single bright white light hurtled towards him. Later, when he tried to recall the events of the crash, it was fortunate that his final memory of the accident was when a large black shape crashed through the windscreen of the stricken Aston Martin.

Just a passenger in the accident as his Honda hit the grill of the approaching car Eric's body was thrown up over the bonnet and with the force of a battering ram burst through the windscreen of the Aston Martin. The closing speed of the two machines had been 120mph as Eric's helmeted body and the head of Linda Young smashed together,

Linda's beauty became just a memory, and young Eric's future ended. Both bright young lives instantly extinguished.

Mat, hit in the face by the boots of the hapless rider, was knocked unconscious. Out of control the stricken Aston Martin spun around and slid wildly along the left-hand grass verge until its tail contacted a massive four-hundred-year-old oak. There was a whaling metallic shriek of protest as the car wrapped itself around the unyielding tree truck.

After the violent noise and action, a sudden, still silence, enveloped the scene. Only the visual evidence of wild destruction betrayed the recent catastrophic event.

It was after midnight before the phone rang in the hall at Sefton Lodge. Mary had not yet fallen asleep, calls this time of night never brought good news, she rushed downstairs to answer it.

"Before the policewoman had an opportunity to tell her, she said. "It's about Mathew, isn't it."?

The call she had received in the war about Williams crash more than thirty years ago remembered as if it were yesterday.

"Has he been burnt." Her next qucstion.

The Marshall family activities were always newsworthy for the British press, but of course, this tragic event escalated things to a new level. The fame of Linda Young ensuring that this time the whole world wanted to know details of the devastating accident.

Mathew Marshall had been unconscious for two days after the crash, his mother always at his bedside. With the invasive press intrusions, Lord William decided he would stay at home. Their daughter Florence flew home from a modelling assignment in France to be with him. Neither had much to say as they sat quietly waiting for news from the hospital. Florence was holding tightly to her father's, hard scarred, hand.

Feeling the warmth of his beautiful daughter close beside him, William was thankful she had remained a level-headed, loving girl. He felt relief that the early praise and fame had not affected her and that they had many good friends who were doing their best to protect them both from the hounds of the press.

Mary was dozing at the bedside when a whispered voice altered her.

"Where is Linda?" Mat had opened his eyes and was looking directly at his mother. Her tears and desperate grip on his hand gave him the only answer he needed.

"Why....what happened, were his first confusing questions; but there was no one to give him any answers.
All he wanted now was to go back to sleep and never wake up.

A day later, two police officers arrived at the hospital to interview him about the accident. But with visible frustration Mat realised there was extraordinarily little he could tell them.

"Just remember driving normally...not fast. Then a large black shape was smashing through the windscreen; I've no idea where from, but after that I can remember nothing."

"Had you been drinking Mr Marshall." asked the younger police officer.

"Of course, he hadn't." Mary had intervened.

"Just a couple of glass of Champagne much early in the evening. Linda can ..." Mat had responded quietly, through sobs that soon escalated into uncontrollable tears.

"Get out now...you bloody people can see he is not ready for this." Mary's pent-up anger erupted.

Incredibly, apart from a concussion, Mathews only suffered two other physical injuries. These were three broken left fingers when the impact of Eric's boots crushed his hand onto the Aston Martins steering wheel, and a whiplash neck injury caused by the stricken Aston's smash into the oak tree.

Feeling the despair, and the helplessness of loss, was a new experience for Mat. Until that night at 11.05 pm on the A3, his life had always been so enjoyable; comfortable almost, his confidence unbounded.

Now, losing Linda, and as he confided to his mother a possible son or daughter, his confidence had been destroyed.

Mary, of course, had unfortunate long experience of loss and knew the only healer was time. But then she thought, even that never heals. The sadness always lurks in the back of your mind, ready to spring out. Often when you least expect it. She had desperate concern about how her son would cope with Linda's death.

Physically Mat healed quickly, within two months his head, neck, and broken fingers healed, but inside he felt emotionally empty; nothing seemed important anymore. Despite encouragement from his family, and constant requests from Reggie, he refused to go near the racing team.

"Don't think I am ever going to drive a racing car again." He had announced to his parents a month after returning home from the hospital.

The situation was made much worse by the attitude of the tabloid press. Gleefully the reporters dredged up the old story of how Mathew Marshall's uncle David had murdered his beautiful girlfriend. While not saying Mat had done the same to Linda, their implied headlines had held Mat responsible for her death.

One of the sensational headlines had been.

Racing Driver Mathew Marshall had been drinking at a party before the accident that killed his girlfriend, famous actress Linda Young".

When Lord Marshall lodged his protests, the general response was a shrug of shoulders and the usual comment

"It's what sells our newspapers." The editor was forced by considerable pressure from Reggie Montague and a host of southern MP's, to issue an apology for their misleading headline. Unfortunately, it was no consolation for Mathew.

The morning after the accident news of it had reached Burlham.

"Have you heard what has happened." Cameron's father said when Cam came down for breakfast.

"There is never any good news, so I've given up listening to the radio or reading the newspaper." a disinterested Cam replied.

"Well, you will certainly want to hear this news, your cousin Mathew Marshall has been badly hurt in a car crash, and his actress girlfriend has been killed,"

Peter told him bluntly. Peter later felt twinges of guilt that he had momentarily been pleased to see that the Marshall's were having some bad luck for a change. He would go to St Mary's church later to apologise for his weakness.

"You had better ring your Aunt Mary to see how he is."

Cam, after the initial shock, like his father had a few seconds of pleasure at the misfortune of his cousin. Then he surprised himself, feeling genuine concern, the racing rivalry with Mat suddenly seeming unimportant.

Chapter23

The Aftermath

The cousins didn't meet, but Mary continued to keep Cam informed on her son's recovery.

It hadn't taken Cam long, once the racing season started, to establish himself as a leading player in the 1972 Shell Formula 3 Championship. His prize for winning the Formula Festival had been a supported drive with the new team, GRD.

The GRD proved to be an excellent car, the small team, mainly made up of ex-Lotus employees, focusing all their efforts on Cam when they discovered he had a natural ability for improving the handling and set-up of the car.

Life for him had completely turned around over the previous six months, and he couldn't help thinking about the massive change in fortunes between him and his cousin.

It was May, the morning after he returned home after victory in a race at Cadwell Park, that he received a phone call from his Aunt Mary.

"Hello Cam, I have been reading in Autosport about your successes this season. Well done."

Then she added, "I am anxious about Mathew, and was hoping you would be able to find some time to visit us later this week."

Cam knew he would always be in his Aunts debt; she had tried to help his racing career when no one else seemed to care. It certainly wasn't her fault Henry Sutcliffe had turned out to be a crook, but he had no wish to go down to Sussex. Despite being close friends when they were younger, in recent years Cam's resentment of his cousin, and his seemingly charmed life had run deep.

"Of course, I'll come, Aunt, if you think it will help." was his reluctant reply.

On the following Thursday Cam drove his E. Type Jaguar to Sussex.

"Lovely to see you Cam; Mat has shut himself away in his cottage and rarely comes out these days. We just don't know how to help him," his Aunt Mary said when she met Cam in the drive of Sefton Lodge.

"He spends most of his days just sitting in the cottage. He will not talk to anyone; our doctor says there is nothing he can do to help him, and that Mathew will have to find his own way out of the depression. But I'm afraid it's getting worse."

Cam went across to the cottage and knocked gently on Mat's door. There was no answer.

"Come on, Mat, its Cam, I know you are in there. " Knocking again,
loudly this time as he shouted through the door. "I just want a chat."
After a while Mat opened the door a couple of inches. His appearance shocked Cam.

"Christ, what have you done to yourself." He said, seeing his unshaven, scruffy cousin.

Through half-closed eyes, Mat replied.

"Good to see you too... Come to bloody gloat, have you."

"No, of course not. Your mother is very worried about you; she asked me to come, I wouldn't have come otherwise. Only doing it for her." His reply was sharp, then added quietly.

"Sorry to hear about the accident Mat...and about Linda."

They just looked at each other for a full minute; before Mat opened the door fully.

"Thanks. You had better come in if you are not going away. Do you want a drink? I've got beer or whisky."

"Just a cup of tea please." Cam replied.

They sat in silence for a while the steady ticking of an old wall clock the only indication of time; Cam held a steaming mug of tea, Mat a bottle of beer. Eventually, Mat said.

"I wasn't drunk, you know, it wasn't my fault...I loved her, the first time I've ever really loved anyone." Mats tears were flowing freely now.

The sudden breakdown took Cam by surprise, but he could easily relate to his cousins' emotion.

"I know, it's the bloody press. Everyone knows that poor lad went round the corner too fast, I heard the police found marks on the road where his bikes footrest dug into it. The bastard hacks have always had it in for both our families. They are never happy unless one of us cocks up."

With Cam's sympathetic response Mat recovered some of his composure and began to talk.

"Yes, I know you're right, but some of the things they print...it does hurt.

I couldn't believe half that stuff they have written about you in the past. You're a bloody diamond smuggler I hear."

Cam smiled and decided not to protest his innocence.

"How about a beer now?" Mat added.

After the awkward start, the boys began to tell each other details of the tragic events that had befallen them. Things they had never been able to tell anyone else, but Cam kept quiet about his diamond.

It almost felt they were back to those carefree early teenage days when they had enthusiastically told each other their mutual dream to be World Champion, racing drivers. It was the year they helped their grandfather when his car, with Mike Cole driving, won the European Touring Car Championship.

"Well, now at least you can reach our dream. I hear you are winning Formula 3 races and have already got a drive lined up in Formula 2 next season. You're on your way to Formula One Cam."

Cam hesitated.

"Yes, I hope so, but there's still a long way to go.

Anyway, winning the world championship without beating you will not be the same. It's time you got back on the tracks before it's too late." He said, smiling at his cousin.

For the first time since the accident on the A3, Mathew Marshall smiled but didn't rise to the bait.
After a short pause, he replied.

"Think I'm finished with racing; I've already told Reggie to get himself another driver."

"Rubbish! You can't let this finish you off, I didn't know Linda but doesn't sound like the type of girl that would want you to give up.

I watched your replacement driver race at Thruxton, and he's not a patch on you. The crash was just an unlucky accident; everyone knows it wasn't your fault."

Cam suddenly had a flash of inspiration. After a pause, he added.

"I'm driving with Mike Coles at Le Mans this year, I'm sure I could get the team to add you as the third driver, it's an all British effort you would fit in well. There would be no pressure if you don't enjoy it, Mike and I can do most of the driving."

Mathew felt surprised by his cousin's concern, and with the familiar, excited, butterflies that rose in his stomach; the spark of desire to return to racing ignited.

The relief to William and Mary Marshall of their son's partial recovery from his depression tempered only by the thought of him driving racing cars once more.

In Formula One so far this season, three drivers had been killed, but both knew, first-hand, about this addiction to speed and danger, and they also knew their genes had passed the passion directly to their son.

"Of course, if we can get him on the team, it will be great publicity for our sponsors." Mike Cole had been delighted when Cam asked the question. "I'll phone Alan Greenham right away."

The car Mike and Cam would be driving at Le Mans was fulfilling the dream of Yorkshireman Alan Greenham. Alan had been taken to the race as a teenager by his father. It was the year that the Cartland Jaguar had heroically finished second. His love affair, many would say obsession, with Le Mans, began then. An amateur racing driver himself, he ran the successful family sand quarry and haulage company that had been started by his father soon after the war.

In 1971 Alan had persuaded fellow young racer and fledgling car designer Jimmy Murray to design a car based around the Ford-Cosworth engine.

For 1972 a change of rules (many thought a deliberate move by the French organisers to ensure a French victory for their Matra cars) prevented the larger capacity engined Ferraris, Fords and Porsche from entering the race.

"By heck, she does look grand Jimmy." Had been Alan's first comment on seeing the finished car. A proud Yorkshireman the pea-green car displayed prominently, on both sides, a large white rose.

Early in 1972 after thousands of hours of hard work by the small team, the Greenham Special was tested for the first time by Mike Cole at Snetterton.
Mike had received a phone call out of the blue from Alan in November the previous year.

"How'd you do, Mike." He said when Mike answered the phone.

"I'm building a new race car. What do you think about driving for me at Le Mans next year? Followed your career when you were with Frank Cartland, that man was me, hero."

When he heard that remark, Mike couldn't say no.

"The car handles well, and it's quick," was Mike's assessment after that first test in the Greenham Special.

"Of course, if we can get him on the team, it will be great publicity for our sponsors." Mike Cole had been delighted when Cam asked if Mathew Marshall could be added as third driver.

"I'll phone Alan Greenham right away."

Reggie Montague had also been delighted when he heard Mat was preparing to start racing again. The young guy they had put in Mat's car after his road accident did not live up to his Formula 3 reputation. In four races so far, he had managed to crash twice causing extensive damage to the car. "Wouldn't bloody mind the money if he was quick, but he will never have the speed of Mat Marshall." Reggie had complained to his team manager.

"When will you be ready to drive for me again?" Reggie had phoned Mat as soon as he had heard the news that Mat might be driving at Le Mans.

"Let's see how this Le Mans race goes first, I'll decide after that," had been Mats guarded reply.

Testing the car at Silverstone for the first time, Mat nervously waited for Mike Coles and Cam to finish their laps. He was aware of the apprehension in the team; no one knew how he would cope with the situation.

"The car is a joy to drive, the same sort of power as your F2 car. Just take it easy and enjoy yourself." Cam had said as he helped the mechanics ease Mat into the driving seat.

What am I doing this for, Mat asked himself as he sat alone in the Greenham Special staring at the concrete expanse of the Silverstone pit straight ahead of him? His heart was pounding furiously, and a trickle of sweat ran down his back. Taking a deep breath, he made himself relax, pushed the small gear lever into first, he released the clutch, and trundled along the pit road and out onto the full Silverstone track.

For three, agonisingly slow, laps he had to force his right leg to press the accelerator pedal down, each time he turns the leather-covered steering wheel to the right into the high-speed Copse corner, Mat lifted his foot as he felt a twinge in his left hand. He was back on the A3. His hands-on the narrow wooden steering wheel of the Aston Martin turning into that right-hand bend.

Then, the fourth time he turned the agile Greenham Special into Copse corner, instead of fear he felt satisfaction as he guided the car to the apex and drew the acre, with his right foot hard down on the throttle, the racing car drifted to the outside of the bend. Suddenly he realised he wanted to do this again, only faster next time. Six more laps and his times were within a second of his teammates.

Car owner Alan Greenham was the first to greet him as the car rolled back into the Silverstone pits.

"Champion job Mat will be delighted to add you to our team...if you want to drive for me."

"Yes, I would like that Mr Greenham." his immediate, smiled reply.

Mathew Marshall was going to be a racing driver once more.

Neither cousin had been to Le Mans before, so the sheer size of the place took them by surprise.

The vast open countryside, sandy, sparsely grassed soil, mixed with the sudden outcrops of tall dense green pines of the Sarthe Forest added to its 'otherworldly' atmosphere.

"Can see why everyone brings bikes here got get around. The place is massive," had been Cam's first reaction.

"Yes, it's certainly big isn't it, you could fit ten Brands Hatch's in here." Responded Mat as he looked up at the vast concrete grandstand.

It had been a great relief when the press began focusing on his racing again after the announcement that he would be racing at Le Mans. The fact he would be sharing a car with his promising cousin

Cameron Cartland and the already well-known Mike Coles added to the interest.

Thousands of British fans had flocked into the circuit to cheer on 'their', plucky little team as they faced 24hours of high speed, drama, and danger.

Chapter 24

Reconciliation at Burlham

"It's a shame that it always seems to take a tragedy to bring our families together."
Mary said to William as she drove them back from visiting her brother at Burlham.

The last time Mary had visited her brother had been for the funeral of their father almost six years previously. Only Mathews accident had promoted Peter to speak to her. The first time for over a year.

She had wanted to take flowers to her parent's graves in St Mary's cemetery, so they went directly to the churchyard. William felt a twinge of sadness as they walked up the old narrow white chalk path to the windswept cemetery. Although his mother was still alive, he knew he would have very few happy memories of his parents. He knew how much Mary continued to miss her father.

He watched from a respectful distance as Mary with head bowed stood over the grey headstone of Frank Cartland's grave. Looking at the name etched into the stone Mary's thoughts were of the passed happier days she had shared with her father, once more she ached to be that little girl again, and feel his strong, sinuous arms around her.

Turning to re-join her husband, she thought how glad she was her father wasn't here to experience the latest family tragedy.

"Let's go and meet my brother." She said, taking Williams arm.

As usual, it had been a tense meeting between brother and sister, they had never been close, but their differences had been compounded by what Peter had seen as Mary's interference in his son's life.

Now, with the latest terrible events, they at least agreed to make up and parted on good terms.

"Peter, you and Grace must come down to see us soon; you are welcome to stay at any time."

She had said as they parted.

Knowing Peter rarely travelled further than Cambridge, Grace had expected this response.

"I'm sure we will, one day, but it is difficult for me to leave the bakery. The villagers need fresh bread every day."

Driving back William was quiet for some time, the deep pulse from the Jaguar engine the only sound. Then he said, something he had also said in the past.

"Don't you sometimes envy your brother. They have such a simple, normal life just living quietly and baking bread most of the day."

Mary lent over and squeezed his thigh.

"No, not for a minute. Besides it's not always quiet and peaceful for Peter and Grace, the press gives them a hard time when one of our boys get into trouble."
William noticed the "our" in her reply; he could sense his wife's growing attachment to Cameron, knowing how guilty and responsible she felt after all his troubles, and her involvement, with Henry Sutcliffe.

Remembering that man always brought bile to William's throat, hatred was not a normal feeling for him, but that man was the one exception.

"Let's call in at Brooklands on the way back." He said.
"Lovely idea." His wife replied.

Back at Burlham, Peter and Grace Cartland were having later afternoon tea in the front room.

"It would be nice to have a day out to visit your sister in Sussex, wouldn't it Peter." Grace tentatively suggested.

"I don't think it is a good idea; they are not our sort, anyway I can't leave the bakery or my church duties." His response was sharp. Then he added, "it would be different if our son had taken an interest in the bakery. Our customers will all go to the new supermarket in Feltham if I'm not here to supply them with bread."

Grace didn't respond immediately, then twenty years of pent up frustrations were released like an explosion into Peter's face.

"What's wrong with you, Peter Cartland, you never want to do anything or go anywhere. You live in the past, most of the shops in the village are closing, even the butcher closed last week. It's time you woke up, we've sent men to the moon, and you still think it's 1950.

At least our son is following his dreams and trying to make something of his life.

You are scared of your own shadow."

It was the most she had said in their twenty years of marriage.

The loud, deep tick of the grandfather clock standing in the hall all that broke the ensuing long silence

"I've got matters to attend to at the church,"
Peter said as he got up and left the house.

Sometime ago Grace had discovered her husband's crossdressing secret, no matter how careful he had been her clothes were often not where she had left them. It was not a secret she could share with anyone and didn't want to confront him with it.

It was a certainty that none of the ladies at the Burlham Woman's Institute would understand.

Chapter25

Le Mans

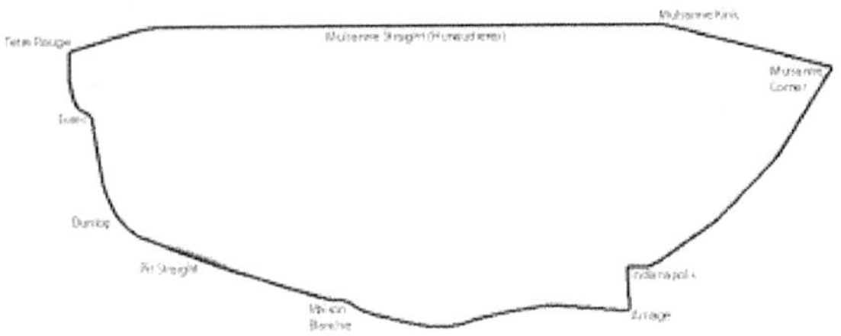

After Thursday practice the three drivers sat in the team caravan behind the Le Mans pits. To qualify for the race, all drivers had to complete at least three laps and produce a time within twenty per cent of the leading car in their class.

Mike Coles being the team leader, started the de-briefing.

"That was a satisfying session we have all qualified within five seconds of each other.

I will always remember what your grandfather told me when his team raced here in the fifties. He had said take an average of the lap times of both drivers and add ten seconds. That should be the pace to aim for in the race. I know there are three of us, but we should still work out that average time.

"That was nearly twenty years ago. Do you think ten seconds is too much?" Mat had asked.

"It probably is these days; I think we should aim for five seconds," Mike replied.

Cam had remained quiet during the conversation, his lap times had been slightly the slowest of the three, and he had been disappointed not to be able to match his cousin.

Cam's old doubts about not being as quick a racing driver as Mat came back to the surface.

Mat noticing his cousins discomfort said.

"Are you ok with that Cam. Conditions were not so good when you had your practice, so I think you would have been quicker than me otherwise."

While he did not believe Cam was a quicker driver than him, Mat would forever feel gratitude to his cousin for pulling him away from his spiraling depression.

"Yes, that sounds fine to me, we can all do that time." Replied Cam.

At 4 pm on Saturday the tricolor dropped and Mike, being the senior driver, started the race in the Greenham Special.

The cacophony of sound from fifty-five racing engines hurt the ears of those who had left out their earplugs as the multi-colored swarm of clamoring cars hurtled around the Dunlop curve and out of sight, heading towards the Esses.

The sudden quiet that descended on the pit area caused a wave of nervous chatter as thousands of spectators, mechanics, managers, drivers, and hangers-on released they had been holding their collective breathes. Ten minutes later the blast of sound began again as the leading cars sped through the pit straight.

For the next twenty-four hours, there would be no escape from the shattering noise of racing engines.

Mike settled into a good rhythm, lapping consistently within a second of the agreed pace.

After three hours the Greenham pit prepared for the first fuel pit stop and driver change.

Cam was ready to take over as Mike arrived at their pit.

"The car is running perfectly but watch out for the oil at Arnage. One of the Porsches has blown up and spread it all over the track."

"Will do," Cam replied as he jumped into the car.

Within two laps he was lapping quicker than Mike.

"What's he doing, bloody kid, is not sticking to the agreed lap times." The team manager shouted.
Give him a slower signal."

For two more laps, Cam ignored the signals, setting a lap three seconds quicker than his practice best. Then he eased back to the agreed lap times. The rest of his session went to plan, and after two hours he pitted for fuel and to hand over to Mat.

"What the hell was that about," Mike shouted at him as Mat roared away on his driving stint.

"Just wanted to show I could go as quick as Mat."

"You're a bloody fool; this isn't about you; this is a team race; it's time you grew up."

Red faced Mike turned away and stormed out of the pits.

Cam was shocked; it was the first time he had seen Mike lose his temper.

Mat drove his stint well and consistently. When Mike jumped in to start his second drive, the Greenham Special was in seventh place. As expected, the works Matra team cars filled the leading three positions.

Mat went to the team caravan to grab a snack and a few hours rest. Cam was sitting alone as he walked in.

"Hi, Cam things are going well...touch wood." He said, tapping the table.

"Yes, but think I cocked things up, not sticking to the plan for a few laps."

Mat sat down next to him.

Cam added. "Sorry Mat, I've really upset Mike, just wanted to beat your time."

"This isn't a race between us. I'm sure that might come in the future, but for now, we have to work together."

"Yes, I know, I just get carried away sometimes."

Getting up he said.

"Better go and see how the race is progressing. Going to apologise to Mike when you do your next stint in the car.

Both looked up as new sound started; it was like the patter of little feet running across the roof of the caravan. "Sod it...hear that, it's starting to rain," Cam said.

Throughout the night, the rain continued. The team worked well, the drivers all being sensible, not pushing the car passed its limit.

With dawn breaking the rain stopped as Mat handed over to Mike.

One of the Matras had crashed in the night, and the leading Alfa had blown its engine. Amazingly the small British team had moved up to the fifth place.
8 am Sunday, and light rain had started again adding to the early morning mist to restrict visibility.

"Mike's ten seconds late." the team manager shouted to the Greenham pit. As he did so, the flashing yellow lights came on, and a claxon sounded indicating there had been an accident.

"It must be Mike," Cam said to Mat as they stood on the pit counter straining tried eyes to see down the road towards the White House Corner.

Unfortunately, Cam was right; it was Mike. The Greenham Special had been part of a massive accident.

Travelling at maximum speed Mike began to lap a slower Ferrari GTB4 at the slight kink on the straight between Mulsanne and Indianapolis corners, the thick forest bordering the track on either side. The Ferrari moved left to take its line as Mike had already committed to overtake before the curve, his car hit the rear corner of the Ferrari at unabated speed and flew 100 meters over the barriers into the trees. A following driver later said, 'the car spun into the air like a helicopter".

The small British team were in complete disarray. By the time the team had managed to find out what had happened, Mike had been extracted from the wreak and critically injured, rushed by ambulance to Centre Hospialier Le Mans.

Over an hour had passed before Cam and Mat piled into the Bentley of Alan Greenham to drive the four miles to the hospital.

Mike died ten minutes before they reached him.

Both young men were in complete shock; even their recent personal experiences of death did not prepare them for the terrible feelings they both now suffered. It was the first time a driver they classed as a friend had lost his life racing. Poor Alan Greenham was in despair, saying.

"It's all my fault something must have broken on the car. Mike never makes mistakes."

When asked later, none of the three could recall their long trip back to England.

Mary had been avidly following the race on the radio, tuning into the BBC for the hourly broadcast updates.

'Isn't it wonderful." She had said to William after the 7 am bulletin. "They are in fifth place."

"It is dear," was his brief reply. The early morning pain from his finger joints his immediate concern.

When she tuned in again just after 8 am on Sunday, the first news she heard was…

'In the last few minutes, there has been a big accident. Unfortunately, the plucky little Greenham Special appears to be involved; we will bring you more news when we receive it. With eight hours still to go the Matras are still leading...' Mary rushed upstairs to tell William, she had an urgent need to share her worry.

In Burlham Grace Cartland had also been keeping up to date with the news from Le Mans, but not with the same enthusiasm as Mary Marshall. Results didn't matter to her, just the safety of her son.

"Their car has crashed." She bluntly told her husband when he came back for breakfast after the early-morning bake.

"Don't tell me Cam has hurt himself again," had been Peter's response.

"They didn't say what happened or who was driving."

"I knew this would end in disaster getting mixed up again with those Marshall's was stupid."

If he had sat in the kitchen of Ivy Cottage more than twenty-five years earlier, he would have heard his mother saying the same thing.

"You had better wait by the phone; I'm going for a walk." He added.

Mary had been more proactive; she immediately rang the news desk at the Daily Mail, she knew their motoring correspondent Donald Benson would be at the circuit covering the race and should be filling a story.

"All we know from Donald at the moment, Lady Marshall is that it was a serious crash."

"Do you know who was driving."

"Yes, it was Mike Coles." When she heard that news, she felt joy and sudden relief. "Mike was driving, not Mat or Cam." She shouted out. William moved to take her in his arms.

Both stood, quietly, feeling guilty in their relief.

"You had both better ring your families." A tearful Alan Greenham told the boys as they stood outside the hospital, "I will make arrangements to get Mike home."

Matt and Cam did as he suggested, almost on automation. Both sets of parents were, of course, relieved to hear their son's voices, their relief tempered with their horror learning of Mikes death.

Dry eyes were in short supply during Mike Coles funeral, and afterwards at the Cambridge, Newmarket Road cemetery.

Over one hundred people have gathered to pay their respects to the popular young man.

"Your son was the best friend I will ever have. I am so sorry Mrs Coles. A tearful Cam told Iris Coles.

"Thank you, Cam, Mike thought a lot of you. He always said he owed your grandfather everything, without him Mike would still have been a garage mechanic." There was no irony in her voice, just sadness. She added.

"You know Mike wouldn't want us all to be sad, he died driving racing cars; the one thing he loved in life."

What a wonderful lady thought Cam, how I wish my parents could feel the same way.

They had not attended the funeral.

When he arrived home sympathy was in short supply at the bakery.

"Very sorry to hear about your friend Mike, he seemed like a nice lad." Was his mother's contribution.

"One day, you might learn how utterly pointless this racing madness is. It could have been you in that dam car." The expected response from his father.

Cam didn't make a comment. Now, two weeks after the accident, he was still in shock. Mike was the last person he had expected to crash. If race driving can take Mike Coles, none of us are safe; this had been the thought that went through the minds of at least ten of the racing drivers that had gathered around his graveside.

Although Mat had attended Mike's funeral, his parents couldn't face the media scrum they knew they would have to face. When a somber Mat returned to Sussex, he sat in the lounge at Sefton Lodge with his parents and sister.

"Not sure how much more I can take, losing Linda, and now Mike." He said, the comment was not directed at anyone in particular.

No one replied for ten seconds, then Florence said.

"You can't give up now, your dream has always been to be World Champion driver, and we all support you. Linda nor Mike would want you to stop." Then she added, "Don't we..."

Looking at her parents as she said this.

After a short pause, it was William who spoke next.

"Your mother and I both lost family and close friends in the war, but we couldn't give up, we didn't have that luxury. Looking back I know we would have carried on with our dangerous jobs even if we hadn't been forced to by the circumstances.

Your mother and I love you both, and would never try to stop you doing the things you love. You are probably unfortunate to have inherited your adventurous spirt from us."

It was the longest speech Mathew and Florence had ever heard their father make.

Mary filled the sudden silence.

Holding Williams, scared hand, she said.

"Your father is right. In the past, our choices have brought low times, but they have also brought many more good times, I have no regrets, only of course sadness now, Mathew, for what you have to suffer recently.

Whatever you decide, we will support you, but give yourself a bit of time before you make a decision you might regret."

"Your grandmother has been ringing ever since your accident, why don't you go to France for a while and stay with her, it will give you time to rest and recover." His father added.

Mathew had no words, just tears. As he got up and they automatically all stood up, first he gave his sister a big hug, then his mother and father walked into his open arms.

Chapter 26

Cam carries on

Cameron never had any doubts about continuing racing, even before the words of Mikes mother.

He knew there was sure to be even more pressure from his parents for him to give up, but he was ready for it.

"I know I've said it many times before, but now even you must see how pointless it is to keep driving these racing cars." his father's comments at every opportunity.

"Without Mike, I would not have even got started in motor racing, and I've only got this far because of him. The last thing he would have wanted would have been for me to stop racing now that I'm getting close to fulfilling my dream."

"I give up, you're still only in Formula 3 aren't you...a dreamer, that's all you are."

At this point, Cam went upstairs, packed a suitcase, and saying to his tearful mother.

"I'll keep in touch, Mum, but sorry, I can't live here anymore."

He moved out of the bakery, unsure of where to go next and decided to spend, at least tonight, in the workshop.

The following morning, he rang Nick, who ran the GRD team.

"So sorry to hear about Mike Cole at Le Mans, you must be devastated, do you think you will be up to driving at Thruxton next week," Nick said when he answered the phone.

"Hi Nick, thanks...yes it was the worse day of my life, Mike was a smashing guy, my best friend, but I will be OK to drive, he wouldn't have wanted me to stop." After a pause, Nick replied.

"Good to hear that Cam...we all know this game doesn't take any prisoners."

"I was wondering if I could come and stay with you in Norfolk, will be great to be close to the workshop, and I can help out."

"Sure, grand idea Cam, I've got a small bedroom you can use for a while. In the week you can drive the van to go and collect all the parts we order; that work will cover your rent."

Being surrounded by like-minded racing people strengthened Cam's resolve. He would keep racing and make Mike proud of him.

By the end of September, he had had two more victories and three other second-place finishes, the Shell Formula 3 Championship was his by just three points.

At the year-end prize awards, Cam gave an emotional thank you speech as he collected his trophy, dedicating his success to the memory of Mike Coles. Afterwards, Nick said.

"It's been a brilliant year, you know we have plans to build a batch of Formula 2 cars for next season, would like you to stay and drive for us Cam, but of course we need money to run the car. About ten grand would do. Think you can raise that?"

Cam, like many other ambitions racing drivers, had become to expect these problems at this time of year. Everyone was wheeling and dealing attempting to secure the best drives for the following season. A wrong decision now, choice of team or car, had been the downfall of many young drivers.

Their dream of reaching Formula One often becoming a nightmare that ended their racing careers.

Cam had hoped that his Formula 3 success would mean being offered a full works drive in Formula 2 and he was still hopeful of a call from other teams. He tried to call Nick's bluff.

"Would love to drive for you again next season Nick, but I'm talking to a couple of other teams; could have another offer."

"OK, that sounds good. There are a couple of South American guys who contacted me, they want to drive for us next year, and they have got a big pot of money, so will need a decision from you very soon."

Don't know where I'm going to find one grand, never mind ten. Cam thought as he drove back to the GRD base. Then he remembered the diamond he had taken from Henry Sutcliffe; it was still in the lining of the old jacket he had left behind at the bakery.

He phoned his mother the following morning. He had been ringing her after each race during the season to let her know he was alright.

"Hi, Mum. The season has finished now; thought I would call to see you this week."

"Are you coming home to stay." She answered.

"Maybe for a short while, if that's OK."

"Of course, it is, your room is just as you left it." Those were the words he was relieved to hear.

After the stained hello's, his father said.

"I suppose congratulations are in order. Your mother told me you had won a championship."

"Yes, well-done son." his mother added, then said, "Mrs Coles called to see us a few weeks ago, said how pleased we should be for you. She said you're doing her son's memory proud and wished he had been here to enjoy your success."

Peter remained silent.

After a quiet evening watching tv, all three avoiding the subject of motor racing, Cam said.

"Think I'll get an early night."

In his room, he went straight to the wardrobe. With relief, he found the jacket and felt the hard stone still lodged in the lining.

Removing it, he studied the sparkling gemstone. I will take a trip to London tomorrow and see if I can sell this, he decided, his first thought had been to ask Mike to go with him, realisation brought a wave of sadness, as he remembered Mike never knew he had taken the stone.

After visiting three shops in Hatton Garden, Cam began to wish he had left the diamond in his pocket. He had thought at least one of the dealers would have been keen to buy the stone, but each one treated him with suspicion.

"It's a good stone, about one and a half carats. Can you tell me where you got it."? This response had been similar in each establishment.

Cam had decided his story would be that he had found the stone a couple of years ago and had only just now decided to sell it. When the third jeweller had said,

"Aren't you Cameron Cartland." He realised he had made a big mistake.

Worried, he soon caught a train back from Liverpool Street to Cambridge. The diamond still in his pocket.

"A policeman phone to speak to you." His worried mother said the moment he walked in the door.

"He wants you to ring him as soon as you get in, I've written his name and number on the pad."

When he saw the name 'Inspector Richard Hurst' he knew he had just made a great mistake.

"What have you done now." His father's predictable reaction.

"Nothing. I will ring later. "he said very sharply.

The previous year had not been a good one for Richard Hurst, his expected promotion after breaking the diamond smuggling ring hadn't materialised.

"You might have got the monkey, but that's no good without the organ grinder," had been his bosses' reaction. The press had poorly received news of Henry Sutcliffe's escape… ' to live a life of luxury', in Spain.

It's funny how some things come in twos he thought; he had just heard that Iris Sutcliffe had died, now he gets a call that one of the stolen diamonds had surfaced and in the hands of Cameron Cartland!

An hour later the return call from Cameron came in.

"Hello Inspector Hurst. My mother said you want to talk to me."

"I hear you have visited a friend of mine, Sammy Cohen in Hatton Garden, Cam. I think we need a chat. I will be at Cambridge Police Station tomorrow at 10 am and think it would be a good idea if you were there. I don't expect you want me to have to come to your home."

"Yes... OK, I'll be there." Cam's reluctant reply.

"Don't forget to bring that diamond with you."

The moment Cam put the phone down, his parents, who had been just outside in the kitchen, came in.

"There's been a development in the Sutcliffe case. He wants me to go to Cambridge Police Station in the morning," he told them.

Cam had woken at 5 am the following morning and unable to sleep went for a walk. At 7 am he found himself sitting on the high banks of the Devils Ditch looking back across the fallow fields to Burlham. He hadn't realised this was the same place his grandfather used to sit when he had his troubles to sort out. The sharp wind made a mournful sound as it blew through the age-old gnarled gorse bushes, their exposed roots like witches' claws.

The problem for Cam was that he had no idea how to resolve his current situation. It is racing that always gets me into these situations; all I ever want is to get enough money together to keep driving.
He wandered back to the bakery to put on his only suit for his visit to Cambridge.

Extremely nervous Cam sat in a sparsely furnished interview room, just a plain metal legged table and two hard chairs. He was quite relieved when the Inspector walked in alone.

"Well, this is a surprise Mr Cartland didn't expect to be interviewing you again. It looks like you were more involved with

Sutcliffe's mob than we thought. I think you have some explaining to do."

"No, I wasn't...I just took one of the stones that fell out of the silencer; I'm not a criminal." A panicked Cam replied.

"Maybe not, but you are certainly a fool, Sutcliffe must have known you had taken a diamond, that's why my whole operation went tits-up."

Cam then confessed how he had pocketed the stone, without really thinking, and admitted he had no idea how to sell it.

"Well, we may be able to turn this to our advantage. You will notice this is not a formal interview. If it were, I would be charging you with handling stolen property by now, at least. Now only you, me and Sammy know you have the stone. I have an idea of how we can still nail that bastard Sutcliffe once and for all, with your co-operation."

"Doesn't look like I have a choice does it." Cam's resigned reply.

"No, you haven't, and I'll look after the diamond."

Richard Hurst had become obsessed with Henry Sutcliffe, to the detriment of his personal life and his job.

"You either start to live like a normal person now, or I'm leaving you," had been his wife's ultimate after the Gallows Wood incident. They had been married five years but had no children.

"Fat chance of getting any" his wife had confessed to her sister. He's hardly ever here, and when he is, he drinks whiskey and falls asleep in the chair."

He was still angry and disappointed over Sutcliffe's escape to Spain, and his response to his wife's ultimatum had been.

"If that's how you feel bugger off." And of course, she did.

The failure to capture their main man also sat very poorly with his police superiors. So far, the Sutcliffe case had cost thousands of pounds and countless staff-hours, this the latest fiasco, the responsibility of Richard Hurst. It became the final nail in the coffin of his career advancement.

With Sutcliffe thumbing his nose at them all, living in the sun and luxury in Spain, the press had had a field day.

'Police cock-up lets another crook live a life of luxury in Spain. ' Just one of the negative headlines.

After that, Richard Hurst' obsession had become a vendetta. He would get the bastard at any cost; he wasn't going to follow the rules anymore.

Chapter 27

Repair and reflection

The South of France proved to be an excellent idea for Mathews recovery and recuperation, the sun and peace being the perfect medicine. For two months, Mathew stayed; gradually coming to terms with his loss.

His grandmother had been pre-warned by her son, not to attempt to involve Mathew in her social scene.

William had no cause to worry. Silvia was now seventy, and the excesses of her life had caught up with her. Arthritis in her hips and knees her worst ailments, as she explained to Mathew.

"It's no fun getting old. I used to make fun of your grandfather's mother as she hobbled around with a stick and complained about her ailments. Mind you; she was always a miserable old bat."

Silvia was happy to spend quiet time with her grandson lazing around her swimming pool, with Mathew encouraging her to tell stories of her early racing exploits at Brooklands.

One day he asked how she had managed to get her converted 120mph badge, now proudly displayed on the mantelpiece.

"I was lucky, had some great help, mainly from your other grandfather Frank. He was a wizard with engines you know."

"Trying for his 120mph badge is what killed grandfather George, wasn't it? " Mathew had asked her.

Silvia didn't answer immediately.

Time had healed many of the bad memories from that period. Now, as she had the time to look back, Silvia felt there had been many things to forget from her wild and reckless younger years.

"Yes, but at least George did achieve his great ambition. He was brave, in the end."

Sensing his grandmother would say no more about it, Mathew said.

"Do you regret getting involved with motor racing...it can bring so much pain can't it. Grandfather, now Mike, and if I hadn't persuaded Linda to go to that bloody party to raise money for my racing, she could be here with me."

His voice trailed away as Silvia watched the utter despair in her grandsons' eyes.

She went to the drinks cabinet and poured two large brandies.

"Get this down you; it does help, in moderation, of course." she smiled.

After a couple of minutes silence, while they both sipped their drinks, and the alcohol began its brain calming effect, Silvia said.

"I've got many regrets, probably more than most people, but we can't change anything that has happened in our past." After a short while she added. "I can tell you racing cars was never one of my regrets.

She stopped to take another drink before continuing.

"You know driving race cars brings joy to your life that every day things can't possibly match. We are the lucky ones; most people never get the chance to experience the incredible euphoric feelings we get when taking risks, whether it is racing cars, climbing mountains or flying airplanes. Not many people want to live their lives to that level…I miss that, so no, I've never regretted my passion for racing, and nor should you. Your grandfather, both your grandfathers, Mike Coles, and all the other drivers that have died doing what they loved would not have changed a thing. They would all do it again if they had the chance." - she did think *but maybe not George.*

"Do you think Linda would have wanted you to stop? if she were half the girl I've heard she was, she would have wanted you to carry on racing and chase your dream to be World Champion."

Mathew took another sip of his brandy and felt the course liquid send a warming glow throughout his body.

"Think I will ring Reggie in the morning and ask if he still has a car for me to drive. Thanks grandmother."

"How many times do I have to tell you, don't bloody call me that. Call me, Silvia."

"Of course I do." Had been Reggie's enthusiastic response to Mathews call to ask about the racing car.

"What about the guy driving for you at the moment."

"He's had his chance...not a patch on you old boy."

When Mat put the phone down, he had a smile on his face; his old self-confidence was returning. He remembered Cam had said much the same thing about his replacement drivers ability before he had persuaded him to drive at Le Mans.

There were just two races left before the end of the season for Mat to show his class.

The Formula 2 drivers of 1971 often included many existing Formula 1 drivers, when their Formula 1 commitments allowed. It gave the promising young drivers a chance to compare their abilities against the skills of the established stars.

The Brands Hatch race demonstrated Mat Marshall had lost none of his exceptional ability to drive racing cars. He finished in fifth place; the first four finishers were all current Formula One drivers.

"Great stuff champ...we had put the Formula One ideas on hold after your accident, but now it's full steam ahead," Reggie announced after the race.

Putting his arm around Mat, he said.

"You, my boy, are going to be a Formula 1 driver."

Mat had not expected that reaction.

"Where are you going to get the money, Reggie. You can't afford to fund it all yourself can you, and my family has none to spare."

"Let me worry about that old sport. We will have you on the grid for the first race, never fear."

"Ok...and I'm sorry about the Aston." Mat had not had a chance to talk to Reggie properly since the accident.

Serious for once, Reggie said.

"I can always get another bloody car. Linda was an exceptional girl; we could all see how much she loved you. I can't imagine

how you are feeling, suppose I've only ever loved myself.
Mat, choking back tears when he replied.

"As my grandmother said, Linda would have wanted me to carry on; I'm just doing this...to make her proud of me."

Chapter28

Hurst's Revenge

It had been more than a year since Terry Thatcher had been locked up in Strangways prison to serve a sentence of twenty years for kidnap, attempted murder and robbery.

Richard Hurst paid him a surprise visit.

He watched the thin, hobbling man- his right leg broken by Danny Glover had not healed correctly, as he approached the wire grill.

"What'd the fuck do you want." Thatchers surly greeting.

"Just thought I'd see how you are Terry and give you some news. I know you still get contact from your boss. Just tell him Cameron Cartland had a load more diamonds than we all thought and that I'm prepared to do a deal with him."

Terry laughed. "He wouldn't fall for that old trick. He's safe from you lot in Spain; I'm joining him when my appeal goes through, and I get out of this hole."
Richard slowly opened his left hand to reveal the sparkling diamond in his palm.

"Tell him there's plenty more... Oh and I'll be in Gibraltar next week on holiday."

He abruptly got up and left, smiling to himself. It would not take long for the news to reach Spain.

"I've got weeks holiday leave due to me, and you are coming with me." He said to Cam.

"Where to.?"

"Gibraltar. I'm going to nail that bastard Sutcliffe once and for all."

"Why Gibraltar."

"I've got an old Aunt who lives there, we can stay with her, and its border is only two miles from Sutcliffe's villa."

Flying into Gibraltar airport is a hair raising experience, the approach over the sea and the runway one of the shortest in the world.

Cam had never flown before, all his European trips being by ferry and car,

"Christ! "He exclaimed to Richard Hurst. "We just dropped out of the sky; my bloody stomach is still up there."

"Yes, that landing shocked me the first time, think it's one of the most dangerous landing strips in the world."

"Glad I didn't know that before."

With legs still wobbly Cam followed the detective into the town, steeply uphill along a narrow, cobbled street to his aunt's house. The looming presence of 'The Rock' dominated his view.

It was undoubtedly impressive the whole of Gibraltar town being building on and around the mountain.

Richard's aunt moved to Gibraltar with her husband when the war ended. He was serving in the British army based on the island. Unfortunately, he had been killed, when he slipped and fell one hundred feet down the rock while on a training exercise. Joan had stayed on and began a bed and breakfast operation.

"Lovely to have you visit me, Richard, and your friend."

"This is Cameron aunt; we have some police business to attend to, will not get in your way."

"Stay as long as you like dear, not many tourists this time of the year, so I've got plenty of room."

Cam had been trying to find out how this entrapment of Henry Sutcliffe was going to work. But all he had got from Richard was vague responses of, 'I'll tell you nearer the time."

Richard Hurst had been obsessed with arresting Henry Sutcliffe ever since Sutcliffe's first wife had died. Babs Sutcliffe had been Richards youngest sister. Her real name was Sally Hurst. They grew up in a small Devon village, where their father was the local postman. Richard had looked after his younger sister, protecting her whenever she had any problems. Her teenage years and changes in her personality saw her leave home, at fifteen, after falling out with their parents.

'I'm going to London. There's nothing to do around here; I'm going to be an actress.'

'She will be back with her tail between her legs.' Her mother had said.

After a couple of months when no one had heard from her, Richard tracked her down to a small flat in Shepherds Bush. Sally was sharing the tiny space with two other girls, also aspiring actresses, they were all doing waitressing jobs to make a little money.

'She seems alright, expect she will have had enough before long.' He had reported back to their parents.

But another year passed, and Sally had moved, without informing her family. Richard was already a police constable by then and had managed a transfer to London intending to track down Sally, but the trail had gone cold.

He had no idea she had changed her name.

The shock when Richard found out about Sally's death much later was immense. It came when he saw a picture of Babs Sutcliffe, his sister, looking back at him from Sutcliffe's file.

As a rising star in the force, he had charge of a small group dedicated to cleaning up the extortion rackets in the West End. Once he knew who Sutcliffe was, he had made getting him convicted his only priority.

The disappointment of allowing him to slip through his fingers and escape to Spain had hit Richard hard. He knew he had blown his promotion chances but now that didn't matter; getting Sutcliffe at any cost, was his only focus.

He planned to play on the greed of the man, sure Sutcliffe would always be looking to make more money, with his UK operations permanently closed and bank accounts frozen.

Richard knew Sutcliffe wouldn't care if the opportunity came via a bent cop; he had had many of those in his pocket over the years.

Now with Cartland's diamond in his pocket this was his great opportunity to put an end to the crook.

Sammy Cohen was an artist; Richard Hurst had first encountered when a batch of paste diamonds got onto the market. Their quality and hardness had been exceptional; Richard discovered Sammy had created them at a time when he had been desperate for money. Richard saw an opportunity to gain a useful contact for the future and managed to keep Sammy's involvement in the scheme to himself.

Now had been the time for Sammy to repay his debt by producing a new batch of one hundred paste diamonds. He didn't ask to what use Richard Hurst was going to put them.

"We will take the cable car up the top of the mountain tomorrow." Richard had informed Cam.

He had noticed two surly-looking young men follow them when they left the airport and caught the taxi to his aunt's house.

He was sure that information would now be with Henry Sutcliffe.

His plan was not without risk, he knew he would have to allow Sutcliffe access to a real diamond, and that he would certainly not just expect to test only one. For that reason, he had also 'persuaded' Sammy to give him two more actual diamonds similar in size and cut to the original.

How's that going to get Sutcliffe to buy these diamonds." Cam had asked.

Richard pulled an envelope from his pocket addressed to Henry Sutcliffe.

“ We are going to leave this for the boys that have been following us to pick up and take back to him. Going to leave two of the real diamonds in it."

"That's madness they will just take the diamond and bugger off."

"Don't think so, they will be too afraid of what Sutcliffe would do when he caught up with them. The rumor is he has been pulling teeth out, with pliers, of a couple of guys that had crossed him recently."

"Bloody hell, what have you got us into."

"You should have thought of that when you tried to sell the diamond you took. You know what he's like; he tried to kill you."

"What about telling the Gibraltar police you've come to arrest Sutcliffe, they would help."

"Fat chance of that, half of them are probably in his pocket; anyway, this is just about him and me."

Cam felt worried, the grim determination on Richard Hurst's face and his erratic manner, making him wish he could be anywhere but here.

They took the cable car up the mountain, and as Richard predicted, two men followed them into the caves at the top, with few tourists about it had been simple to leave the envelope which said 'Take to your boss Henry Sutcliffe'.
Once they knew the men had taken the envelope, Richard and Cam returned down the cable car.

"Let's go down to the harbour and get a coffee. Those goons will be rushing back to Sutcliffe by now."

"What did you say in the note," Cam asked as they sat by the waterfront sipping the strong black coffee.

"I told him if he wanted another twenty-two of these he should meet me at 5 pm tomorrow at the top of the Moorish Castle, he should bring five thousand pounds with him, and to come alone."

"You can't be serious. You can't trust Sutcliffe; you know he wouldn't bring any money, he'll just come to kill you, and me. Then just take the diamonds."

"I know that will be his plan, he's sure to have a gun...but so have I."
He opened his jacket and showed Cam the police issue hand gun.
Cam didn't know what to say; eventually, he said.

"This is a bloody nightmare; you intend to kill him, don't you."

"If I have to."

-Looking behind him, Cam said.

"Is that the castle up there." He pointed to a grey castellated tower high on the rock face. "It looks like a ruin."

"It is, pretty much, but the steps to the tower are solid, very narrow only one person at a time can come up or down. There are two hundred of them; halfway up is a disguised ledge where someone can hide." Before he could continue, Cam asked.

"How do you know all this."

"When I was fourteen, I came to stay one summer with my younger sister Sally. We used to play in the castle, and I discovered the ledge then. Sally loved playing hide and seek..." His voice trailed away.

Cam didn't pick up on the wistfulness in Richard's voice.

"So what's the plan, not that I want anything to do with it."

"All you have to do is stand at the top of the tower alone and look down. It will be almost dark, and Sutcliffe will think it's me waiting for him. I'll be concealed in the hidden alcove then when he goes past, I'll come out and cut off his minders, one shove and they will fall back down the steps. Sutcliffe is sure to try to turn around when he hears the noise, expect he will have his gun in his hand so I'll shot him before he shoots me."

Cam was quiet for a long time, then said.

"Think I am going to need something a lot stronger than this coffee."

Chapter29

Silvia returns home

For the Marshall family, and Mathew particularly, Christmas was tough. The previous year with Linda had been magical; he knew that all future Christmas's would never have the same appeal for him.

One thing had helped lift the gloom surrounding the Sefton estate, that was the arrival of Silvia. In her later years, the whole family looked forward to seeing her.

They had been immensely grateful to her for being instrumental in helping Mathews recovery from the tragedy. Mary had almost forgotten how uncomfortable this woman used to make her feel.

"I have decided to sell my French home and move back here to England." She had announced at dinner on Christmas Eve.

"Where are you going to live mother." Asked a slightly apprehensive William.

"I though here on the estate if you will have me."

"You can have my cottage grandmother." Mathew quickly responded.

The look she gave him made him add. "Sorry...Silvia."

He had not stayed there much after his depressive period and knew without

Linda that cottage could never again become his home.

"Wonderful, but will that be alright with you, Mary," Silvia asked.
With everyone looking at her, Mary thought; Is this the same women I used to know.
Then said

"It sounds like a lovely idea, I will be pleased with the company, Florence is away most of the time, and William spends nearly all his time at Brooklands."

"Let's drink to it." Silvia raised her glass. "But only in moderation these days."
They all laughed; even Mathew managed a rye smile.

"A'h Brooklands. I would love to come up and revisit the old place, I had some great times there. Then remembering George, she added, but not all good of course. I hear you are working wonders to restore Brooklands to its former glory William."

"We will never be able to do that, unfortunately, too much damage has been done, but we are trying to save the parts that haven't been destroyed and cut up. There's an open day for the public next year, and we are inviting all the old drivers that are still around, so I suppose that includes you, mother."

Mary smiled as she saw William looked at his mother with a twinkle in his eye.

"Wonderful, I can tell them all about my adventures."

The twinkle left Williams eye; he was a little worried by that remark. Silvia had quite a reputation from those pre-war days.

Chapter30

Showdown in Gibraltar

Cameron Cartland stood looking down over the harbour from the top of the Moorish Tower.

Not for the first time in his life, he thought what the hell am I doing here. Once more, his blind passion for furthering his racing career had landed him in a difficult situation.

The sudden appearance of three dark figures walking up the path far below brought him back to the moment.

He stood at the edge of the battlements, it was a clear evening, and he was sure the figures had noticed him silhouetted against the darkening sky. Although it was warm, he shivered, waiting for the events to unfold.

Although the tower closed to visitors at 5 pm, Richard had used his police authority to obtain the key from the caretaker, explaining he had needed to use the tower for a few hours' surveillance. The ten pounds offered for his cooperation helped with the caretakers' compliance.

Richard Hurst felt remarkable calm as he heard the first footfall on the stone steps below. Concealed in his nook, he waited as the breathless sounds of effort, and

heavy footsteps grew louder. The first grey figure passed by continuing to climb.
Richard quickly stepped out directly in front of the second figure as it appeared around the twisting corner.
There was a mutual look of shock and surprise on the faces of Richard, and Henry Sutcliffe now inches apart.

Sutcliffe's gun arm started to raise as Richard gave him a mighty push. The shattering sound of a gunshot invaded the confined stone staircase, shards of sharp stone ripped into the cheek of Richard as a bullet smashed into the wall inches from his head. Helpless, Sutcliffe fell backwards, collecting a following body as they went tumbling down the twisting stairs. Their soft flesh and bone no match for the hard granite stone steps and flint lined walls. The crunching, wailing, snapping sounds growing fainter as they spiraled down to their deaths. Richard had his gun raised as the first of Sutcliffe's henchmen turned back to investigate. The gun in his face insured he offered no resistance.

Cam had remained frozen to the edge of a buttress since the gunshot. *It's funny all the other dangerous situations I have got myself into; racing, the North Sea, Gallows Wood, I have never had time to be frightened, events usually happened too fast for fear. But here I have time to think, what if Sutcliffe has shot Richard and is on his way up to kill me,*

"You can come down now, Cam; it's over." A welcome voice shouted up from below. The sound of Richard's voice caused Cam's knees to buckle, as he slid down to the floor.

The flight home to England was a great relief for Cam; even the tricky take off didn't bother him. He reflected on the events, just relieved to have got away from Gibraltar in one piece. The fact he had lost the diamond and would have no money for his drive the following year was of no importance at that moment.

Even when he had seen Sutcliffe's twisted and broken body at the foot of the Tower stairs, he still needed Richards assurance that the man was dead.

With blood dripping from his damaged face and a look of wild excitement in his eyes Richard said.

"Yes, look at them; there is no doubt they are both dead. A real bonus, I had expected Sutcliffe to come up first." With his gun still pointing at the remaining crook, he had added.

"Bugger off back to Spain, or I'll shoot you now; your boss is dead, you can all fight amongst yourselves to be new top dog."

Without hesitation, the crook turned and ran out of the building, heading for the Spanish border.

"Why did you let him go, the police will want to interview him," Cam had said.

"You just let me handle this with the Gibraltar police, I'll tell them I had tricked Sutcliffe here to arrest him, he resisted, and they both fell down the stairs.

We don't want any witnesses to say different. I intend to stay on here until it's all sorted out, you can catch the next flight back in the morning. And remember should anyone ask; you had gone for a walk out to the lighthouse alone, you weren't here."

After he had been home for two weeks and had no police knocking at the Bakery cottage door, Cam began to relax a little.

"There's a card for you." His mother had said a few days before Christmas.

"It's got a foreign stamp on it."
Under the usual Christmas messages, there was a handwritten note.

'Hi Cam greetings from Gibraltar, you will note I've decided to stay here and help my aunt run the B&B. There will be no further problems for you to worry about, the

Gibraltar police have closed the case. Getting rid of that bastard means I can retire happy. Happy Christmas, Richard.'

I bet you can, thought Cam, you kept all the diamonds.

"Aren't you going to put that card on the mantelpiece with all the others." His mother asked.

"No, it's not from anyone you know." He had dismissed her question.

Cam certainly wasn't going to allow his father the start questioning him about what the note meant.

Chapter31

Formula One for Mathew

The 1973 Formula One season had started in South America, but it was April before Mathew Marshall, achieved the first part of his dream and became a Formula One driver.

Reggie had "done a deal, old boy." with the March Formula One team and brought one of their previous year's cars, plus two Ford Cosworth DFV engines.

Having driven the Greenham Special, Mat had an experience of the power of the Ford three-litre engine and soon settled into the new March of the Montague Formula One team.

Testing at Silverstone had gone very well, and the whole team were confident when they travelled to Monaco for their first Grand Prix.

The trip to Monaco was the moment Reggie had been looking forward to; he had chartered a 140 feet yacht for his wealthy friends and their gaggle of glamorous girls to enjoy the delights of Monte Carlo. It also allowed the masses of press, English and continental, plenty of "topless" shots.

Despite the obvious temptations, Mat focused all his attentions on the race.

One of the seasoned Formula One drivers said to him.

"Bloody hell Mat, your boss certainly knows how to enjoy himself. I would have thought you would be in there helping yourself."

"I'm just here to race the car; I've no interest in anything else, " Mat's curt reply.

Before Linda he had dipped his toes into Reggie's hedonistic world and found it too hot for him.

I can see why Linda had become tired of all the glitter and glamour, I wish she could be here with me. But he knew he couldn't allow himself self-pity.
He had a job to do.

The small British team surprised many, with their year-old March performing well, and Mat driving superbly. They were in the seventh position with just ten laps to go when the engine blew up.

Everyone agreed it had been an encouraging first race.

More successful races followed along with some disappointments. Mat managed to crash the car in final practice at Zolder. He was unhurt, but there was not enough time to repair the March before the race, so the team non-started.

It didn't stop Reggie from enjoying himself; at the prize-giving dinner bread rolls were flying across tables and the battle between Italian and English tables began to get out of hand.

Reggie and two of the team mechanics had placed a jumbo firecracker with a built-in timer, under the table of the Ferrari team. A loud bang accompanied by smoke caused pandemonium. Wild Italian shouting and arm-waving followed, especially when they noticed the carpet had been set alight. Very soon they were pointing, and gesturing using abundant Italian expletives towards the Montague table who sat almost unmoved by the whole event. Just slight smiles on all their faces.

One of the old English team owners commented.

"I wish I had thought to do that, years ago."

At the time Mat had been experiencing the high life in Monaco Cameron Cartland was sweeping the floors in the GRD workshop in Norfolk.

He had let the team know he would not be able to raise the money for a Formula 2 drive.

"That's a great shame, Cam," said Nick. "I will have to commit to the two Brazilian lads then. You could stay on as reserve and test driver in exchange for acting as a mechanic on one of the cars and teaching these new boys the circuits."

"Thanks Nick, I'll let you know." The despondent Cam had replied. I must be able to get a drive somewhere, I'm the bloody Formula 3 champion after-all, he thought.

Unfortunately, it was a difficult time for everyone, a three-day working week was in operation, all the racing teams were struggling to find sponsorship, and most had reverted to using paying drivers for their Formula 2 cars.

By early February Cam rang Nick.

"Hi Nick, if the offers still on I would like to take the role of test driver," he couldn't face saying 'and mechanic.'

The Brazilians arrived in England during a mid-March snowstorm. Nick had sent Cam to pick them up from Heathrow airport.

When he noticed the lads coming through the arrivals gate, he couldn't help feeling sorry for them. Both were struggling with two large suitcases and were wearing clothes suitable for the 70degree heat they had recently left behind.

Carlos Silva, the taller and slimmer of the two, walked with a confident swagger, he had a mass of wavy black hair, and dark, intense brown eyes. Elmo

Domingo, fairer skin, and two inches shorter looked around nervously. Both boys were from wealthy families and had been racing in Brazil since they were eight years old. Firstly, on go-karts and recently in the Brazilian Formula 3 Championship.

Still teenagers, their confidence and money soon stirred the recently dormant green-eyed monster in Cam. I'm twenty-two, these boys swan over here and buy themselves straight into Formula 2, bloody unfair.

Three races into the season and it was apparent Carlos Silva was an exceptional talent and a quick learner. Cam had tested, and set up, both cars at Snetterton. He had enjoyed the experience.

"The Norwich Straight suddenly doesn't seem very long." He joked to Nick. The speed of the nimble little cars with their two-litre engines being much quicker than the Formula 3 cars he had become used to experiencing.

During the Brazilians first test at Snetterton, Carlos had set a time one-tenth of a second quicker than Cam's best on the same day.

That test session showed Elmo to be almost a second slower than his countryman, and that difference continued when the racing season started.

"Looks like we have a real star on our hands." A delighted Nick said to the motoring press.

After the fourth race, it became apparent Elmo was disillusioned and disappointed with European racing, he hated the cold weather and was also homesick.

"I think I shall go home and carry on racing in Brazil." He had announced to Nick as they watched Carlos on the Thruxton podium collecting his second-place trophy. Elmo had retired from that race when he had missed a gear in his desperate efforts to keep up with the leaders. The resultant excessive revs had blown-up the engine.

His best result so far had been tenth at Estoril in the Spanish round of the Formula 2 Championship.

"Can't afford to refund your payments," was Nick's first reaction." Elmo's father had transferred funds to cover nine races, but with this engine blow-up, about half the remaining money would have to go towards re-building it.

"Is OK, my father can afford it." Was all the despondent lad said before leaving the pits and packing his bags.

Elmo was on a plane home to Brazil the following day.

Cam had been standing next to Nick and listened with interest. He had been acting as the second mechanic on Elmo's GRD, growing increasingly frustrated knowing he could be doing a much better job than its driver.

Nick turned to Cam and smiled.

"Well, I can give you the next three races Cam then we will need more money to finish the season."

“Smashing, thank you Nick, I will not let you down.”

Cam didn't disappoint the team as he regularly proved to be as quick as Carlos, who the motoring press had already tipped for a top Formula One drive in future. Although Cam was pleased with his performances, being as quick and occasionally quicker than his younger teammate, he knew what an effort it was for him to produce the fast lap times. For Carlos, he could see it was effortless; he had a natural, confident arrogance. He just knew he was a quicker driver than anyone else.

After the seventh race, in which Carlos won and Cam finished third, Carlos was the joint leader in the Championship, two other drivers German Hans Holast, and

Italian Gino Mordelli could both still beat him.

"You're doing a great job Cam. Carlos has told me he wants you to stay in the car for the remaining three races, we both think you can take points off his closest rivals in the Championship. He has spoken to his father, and Carlos says he is sure he will provide extra funds to run your car."

"That's brilliant news, Nick. I think if we have a test at Snetterton before the next round, we can improve the cars some more. We should try to lower the rear ride height and put stronger springs on the back-end."

"OK, the next round is three weeks away, Carlos is going back to Brazil this week to butter up his father.

"You are the set up magic man," Carlos said to Cam after their first practice at Imola. He had flown straight to Italy from Brazil; Cam had driven down with the mechanics in the team transporter.

They were first and second fastest, Carlos two tenths quicker than Cam, and the race went to plan, the GRD drivers finishing first and second.

The following race with Carlos in second place, and only five laps left, he tried a rash pass on the inside of the leader Hans Holast as they braked for the hairpin.

"Bloody Hans, should have let me through." Carlos threw his helmet down after the race.

The resulting spin when they touched had sent them both the tail of the field, ensuring neither scored points. Cam, suffering from a heavy cold, had only managed fourth place. Unfortunately, Gino Mordelli won the race and took maximum championship points.

Going to the final round at Brands Hatch Carlos was just two points behind Gino and two ahead of Hans.

"I can win, but you have to stop that bloody Italian finishing second." Carlos had said to Cam after practice. If that were the result, they would equal on points, but the Italian would be Champion with three wins to Carlos two.

Carlos had set the fastest time so was on pole position Cam had managed third. Gino second quickest.

The start was very even the whole pack getting through Paddock bend without incident. Braking uphill to the Druids hairpin Cam saw a small gap on the inside of Gino, he braked very late, locked up his front wheels and slid into the side of the Italian's car, both cars spun, and the rest of the field took drastic avoiding action. Amazingly no one hit them, both resumed the race, but now well out of contention for victory. Carlos had a substantial lead after the first lap incident, and he increased it on every lap. With arm raised in delight as he acknowledged the chequered flag he eventually won by five seconds from the Hans Holast.

During the celebrations, champagne was flowing, Carlos had his arm around Cam saying,

"This man he won the Championship for me!"

At that moment, a very angry Gino Mordelli arrived, after much shouting and posturing he threw a punch at Cam but hit Carlos instead.

Chaos followed with much pushing and shoving between the English and Italian mechanics; eventually, the Italians broke away and dragged there still vocal driver with them.

Carlos, rubbing his bruised chin, said laughing.

"Expect that will happen again next year in Formula One, shame I will not have you as a teammate to knock him off."

"Have you got a drive already then," Cam asked.

"Yes, I've signed for Lotus next year, and I know the Italian has a contract with Ferrari in his pocket."

"You're quite Cam, " Nick said as they drove home from Brands Hatch.

"Yes, wondering about next year, think my cock up today has blown any chance of a Formula One team wanting me."

"Well, you've got a job with us as long as you want it. We've got orders for six F3 cars and four F2 cars already for next year thanks to you and Carlos. He is something special, isn't he? Sure, he is going to be World Champion in a few years."

Nick was unaware of how much that remark hurt Cam.

I can still be World Champion myself if someone will give me a bloody chance.

He brooded watching the Essex countryside flash by as Nick drove them back to East Anglia.

This season racing in Formula 2 had raised the profile of Cameron Cartland, and in Cambridgeshire at least, he was now well known and had a large following amongst the local racing fans.

Of course, his past escapades also meant the general public took an interest, but usually only when things went wrong, like today.

The BBC televised the race at Brands Hatch, and unfortunately for Cam, his parents had watched it.

"Looks like you got yourself in trouble again." Was his father's comments as Cam walked into the room.

"I expect we will have the press at the door again tomorrow."

Cam's frustration boiled over.

"You can never give me any credit, can you," Cam shouted at him as his mother started to cry.

"If you knew, or cared, anything about my racing you would know I've had a brilliant season. Not going to let you drag me down anymore. I'm leaving for good this time."

With his mother pleading with him to stay, his father said to his sons departing back.

"Don't worry, he will be back again when something else goes wrong. *Not this time.* Cam thought as he slammed the door behind him.

Chapter32

Ambitions plans

The 1972 season had been a steep learning curve for the Montague team. Most of the established Formula One teams had been amused and upset, in equal measure, by the brash young team upsetting their cozy world. The best result for the team was Mat's seventh-place finish at the German Grand Prix. The fact that he had managed even to finish a race at the daunting, more than 14 Mile length, Nurburgring track was considered an excellent achievement. The circuit with its one hundred and eighty dangerous corners was the most difficult in the world. In two other races his March broke down when it looked like he would pick up a few points.

After the last race of the season, Reggie said to Mat.

"Right 'o old bean, it has been a bloody good year. Next year I'm going to give you a car that can win races."

"Appreciate your confidence in me Reggie, but don't want you to overstretch yourself. A couple of teams have asked me to go and see them about next year. Should be able to get a seat with a little sponsorship."

"Not bloody likely, I want you winning the World Championship in a new Montague car. It's only money, can't take it with you."

When Mathew told his parents of Reggie's plans, William said.

"His poor old father will be turning in his grave. That estate has been in the Montague family for generations; I hope he knows what he is doing."

Mary said nothing; she understood the addiction only too well.

"Wow, that looks stunning." Had been Mats first reaction on seeing the
new RAM Ford. He quickly slid himself down into the seat.

Standing over him a proud Reggie said.

"Yes, isn't it, the boys have done a great job, working all hours; cost me a fortune in overtime. I've given it chassis number RAM01."

Completion of the RAM01 Formula One car had taken only four months from drawing board stage to its Cosworth engine bursting into life. Reggie had raised some sponsorship to get the season off the ground but admitted more would be needed, much more, to get them through the whole season.

Although he had not confessed it to anyone, he had borrowed heavily from his mates in the city to get this far; many acres of prime Montague farming land pledged as security.

At the first race in Brazil Mat finished in third place, a brilliant result for the team.

"This car is outstanding so much easier to drive on the limit than the old March," had been Mats excited comments to the Motor Sports reporter after the race.

Julian Jacks been reporting on Formula One since the 1950s. He had said in the Motor Sports end of season Formula One review.

'It does look like Mathew Marshall, the grandson of famous engine tuner Frank Cartland and son of World War 2 fighter ace Lord William Marshall, has a promising future in Formula One, but not with his current team. If those Montague playboys win any races next season, I'll shave off my bread.'

The little man had had a long, unkempt, ginger beard for as long as anyone alive could remember.

"Watch out; I've got a razor ready Julian." Said Reggie, butting in on the interview in Brazil.

"Fuck off Lord Muck, still don't expect you lot will win any races." The little man replied.

It was at the Dutch Grand Prix at Zandvoort that Julian worst nightmare happened. Mat had picked up points in Spain and finished third in his home Grand Prix at Silverstone. He was lying fourth in the Championship points standings as they went to Holland. Here both car and driver had a magical weekend.

Mat had been fastest in practice and went on to win the race by ten seconds.

"Amazing this game seems so easy when everything clicks into place." Said Mat to the gathered reporters after the race. There was no sign of Julian Jacks.

"Don't mind reporters at the gate this time." Had been Mary's reaction on noticing the group waiting to interview her son on his return home from Holland.

"It does make a pleasant change," said William.
Neither had attended the race but watched it live on the BBC. They had opened a bottle of champagne to toast their victorious son.

There were only three races left in the season, the German, Belgium, and Italian Grand Prix; all run on dangerous and demanding circuits.

Mat had arrived at the Nurburgring full of confidence, but the weather soon put a damper on everyone's spirits. The famous castle was shrouded in a heavy mist from the moment all the teams gathered in the German paddock on Friday morning, the twisting tumbling track as slippery as an oil slick.

"It's just going to be a matter of survival out there. Take it easy," had been the advice from all the team managers to their drivers.

But once you have slid your body into your figure-hugging seat, pushed in your earplugs, pulled on your balaclava, and slipped on your crash helmet, a racing driver becomes a changed person. Oblivious to everything but the road ahead. When the engine starts, and you begin to control a roaring, angry, three hundred horsepower beast, there is no room for trepidation or fear.

It happened on the first lap at the Flugplatz jump. American Peter Austin had been drafted into the US Racers team to drive their hired March after Danny Unser had to pull out after breaking his arm in an Indy car race.

With little practice on the track Peter had approached the daunting turn too fast, he lost control as the car landed from its flight over the hump. The March careered into the hedges and trees to the left of the circuit, ripping off its left front wheel against a tree. The wheel smashed into Peter's crash helmet before rebounding across the track directly into the path of Mat's RAM.

Mat swerved right, but the car took control and dived into the ditch at the edge of the road.

The accident was not Mat's fault, but the resultant crash destroyed car and a broken right leg ended his season and Championship hopes.

Returning home after a week in Adeuer hospital Mat received a phone call from Reggie.

"Afraid that's it, old boy... can't afford to rebuild the car, the dream is over. Wanted to let you know before you read it in

the press. I am stoney broke, had to let all the boys go and I'm going to have to sell the old family pile. The bloody place is crumbling down anyway."
The subdued Reggie that had informed Mat as he convalesced at Sefton Lodge.

So far it had been a lousy year for Formula One accidents, with the death of Peter Austin in the collision with Mat three drivers had now been killed so far this season.

"Why do you think it is now so dangerous to be a Formula One driver." A reporter from the local Chichester paper had asked Mat when he came to interview him. His leg in plaster.

"Formula One has always been dangerous, but modern cars are faster, and little thought given to safety at the tracks." Mat had replied.

'Race circuits are too dangerous says Mathew Marshall.'

This quote became the headline in Autosport magazine the followings week.

"I expect you will be retiring now Reggie's had to pull the plug." William had said to his son after reading the article.

Mary could have predicted her son's response.

"Not unless I'm forced to, I've got unfinished business, so I can't pack up yet.

As soon as the leg heals, I'm going to look for a drive for next year." Mats answered.

Williams question had been more in hope than expectation; he had also expected that answer. In the war, life was quite different when he had been his sons' age, even though he knew his fellow pilots were getting killed, daily, he would willingly jump into his Hurricane. Wistfully he thought, *I would tomorrow if I could.*

Cam had phoned his Aunt Mary as soon as he had heard about Mats accident in Germany.

He was concerned about his cousins' health, but he did have an additional motive. *If Mat can't race for a while maybe Reggie Moncrieff will need another driver.*

But it had been the following weekend that Elmo had decided to return to Brazil, so there was little disappointment for him when he heard the Formula One Montague team had closed its doors.

Chapter33

Fate lends a hand

The Christmas period in 1973 had not been a happy one for either Cameron Cartland or Mathew Marshall.

Mats' left leg had completely healed, but despite speaking to all the Formula One teams, there seemed little chance of a drive being available for him for the 1974 season.

"Sorry Mat we have fixed our drivers for next season" had been the typical response.

His cousin had found the same reaction to his requests and had resigned himself to putting his Formula One dreams on hold for another year.

"At least you have F1 experience and have won a race, I haven't even managed to drive a bloody Formula One car yet." had been Cam's response when they meet at the Racing Car show in January.

Cam was working on the GRD stand at the show, enticing young men and their rich fathers to buy a new Formula 3 or Formula 2 car.

Also, on the stand was the new 2 Litre sports car the company had recently announced, Cam was due to give the car its first test at Goodwood later in the month.

"Who's driving the new sports car this year." Mat had asked him.

"Not sure, it will depend on how the testing goes."

Looking at the sleek deep blue sports car Mat added.

"As we've got nothing else organised, why not ask Nick if we can drive it."

"Together, you mean?"

"Why not, we got on ok at Le Mans didn't we...until Mikes accident."

Both remained quiet for a while remembering their lost friend. Nick came along to break the silence.

"Hi Mat, good to see you have recovered from your accident. What are you driving this year?"

"Afraid there are no F1 seats available, so not much, now. Just been admiring your new sports car with Cam."

"Well if you get some money together why don't you two drive it. About 5k should seal it."

Mat shook Nick's hand, "I'll see what I can do."

"I've got no money to contribute." Cam butted in.

"You sort the cars; you're right bloody good at that, sell a few of these, he said as he looked at the gleaming Formula 3 cars, and keep sweeping the floors for me, that will be enough if Mat can come up with some cash." Nick laughed.

Mat broached the money subject with his mother when he got home. He didn't want to approach his father; money spent on racing had always been a difficult subject with him.

Mary couldn't hide her excitement for the project but had her reservations.

"Would be lovely to see you and Cam drive together again, your grandfather would have been so proud, but after Mikes accident at Le Mans, are you sure it's what you want to do."

"Yes, I'm sure. You know what it's like, when you get an opportunity to drive a racing car, you must go for it.

Mary did know...her primary emotion was of jealousy.

"Why don't you pop round and see your grandmother. Tell her if she puts some money in the pot, I'll match it."

Mat was able to phone Nick and Cam the following day to say they had enough money.

The sports car Championship was run over seven rounds using many of the Formula One circuits.

The first round at Dijon went perfectly. Despite both men driving well within their limits, their GRD won the 2 Litre class with ease.

"If the rest of the year is like that, I'll be happy." Nick had said as he congratulated the pair.

Unfortunately for him, within three weeks, two tragic events in Formula One caused him to lose both his star drivers.

Carlos Silva had been disappointed with his Lotus experiences so far. Neither he nor his teammate had managed to sort out a satisfactory balance for the car's handling. Both were rapid young drivers but didn't have the mechanical knowledge or experience to sort out the cars. So far, they had lapped over a second a lap slower than the Ferraris and McLaren teams.

The Lotus boss Ken Champion was becoming frustrated with his young chargers.

"You're two are supposed to be the fucking bee's knees, that's why I signed you, but you can't sort out a bloody pushchair."

"I want Cam Cartland. You sign him as a test driver; he was great with my car last year." An angry Carlos replied.

"That was a Formula 2 car, not letting him loose in one of my cars. He crashes most of the bloody time."

"If you want to keep me, you get him this week, Williams has told me I can always drive for them."

Ken was fuming as Carlos stormed out of his office. He was not used to his drivers dictating terms to him.

There's a call for you Cam, Nicks young secretary had shouted to him across the workshop floor.

Ann Gardner was nineteen; she had taken the job only one month earlier. Ann had grown up in Thetford, less than ten miles from the Snetterton circuit, with a father passionate about motor racing.

She had gone with her father to Snetterton race meetings whenever he could afford it.

When Ann first met Cam, she had said. "I saw you crash your Mini, Mr Cartland, and thought you were dead. I cried all the way home and made my Dad phone the hospital." Embarrassed, she stopped talking.

"You must have been very young." Cam had replied smiling at this lovely young girl.

"I was twelve, I've got a scrapbook with all your cars in." she excitedly replied as she smiled back.

It was Cam's turn to be embarrassed; he didn't know what to say; he just mumbled. "That's nice please call me Cam."

"Hello, Cam Cartland here." He said as he picked up the receiver.

"It's Ken Champion here Cameron. I'm inviting you to test one of my Formula One cars at Snetterton next week."

"Is this a bloody wind-up."

"No. I want you to be at Snetterton next Thursday at 8 am. Don't be late." Ken hung up.

Seeing the confusion on Cam's face, Ann said.

"What's the matter Cam."

"It...it was Ken Champion boss of Lotus; he wants me to test the F1 car next week."

Excited, Ann ran around the table and put her hand on his arm.

"That's wonderful news."

"Yes, it is isn't it," Cam replied, he turned towards her and kissed her gently on the cheek.

Both pulled away, embarrassed.

Thankfully, it was a dry morning as at 7 am Cam drove his old E Type from his rented flat, closed to the GRD base, the twelve miles to Snetterton.

The Lotus mechanics had already unloaded two Lotus 72 cars from the transporter. John Player had sponsored the sleek racing cars for this year, and with their black and gold colours, they looked sinister, sitting quietly on the concrete pit road. Cam shivered knowing he was about to achieve one of his childhood dreams and drive a Formula One car.

Two hours later, after a seat fitting and long lecture from chief mechanic Rex Taylor, Cam carefully accelerated the black projectile out on the circuit and headed to Riches corner. Although it was the first Formula One car he had driven, his experience with the Greenham special at Le Mans meant the power of the Ford Cosworth engine was not too much of a shock.

He spent the morning settling into the car, getting used to the wide tyres with their extra grip and his brain adjusting to the immense speed the Formula One car generated.

During the lunch break, Rex had said.

"It's very difficult knowing how to set up this car when you get no useful feedback from the bloody drivers."

"I'll have a bit of a go this afternoon and should be able to give you some." Cam had replied.

After lunch and a dozen hard-driving laps later he rolled the Lotus into the pits.

"It's got too much understeer when you turn into the slower corners, the only way to stop it is to flick the wheel to induce oversteer, but that's not quick, although it looks good in the photos.

For the next hour Cam would complete a few quick laps, call back to the pits, and get Rex to alter settings, first the front wing angle, then softer springs. Each change made slight improvements.

When the session finished, Cam had managed to lap the track point four of a second better than Carlos best.

"I think you need to get some softer front anti-roll bars made up. If we tested again, I think you will gain a bit more time."

Cam had said as he left Rex and the other mechanics packing away their cars.

There had been no sign of Ken Champion all day.

Driving home Cam smiled to himself, his body ached all over and his neck muscles felt like they could hardly keep his head upright, but without a doubt this has been the best day of his life. And it got better, when he arrived home Ann was waiting outside in her old red Mini.

The following weekend Cam, with Ann snuggled up to him on the old sofa in his flat, watched on television as Carlos and his Lotus won his first points of the season by finishing in fourth in the Spanish Grand Prix.

The following day he received another call from Ken Champion.

"Hello, Cartland its Ken here. Could you come to Snetterton again next Tuesday we have new front Anti-roll bars for you to try, and I have a few other ideas I would like you to test. "

When he put the phone down this time, Cam smiled and said to the happy girl by his side.

"He seems much more friendly than last time."

The test again went well; this time, Carlos was also in attendance.

Most of the changes recommend by Cam were positive.

"The car is easier to drive at the limit now." Carlos had explained to Rex after he had a run in the car. He had just produced his best lap around Snetterton, four-tenths quicker than Cam's best time.

"You are a genius, my friend. I wish you were my teammate again." Carlos told Cam in front of the whole team. Everyone knew that he and his existing teammate didn't get on.

The next Grand Prix was in Holland; Ken Champion had phoned Cam to congratulate him for his work with the car and to invite him along the Grand Prix.

"Just as a thank you... it's not a contract." He had added quickly.

There was no sports car race that weekend, and as Mat was a previous winner at Zandvoort, he had also received an invitation.

The boys stood together in the euphoric JPS Lotus pit as Carlos flashed across the Zandvoort finish line to win the race. Behind the paddock area, unseen by those enjoying the Lotus victory, a vast pall of black smoke was rising at the back of the circuit between the dunes. Carlos teammate Peter Carlson had been in fourth place; he had also benefited from the handling improvements made to the Lotus cars by Cam. On the last lap coming through the downhill flat out right-hand bend halfway around the circuit, a link on the front suspension had broken. Out of control, Peter just a passenger, the stricken car, travelling at over one hundred miles per hour, hit the guard rail, its' narrow nose split the two layers of Armco and sliced into the cockpit of the Lotus. Thankfully, Peter was killed instantly by the metal barrier. With volatile fuel gushing from the ruptured fuel tanks sparks ignited the stricken machine.

Eventually marshals reached the crash and managed to extinguish the burning remains

Travelling back to England on the ferry to Felixstowe, the cousins were in a reflective mood. The euphoria of the Lotus victory had quickly turned to sadness when news of Peter's death filleted through to the paddock. All the teams packed up their cars and mountains of spares eager to return to their bases. It was only two weeks to the French Grand Prix, and as one mechanic put it 'the bloody show must go on."

"Not sure I can carry on race driving after this, it's like playing Russian roulette out there." Mat had confided to Cam as he dropped him off in Norfolk.

Mat gave Ann, who came to the door the moment she heard the car, a wave and drove straight off.
He didn't want to talk to anyone just drive home alone and think.

Tearfully Ann hugged Cam.

"Heard the news, I'm so sorry about Peter; but does that mean you get his seat." She said.

"Don't know yet, they could draft in someone else." Looking at his cousins departing Jaguar, he added.

"Ken Champion might give it to Mat. I know he rates him as a top race driver."

Mat did not discuss the tragic events at Zandvoort with his parents, and they didn’t want to raise the subject. By Tuesday morning he had decided he was going to retire from racing and devote his time to helping with the estate farm. He knew the workload for his parents was growing burdensome; he felt he had taken all their goodwill too far. I'll tell them this evening he thought.

Then the hall phone rang.

"It's Ken Champion here Mathew; I would like you to drive for us in France next weekend."

Mats brain tried to compute all the implications of this offer; his plans had suddenly turned upside down, but of course, he could refuse the offer.

"Thank you, Mr Champion, but what about Cam he thought you would offer the drive to him.

"Ah yes, Cartland is an excellent test driver, but he's got no Formula One experience. Need a safe pair of hands in the car after what's just happened."

"Can you give me some time to think about it."

"Need an answer by tomorrow at the latest. Got a queue of young guys knocking on my door wanting the drive, and some have money to bring." He said in his usual abrupt manner, then Ken Champion put the receiver down.

Mat stood holding his receiver in his hand for another minute until the sudden harsh continuous bleep from the phone brought him back to his senses.

The conversation with his parents that evening took a different direction to the one he had early planned. When he told them about the offer, he could see they were concerned.

William spoke first.

"Are his cars safe, I read something broke on the car last Sunday."

"Breakages can happen on any racing car; we all know that" had been Mary's first comments.
Then she added.

"It is a great opportunity, something you have wanted all your life. But it's your decision; we will support you whatever you decide. Wouldn't we William."

"Of course," was her husbands' automatic reply.

"The other thing that worries me if I accept is Cam's reaction. I'm sure he will be expecting to get the drive."

Suddenly he made his decision.

"I had better ring Cam and let him know I am accepting the Lotus drive."

"Fuck, fuck, fuck." Was Cam's reaction when he put the phone down after his cousin's call. He didn't usually swear much, but this time it felt justified. Although he had half expected it as he had told Ann, the disappointment was profound.

"What have I got to do to get a Formula One drive." He shouted. Fortunately, Ann was out when Mat had called, so no one heard his cry or felt his pain.

"Another drive will turn up." Ann had said when she came home and found him drowning his sorrows with his third bottle of beer.

"You still have the GRD drive, and you still have me, I know you are going to get the break you deserve soon. You have proved how good you are, so don't even think about giving up."

Slipping out of her dress, she said." Now come to bed."

The following day in the GRD office, with Nick and Ann giving him positive encouragement, Cam realised how lucky he was to be surrounded by people who believed in him. All his life had been a struggle, trying to reach his dreams alone since his grandfather, and then Mike's death. Now at last he had support.

He smiled when Nick said.

"For what it's worth Cam if I had a Formula One car out there in the workshop you are the only guy, I would want to drive it."

"Me too" Ann added.

The remaining racing season proved successful for both Cam who, with his replacement co-driver won the European Sportscar Championship; and for Mat who drove quickly and well. Although he did not get any race wins his consistent finishes saw him fourth in the World Championship table. Carlos managed three race wins and ended second in the Championship ten points behind the new World Champion' Ferrari driver Jake Carpenter.

At the press conference after the final race Carpenter announced his retirement from driving. It was Jake's third Championship victory; he was thirty-eight years old.

"I've been lucky, so many of my friends are no longer with us, and I promised my wife this would be my final season. It is time to let the younger guys take over."

During the season Carlos had made it known he was unhappy with Ken Champion and Lotus.

"Why you bring in a quick driver, you give Marshall same cars like me. I am the number one driver, should always have the best car." Carlos made this complaint often when things didn't go well for him.

As had been widely predicted, Ferrari offered Carlos a lucrative contract for the 1975 season, to take the place of the retiring Jake Carpenter. Much to the disgust of Ken Champion, his star driver accepted the offer without allowing him to make a counteroffer.

Two weeks after the end of the season Ken Champion made another phone call to Cameron Cartland.

"Hello again Cartland, congratulations on winning the sports car Championship this year, I hear from Nick Fellows you have been driving extreamly well.
My new number one driver Mathew Marshall thinks I should offer you the seat in my second car, Nick, your GRD boss, thinks you are the man for the job, even your bloody girlfriend has been annoying me all week to give you the drive.

Not much time until the start of the new season, so I've got to make a quick decision. I will give you a contact to drive my Formula One car next season; but only for the first three races, with an option for me to renew after the third race. How does that sound."

"Sounds bloody marvelous Mr Champion...I accept." Cam's immediate, enthusiastic response.

"Good, I've got a two-day test booked next week at Snetterton. I want you to try out some fresh ideas I've got to improve the car."

"How much is he paying you, Ann asked when Cam put down the phone.

"Hell...forgot to ask." He replied, picking her up and whirling her around the room.

"What on earth did you say to him."

"I just told him you would be the best driver for him. That you would do a brilliant job, and he would be stupid if he didn't sign you."

"You are an amazing girl; I love you."

She put her feet down to stop him swinging her.

"Do you mean that...or is it just the excitement," Ann asked...serious now.

Cam looked down into the, young, bright brown optimistic eyes looking into his.

"Oh...I mean it, I've never said that to anyone before, I have always just thought of myself. Finding someone that cares about me is… is wonderful."

"All I want is for you to reach your dream and become World Champion."

"Now I've found you; I think I can."

For both aspiring World Champions Christmas, 1974 saw them in a much happier place than the previous year.

The Marshals invited all the Cartland family to Sussex for Christmas Day, and to everyone's surprise and delight Peter and Grace had decided to accept. They travelled down with Cameron and Anna.

"Do not expect it will hurt the bakery if I have one day off," Peter said to his sister when they arrived.

Mary was delighted to see Mathew and Cameron together and to meet Ann for the first time.

"It is lovely to see Cam so relaxed; I've never seen him so happy. He is lucky to have met you." She told the young girl.

"I'm the lucky one; I'm so proud of what he has achieved. He told me how much you have helped him in the past. He thinks a great deal of you."

Mary smiled. *It's a shame Mat can't move on and find someone lovely like you,*

On Boxing Day, the boys, now Formula One stars, caused excitement at Brands Hatch by deciding to attend the annual Boxing Race meeting. Both were given the honour of starting a race. Ann, and Mat's sister Flo, added beauty and glamour to the party. The girls had hit it off immediately and, despite their different backgrounds, soon became friends.

Both young men were by now well-known racing drivers, carrying on the racing legacy passed from their grandfather Frank Cartland. The official announcement by Ken

Champion at the January Earls Court Racing Car Show that he would be an all British driver team for 1975 caused headlines all around the world.

It was inevitable that the past histories of these two; already famous motor racing families, would be pulled out of the archives and republished with a more modern spin.

William Marshall and Peter Cartland again had something in common, anger and discomfort over the additional intrusion into their private lives.

"I see the motoring mags are building us up as bitter rivals." Mat had said to Cam as they took on the rounds of media appearances and interviews.

"Don't want to have to fight you, I think it's high time we worked together...for the team. It's going to be a long season with twelve rounds, and it will be hard enough beating all the other bloody teams; the Ferraris and the McLaren's look like they are going to be very quick next season." Cam had replied as he put out his hand for his cousin to shake.

My cousin has changed, thought Mat as he accepted Cam's hand.

Chapter 34
The season begins

At the start of the 1975 season the leading players were:

No.1 - Renzo Mantova - McLaren M23
2 - Jochen Roos - McLaren M23
3 - Jody Clarke - Tyrrell 007
4 - Patrick Prost - Tyrrell 007
5 - Mathew Marshall - Lotus 74
6 - Cameron Cartland - Lotus 74
7 - Alex Rossi - Brabham BT44B
8 - Danny Brise - Brabham BT44B
9 - Carlos Silva - Ferrari 312T
10- Nicki Wagner - Ferrari 312T

Ken Champion had entrusted Cam with much of the early testing of the new car as it was widely accepted, he had developed into one of the best drivers in the world to sort out race car handling issues. Cam had spent two days testing and changing the set-up, working with chief mechanic Rex they produced an improved car which Chapman named JPS Lotus 74.

"It's doesn't feel as easy to drive as the old 72, and it's tricky to set up," Cam confessed to Mat as he prepared to test the car.

"I must say I still prefer the old car." Mat had said after his first run.

Neither of the young men was confident enough to confront Ken Champion with their reservations about his new design.

"Right, that's it, time to get the cars and spares packed. The plane leaves for Argentina in two days."

The Lotus team manager Peter Laws had instructed at the end of the final test session.

“See you, boys, at the airport, speak to Sally in the office she has got your timetable and tickets. Now, take a few days' rests, you're not going to get much in South America."

"What an adventure this is going to be, racing in eleven different countries between now and October!

"Cam had announced to Ann that evening.
He was surprised when she remained quiet.

"What's the matter." He asked.

"I wish I was coming with you to South America."

"So, do I Ann, but you know none of us can take partners for these early meetings. The fourth race is back in Europe you will be with me at all the races from then on, I promise."

"I know, stay safe and do your best. If you get some points, Champion must extend your contract after the third race in South Africa."
Cam had forgotten he was only under contract for three races.

"Don't worry; I'm not going to blow this chance. I'll make you proud of me."

"I will always be proud of you." She replied, as she took his hand and led him to the bedroom door.

12th January Argentine Grand Prix at Buenos Aires -
1st - Carlos Silva - Ferrari 312T
2nd - Nicki Wagner - Ferrari 312T
3rd - Jackie Collins - Shadow DN5

Not a good start for the Lotus team. The car proved to be slower than their main rivals. Mat managing 5th place when two quicker cars retired with mechanical problems, and Cam having to retire from a seventh place when an oil pipe broke and wrecked his engine after only twenty laps.

When teams left Argentina and moved up to Brazil for the second round, the Lotus team knew they had a great deal of work to do. Cam and Matt were not in the mood to enjoy the delights of Copacabana Beach.

They preferred to spend their time assisting with the necessary rebuilding and making modifications to their race cars.

26th January Brazilian Grand Prix at Interlagos -

1st - Jochen Roos - McLaren M23
2nd - Patrick Prost - Tyrrell 007
3rd - Mathew Marshall - Lotus 74

A slightly better race for the Lotus team, with Mat picking up four points for third place, and Cam managing 6th place to pick up his first World Championship point. But the results were flattering. Rain caused several incidents, forcing the retirement of quicker cars, and both Ferraris retired, Carlos with a fuel blockage and Wagner with suspension damage after a first-lap collision.

Flying back from South America, the mood in the Lotus camp was reflective. While not getting the results, they wanted at least they had picked up some points.

"South Africa is only one month away; we need to find some bloody improvements, so you lot need to pull your figures out." Had been Ken Champions response when the team gathered back at their Norfolk base.

"Cartland, you will be driving every day at Snetterton until we find the extra speed, I've been working on some more mods for the car."

"You will have to tell him Mat...he's more likely to listen to you," Cam told his cousin at the end of the second day's testing.

"We need to go back to the 72 this car is never going to be quick enough."

Fortunately, by now Ken Champion had come to the same conclusion.

"Shakedown two of the 72's tomorrow boys, we will revert to them for the South Africa race."

The relief in the Lotus team was palpable.

1st March -South African Grand Prix at Karilarmy

1st - Jody Clarke - Tyrrell 007
2nd - Carlos Silva - Ferrari 312T
3rd - Mathew Marshall - Lotus 72D

More points for Mat, but poor Cam picked up a puncture towards the end of the race, the resultant pit stop to change tyres dropped him down to twelfth place after running as high as sixth. Ken Champions had not travelled to South Africa, concentrating his time on producing new parts for the car.

The Lotus 72 had been "state of the art" when newly introduced in 1970, Champions design well in advance of his rivals, but now it was looking dated.

The apparent failure of the 74 models, had left him no choice for 1975 but to revert to the existing car.

"Doesn't matter if we have to write off this year." He told the team manager. Peter Laws.

"We only have two rookie drivers, no superstar, so we can blame them for poor results. Think Carlos did me a favour by leaving. Might as well keep Cartland he does have great testing skills." Peter didn't respond. He felt sympathy for Mat and Cam but knew his boss was probably right.

Since he lost his star driver, and friend Ronnie Clark in a Formula 2 crash six years previously, Ken had not allowed himself to get too attached to his drivers.

"It's six weeks until Spain; I have a couple of ideas I'd like to try out," Cam said to Peter Laws when they arrived back from South Africa. Somewhat apprehensively, he added," If the boss intends keeping me on the team."

"He is Cam, says he rates you as a test driver, so let's get testing."

Cam's relief was so high he hugged his surprised team manager.

While Cam concentrated on trying to improve their cars, Mat went back to Sefton Lodge for a short break. While he was happy to have gained some points in the first three races, he was under no illusion about the task they would face to win any races.

"I'm a bit disappointed, to be honest, had hoped the new car would be competitive but looks like we will have to use the old 72 for the rest of the season." He told his parents at dinner.

"Maybe Cam can improve it some more." His mother replied.

"Hope so, he is far better at that testing than me," was his less than an optimistic reply.

William had remained quiet during dinner and excused himself soon afterwards, saying he was tried and would have an early night.

"Is father, alright?" Mathew asked his mother when William had gone upstairs.

"I'm concerned about him, although he doesn't tell me much because he doesn't want to worry me, but that makes it worse."

"Is it his war injuries, or something else."

"It is the burns, seems everything is getting harder for him, especially his breathing, sometimes at night, he coughs up blood, but tries to hide that from me."

"What do his doctors say, they must be able to help him."

"I've at last persuaded him to go to a lung specialist in Harley Street. We have an appointment next week."

"I would like to come with you," the worried Mat said.

After the consultation and tests carried out by Doctor Yates, William and Mary were called back into his office, relieved their son had been called to Snetterton to try some changes Cam made to the set-up of the car.

"It is not good news I'm afraid Lord Marshall." Doctor Yates began.

"Your right lung is in imminent danger of collapsing, and unfortunately the left is not in much better shape. The only cure would be a transplant."
Mary spoke first.

"Is that possible."

"Well...it's a very new and experimental procedure, my college in Belgium Fritz Gerom is the leader in the field."

"Can you contact him for us," Mary said immediately.

Doctor Yates looked at William, who had remained silent.

"I don't think it will be worth the effort," William said, in a low voice, the others struggled to hear.

"Of course, it would...if it saves your life." Was Mary's angry response.

William looked at her. His soft blue eyes showed the only emotion possible for him. She could see they were moist.

"I'm sorry darling, but the constant pain has worn me out."

Then looking directly at Doctor Yates said.

"How long have I got before these lungs finally give up."

"To be honest Lord Marshall, I am amazed you are still with us. Your strength is all that's keeping you going, so could be weeks or months."

William got up and held out his gnarled hand.

The doctor took it and wrapped his other hand over it. There were no words.

On the way home, William says

"Don't tell the children darling; this is just between us."
Mary remained silent; only her tears betrayed her.

Ken Champion had been surprised but delighted with the improvements in the Lotus 72.

Working closely with Cam, they had tried a succession of new parts and eventually improved performance by almost half a second.

"Bloody good show Cam. Didn't think we would get the old girl to go so quick. Going to rename this car Lotus 72C."
"Thanks 'Mr Champion, those changes to the aero have improved the car." *Wonder if he thinks the C stands for Champion or Cam.*
Mat, who had covered less than a quarter of the testing miles, also prised his cousin.

"The car is the best we've ever had. I couldn't have done that Cam."

The team packed for the First European round in Spain with renewed confidence.

27th April Spanish Grand Prix at Barcelona

1st - Jochen Roos - McLaren M23
2nd - Patrick Prost - Tyrrell 007

3rd - Cameron Cartland - Lotus 72E

The race was dramatic and stopped before sixty per cent distance due to several accidents; one including Mat Marshall, but although no drivers were injured, parts of damaged cars had flown over the low guardrails and killed two spectators. Everyone sighed with relief when they left Spain; no one complained when the race carried only half points.

Then came a rush of five races during May and June. After Monaco, Belgium, Sweden, Netherlands, and the French Grand Prix's. All teams had mixed results from these races after France the leading points situation were as follows:

Carlos Silva 40
Jochen Roos 35
Patrick Prost 28
Jody Stewart 27
Mathew Marshall 23
Nicki Wagner 22
Cameron Cartland 20

With only twenty points covering all these drivers it was turning out to be the most open World Championships for years, although Carlos was favourite to win having a lead of five points.

The next race was the home Grand Prix for the British drivers at Silverstone.

Jody Stewart received most of the attention being the senior English driver and ex-World Champion, but considerable newsprint was also devoted to Mathew Marshall and Cameron Cartland.

'The rising Formula One stars of British Racing.'

Had been a typical headline, and always looking for an angle the tabloids tried to stir up trouble between the cousins.

They had managed to take a picture of Mat having dinner with, and in intermate, conversation with, Cam's girlfriend, Ann. The photograph splashed over the following days' newspaper with the headline.

'Is Mat Marshall a rival for Cam Cartland off the track as well as on it?'

It had been an utterly innocent dinner; Cam had gone back to the Lotus factory to discuss set-up ideas for Silverstone.

If the press had been able to hear the conversation, they would have heard Ann sympathetically listening to Mat.

"I cannot get over losing Linda; I blame myself for her death every day. The only time I can forget is when I'm strapped into the race car."

Ann had reached across the table and took Mats hand. It had been the photo the press had hope for and gleefully used.

"I love you, of course, I don't want to be with Mat. He just needed someone to talk to about Linda. Ask him if you don't believe me."

"I will, don't worry," had been Cam's reaction.

It was the first disagreement the couple had had. The old jealously of Mat was never far below the surface for Cam.

The next time the cousins met was for the press conference on the Tuesday before the race. Matt spoke first.

"Cam, I hope you don't believe any of that rubbish in the press about Ann and me. She is a lovely girl, and you are truly fortunate. Make sure you don't lose her."

Cam didn't notice the tears in his cousin's eyes.

"I'm not going to, to you or anyone else," had been Cam's curt response.

The British Grand Prix at Silverstone.

1st - Carlos Silva - Ferrari 312T
2nd - Jody Stewart - Tyrrell 007
3rd - Nicki Wagner - Ferrari T312

Disaster for the Lotus team.
"Don't crash with your teammate. I've warned you so fucking often."

Ken Champion shouted at his drivers as they arrived back in the pits after coming together at Copse Corner on the first lap. Qualification had been promising, both starting on the third row of the grid with Cam fractionally quicker.

The accident had not been either driver's fault, Jochan Roos had made a bad start, and Cam had managed to squeeze inside him going into Copse, Roos tried to "close the door" on Cam, they touched, both spun and collected the hapless Mat in the ensuing accident. All three cars eliminated immediately.

Reviewing a film of the incident after race Chapman had to admit neither of his drivers was to blame, but of course, he didn't apologise.

Further disappointment for the British fans as Jody Stewart was beaten into second place by the Ferrari of Carlos Silva.

"It's the Nurburgring in two weeks, another fiasco like Silverstone and that will be it for both of you. There are half a dozen hungry young Formula 2 drivers waiting to take your places, and they have money. Bring me back some points or else."

Ken Champions ultimatum at the meeting back at the Lotus Norfolk headquarters after the Silverstone race had quite an impact.

3rd August German Grand Prix at The Nurburgring

1st - Cameron Cartland- Lotus 72C
2nd - Nicki Wagner - Ferrari 312T
3rd - Mathew Marshall - Lotus 72C

The turnaround in fortune for the Lotus team, brought Cam his first Formula One victory.

The daunting track, as usual, claimed its victims March driver Bruce Bevan crashed in qualifying at Pflanzgarten, breaking both his ankles.

The race had started in heavy rain, visibility, unless you were at the front of the grid, was restricted to a few feet, the wide tyres from the car ahead throwing up an impenetrable wall of dense water spray.

"They are driving at 140mph in thick fog, sure if they are just brave or completely mad."

Murrey Walker had commented to the millions of fans now glued to their television screens.

Starting cautiously Cam and Mat had remained in their sixth and seventh starting positions. Then after eight of the fourteen-mile laps, the track begun to dry in many places. With the leading Ferrari of Carlos Silva diving into the pits, the other leading drivers followed him to change to dry weather tyres. Peter Laws, the Lotus team manager, decided to leave his two drivers on wet tyres for one more lap. Gambling, the grey sky still heavy with dark clouds, would soon deposit another rainstorm.

As they flashed past the pits Mat and Cam found themselves in first and second places. But it didn't make them happy; both could see chunks of their wet tyres lifting, overheated by the drying surface. Both desperately searched for the remaining still wet parts of the track to cool the tyres. With Cam taking more risks than his teammate, he slid past Mat as they turned into the Bergwerk turn and took the lead. Seven miles around the lap it was apparent their dry tyres rivals were catching the Lotus pair; rapidly.

The Ferrari pit stops to change Carlos Silva's tyres had been slow, caused as a wheel spinner became cross-threaded. When he pitted, he had been leading the race by five seconds. now he was back in seventh place. His frustration was made worse by the fact that his teammate had emerged third. Everyone expected the rest of the field would quickly catch the two wet tyred Lotus drivers.

Carlos had left the pits with spinning wheels and smoking tyres, angry at the delay.

Driving at ten-tenths, right at the limit, he left no margin for error. Entering the right-hand winding descent of the Wehrseifen turn slightly too fast, instantly the Ferrari drifted inches off-line. The outside rear wheel found the still wet strip of track and immediately lost adhesion. Even the lightning reflexes of Carlos couldn't save the Ferrari from slamming backwards into the guard rail. The blood-red car turned over as it bounced back across the track, sparks set alight the gushing fuel from the ruptured fuel tanks as, like a child's spinning top, the wrecked car continued its fiery descent down the hill. Following drivers managed to stop and rushed to help the ill-equipped marshals, but it took five long minutes to extinguish the inferno and right the car. The unconscious Carlos was dragged from the wreckage to the grass verge at the side of the road.

When Cam, now followed by the fast-closing Ferrari of Nicki Wagner who had passed Mat, reached the finishing area the red flag was displayed to stop the race. Only twelve of the twenty-six cars that started the race completed that lap.

"What has happened." a remarkably calm Cam asked Peter Laws as the cars pulled into their respective pits.

"There's been a terrible accident apparently; cars are blocking the track."

"Who is it."

"Don't know yet but looks like Carlos is involved."

For fifteen minutes, the drivers were left alone with their thoughts strapped in their cars.

There followed a delay of more than an hour during which Carlos was taken by helicopter to Coblenz hospital, and with darkness closing in, the race declared a result.

Unlike the Spanish round this time, as more than half the race had finished, full points were awarded.

The podium presentation was a somber affair; this was not the way Cam hoped his first victory would happen; Cam's quote to the gathered press.

" I am delighted to get my first victory, but the accident of Carlos has spoilt it. He is a great driver."

It was with mixed feelings the team arrived home, the Lotus teams' celebrations tempered by the news that Carlos had died in hospital on Sunday evening.
Mat had gone straight home, knowing his parents would be anxious for him.

"Third is a good result, Mat." his sister, the first to comment.

"Are you alright son, so sorry to hear about Carlos." His father managed to say. Mat was shocked to notice how difficult it was for his father to speak.

"Glad to have you safely home." Was all his mother could add?

With the American round of the Championship cancelled after start money disputes, it meant there were only two rounds left in the 1975 World

Championship. The death of Carlos had thrown the race to be world champion wide open. Five drivers could still win it; one being Carlos who was still leading on points.

27th August Austrian Grand Prix

1st - Mathew Marshall - Lotus 72C
2 nd - Cameron Cartland- Lotus 72
3rd – Patrick Prost – Tyrrell007

The penultimate round was the Austrian Grand Prix, and it rained the whole weekend.

" Have you lot been doing a bloody rain dance." Julian Jakes asked Cam in the paddock after practice. The two Lotus drivers had qualified second and fourth for the Grand Prix.

"The car is working well in the wet. Mat told the gathered press. "It's all thanks to Cam's hard work during testing."

Unfortunately, practice for the race brought another serious accident when a March driven by a guesting American driver lost control and hit the barriers on the Bosch curve. The left front wheel was ripped from the car and careered into the spectators, killing one of them.

The two Lotus drivers powered into the leading positions on the first lap and

stayed there for the whole race. This time Mat won with Cam a dutiful second. He did comment after the race that he felt he could have passed Mat but was obeying team orders.
The happy Lotus team travelled home to Norfolk to prepare their cars for the final race in three weeks at Monza.

When Mat arrived home, clutching his silver winner's trophy, his mother was at the door waiting for him. They did not need words; she just opened her arms and Mat rushed into them.

They held each other for at least a minute. Mary broke away first and led him into the lounge of Sefton Lodge.

"Mat, I'm afraid your father is extremely ill. He is upstairs; there is a nurse with him; his lungs are finally giving up."

"Why didn't you let me know earlier, I would have come home."

"William didn't want to add to your worries before the race, he had told me not to call you or your sister."

"He is far more important than a bloody motor race." When Mat said this, he realised that was true. *All events of the last two years, the death and misery, that had started with Linda, are all connected with my passion for racing. Well no more, whatever happens, I will retire from racing after Monza.*

His shock when he entered his parents' bedroom was strong. A large machine was nosily helping his father to breath. His sister and nurse were at the bedside.

Mat took his father's firm hand, and William opened his eyes.

"Glad you are alright son, congratulations on a great win." He managed to whisper.

Mat had no response only tears.

Chapter 35

Reconciliation at Burlham

The dramatic, and often tragic, 1975 Formula One season had captured the imagination of the public worldwide, and nowhere more than in England.

Two young English drivers from famous racing families would be battling from the ultimate prize in the capital of Italian motor racing at Monza. Their two main rivals were both Ferrari drivers. Although Carlos had died in Germany, he could still win, and become the first posthumous World Champion.

The permutations for the outcome of the 1975 World Championship were endlessly discussed and written about in the motoring press.

One of the Lotus drivers would need to win the race to be champion, while Ferrari driver Nicki Wagner could finish first or second to take the title. If none of the three managed to win, Carlos would be champion. There were three other drivers capable of winning the race.

"Sorry to hear your father is ill Mat." Cam had greeted his cousin when they met up at the Lotus factory one week after the Austrian race.

"Thanks, Cam." Was all Mat could say.

There was understandable tension between the two men, although they had resolved the misunderstanding over Ann, they both knew they were now facing the most significant event of their young lives. The one thing they had both been dreaming of since childhood was in touching distance for both of them...but only one could win.

"Don't care which of you wins but bring the bloody cars back in one piece. If you both finish in the top four, Lotus can win the constructors championship. That's far more important than the drivers' championship."

Ken Champion had told them at the post-Austrian briefing.

Cam was now in the far better mental place than his cousin, thanks to the increasing influence of Ann.

"I've been in touch with your parents Cam; we are going to visit them on Sunday," she announced.

"They, or at least my father, wouldn't want to see me." He had protested.

"That's rubbish they are proud of what you have achieved, and I want you to get over your differences with your father, please do it for me."

Grace had been excited by Anna's call and prepared a full roast Sunday lunch for their visit.

"She is a lovely girl, so pleased Cameron has met her." She said to Peter.

"Let's hope she can control him," was his only response.

Thanks to Graces excitement telling her friends at the Woman's Institute; the whole of Burlham knew the famous racing driver was visiting on Sunday.

After Cam had spent ten minutes signing autographs, they managed to get into the bakery and shut the door.

"That was a wonderful dinner, Mrs Cartland, I will help you with the washing up," Anna said. The two women got up, leaving the men together in awkward silence.

Eventually, Peter said.

"Congratulations son, Ann is a lovely girl." Cam smiled, for a second, he had thought his father was going to praise him for his racing success.

"Yes, she is isn't she. Meeting Ann has made a big difference in my life. You know that you and Mum are welcome to come to Italy with us for the final race."

"I don't think it would be good for your mothers' nerves; she worries about you." His additional remark was a pleasant surprise for Cam.

"And so, do I, every race someone seems to get killed, we don't want the next one to be you...we love you."

Cam held out his hand which his father took in his.

"Thank you, Dad, that means a lot to me."

When the young couple had left, Peter couldn't help remembering the final meeting he had had with his father when they had made up their differences. The following day he had discovered his grandfather had died in his sleep.

Chapter 36

The final flight for William

Ten days before the final Formula One race at Monza, Lord William Marshall finally gave up his fight with life and died. It was the end of an awfully long battle that had started in a blazing Hurricane thirty-five years earlier. Every day since then, William's life had been blighted with pain; and each time he noticed the reactions to his appearance had always compounded the hurt.

Mary, Mathew, Florence, and his mother, Silvia were at the bedside as William Marshall released a final long sigh and closed his eyes forever.

Then he flew...in 'Harry' higher and higher, their Merlin engine screaming with delight, in that last breath William pulled the joystick fully back, opened the throttle wide and together they tore straight up through the atmosphere until they reached the heavens.

The heartbroken family lent over the body of William in turn and gently kissed his forehead before leaving the room. His scared face left awash with tears.

Mary broke the silence downstairs in the lounge.

"William requested his ashes be scattered in the trees above the test hill at Brooklands. He made me promise to make sure it happened."

"But no Marshalls have never been cremated, they are have always gone into the family crypt," Silvia said.

"Well, that tradition has ended with grandfather, George," Mathew added.

"I agree with mother we should respect our father's wishes."

Well, you are Lord Marshall now Mathew, so you are free to make all the decisions." his grandmother replied.

That sudden realisation hit Mathew hard.

"I suppose I am, but nothing changes, mother always made joint decisions on the estate with father. She will still do that with me. But one decision I am making now is to retire from motor racing immediately."

"No, you can't." All three women spoke at once.

"You are so close to being world champion this year; your father would never have wanted you to give up now." His mother added as Florence and Silvia nodded in agreement.

Mat looked at the three, tear-streaked, concerned faces; all experiencing their private grief. He added after many seconds.

"Alright, but Monza will be my last race whatever happens. I had already decided to retire, my love for driving has not been the same since I lost Linda.
Then there was Mike, and now father..." He could say no more, his chest heaving with his own suppressed grief.

The funeral of Lord William Marshall brought the town of Chichester to a standstill. It was flooded with people. despite the families request for a quite ceremony, hundreds lined the streets to pay their last respects.

After a service in the medieval Cathedral Williams coffin was taken to Chichester crematorium for a private service.

As William had requested, the following day close family and his friends from Brooklands gathered at the top of the Brooklands Test Hill.

Mary walked to the study pine were she and William had first declared their love.

"One day I will join you here." she softly whispered as she gently spread her husband's ashes at the bases of the tree.

Chapter37

Showdown at Monza.

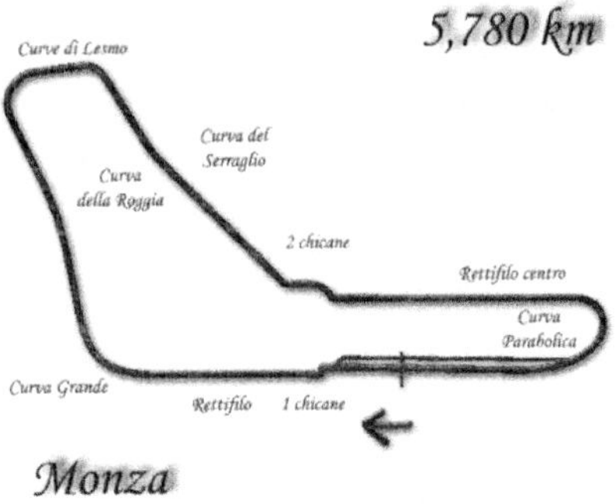

The five cars were wheel to wheel at 180mph as they approached the Curva Parabolica for the final time, lap after lap they had traded places never more than a second separating them, inches apart they diced with disaster. At the end of each lap, they had crossed the finish line constantly swapping places as they began another high-speed lap.

Murray Walker's voice, now nearing hysterical pitch, being transmitted to millions of homes continued his commentary.

"This Italian Grand Prix has been the most dramatic race I can remember, the fastest in Formula One history, one of the greatest races I have ever seen. Two hours seem to have gone by in a flash. Now the whole season had come down to this moment. If Marshall, Wagner or Cartland appear out of this last corner in the first place and across the Monza finish line they will be world champion driver, or if it's Prost or Roos, Carlos Silva will be posthumous world champion."

At the 300-yard board marker that signalled the approach to the final corner, the Lotus of Mat led the pack. A glance in his right-hand mirror and he saw it filled with the bright red nose of Nicki Wagner's Ferrari attempting to pass on his inside. Mat knew Cam had used his slipstream and was tucked under his gearbox waiting to pull out at the last moment; Mat also knew Cam would never be prepared to give way…ever.

Instantly he realised he didn't need this victory as much as his desperate cousin; Cam would rather die than lose the chance to be World Champion driver.

Mats brain computed all these actions and thoughts in a split second as he eased his Lotus to the right to block the charge of Nicki forcing the Ferrari driver to lift his right foot slightly to avoid a collision. As he did so, he also raised his right foot a fraction off the throttle pedal. Cam moved inches to his left and delayed his braking until the last possible moment, with his wheels locked and tyres smoking as the rubber franticly searched for some grip on the Italian tarmac.

All his hours of testing came to his aid as instinct took over, he held the sliding car on the edge of the track. Cam turned late into the bend with the black nose of his Lotus leading the snarling pack; around the long right-hand corner, he retained his slender lead. With Cam on the outside carrying more speed, Mat who had dealt with the charge from Nicki, eased his car back across the open expanse of the Monza concrete pulling behind his cousin to block the other two drivers attempting to slipstream past. Prost managed to pull out and inched passed his Lotus feet before the finish line. All five drivers had their right feet pushed hard to the floor of their cars, straining every muscle to obtain some advantage, a blur of black, blue, black, red, and green racing cars flashed under the welcoming chequered flag in a blink of an eye to finish the race.

In millions of homes around the world, fans had been fixed to their TV screens and radios, watching, and listening to excited commenters in many languages.

In the United Kingdom, fans continued to hear Murrey Walker's passionate voice.

"I've never seen anything like it, and unless I'm very much mistaken the Lotus of Cameron Cartland crossed the line a nose ahead of the blue Tyrrell of Patrick Prost which means Cameron Cartland is our new World Champion driver."

Sitting in Sefton Lodge Mary Marshall released a long breath, she hadn't realised she had been holding it for most of that last lap. She hugged her daughter, thinking of William, and that how her father's lifelong ambition has been achieved, no matter that it wasn't her son. Mary was just thankful Mathew had survived and would be coming home.

In the village bakery of Burlham, even Peter Cartland allowed himself a smile, as he said to Grace.

"I said he would either kill himself or be world champion, thank goodness that's all over, hopefully, we can have some peace now."

"Why can't you just for once in your life be proud; our son had an impossible dream, but he has fulfilled it. I'm sure he is going to continue racing, and I will always support him."

Grace then got up and left her husband, open-mouthed sitting in his old armchair.

Peter had no way of knowing that his son, with his arm around Ann, was currently enjoying the wild adulation Italian race fans. No matter that it wasn't an Italian hero, they always enjoyed a new world champion. Or that he would soon sign a two-year deal to be number one driver for the Lotus Formula One Team.

An hour after the race Cam and Mat had managed to get a quiet moment together in the Lotus transporter.

"Well done, Champ." Mat said, putting his arm around his sweat, and champagne-soaked, cousin.

Cam looked directly at him.

"I know what you did out there on the last corner...thank you Mat. You had a chance to win this World Championship for yourself. I'll return the favour next season, and help you be the next world champion."

"No need Cam... that was my last race. I've found my desire to win is not as strong as yours; you deserve it; our grandfather would be proud of you."

"Of both of us," Cam added as he gave his cousin a long, and sincere hug.

Far, far above the Monza circuit, a shaft of sunlight had broken through the overcast sky as the mass of crowds began to drift away from the famous old track. As they did, some people swore they had heard a clap of thunder. But could the disturbance in the sky be Frank Cartland being thumped on the back and having his hands shaken by Freddie O'Hare, Eddie Swift, Mike Cole, and the hundreds of other drivers killed by their fatal addiction to speed. You're a lucky old bugger Frank, Freddie seemed to whisper, now you've got a world champion at last.

Frank just smiled.

Inspiration! Some of the Reference books and recommended reading

Adventures Fen : E. Ennion

Brooklands Part 2: W. Boddy

From Brooklands to Goodwood: R. Walkerley

Silverstone the first 40 Years:

Formula 3 Racing : P. May

Archie and the Listers: R. Edwards

Starting Grid to Chequered Flag: Paul Frere

Alf Francis Racing Mechanic: A. Francis

Hurricane Combat : K W Mackenzie

The Battle of Britain: P. Bishop

V 1 Flying Bomb 1942-52: S. Vologa

Le Mans: A.Clausager

The Le Mans 24 Hours: D. Hodges

Powered by Jaguar: D. Nye

Sports Car Racing: D.Jenkinson

Other books in the trilogy

Book 1 of A Fatal Addiction

The Seduction of Speed

'He was grinning as the car roared on to the Home Banking, flashed under the Members' Bridge and across the white timing line. His last thoughts were that the lap must have been much better than 120mph. Then, as he came into full view of the packed paddock, the engine unable to take any more abuse gave up the struggle and blew apart'

Book 2 of A Fatal Addiction

The Trumphs and the Tragedies

'The unpleasant smell that invaded him when he finally managed to open the door was a mixture of dampness and decay. His torch illuminated a layer of inky black water, much as he had been expecting, but as he moved the light across the slick surface, he noticed a flash of white.

He concentrated the beam on the spot,
and an involuntary shriek of terror left his mouth. The sockets of an eyeless skull were looking up, straight at him'.

About the Author

Maxwell Mark Power's life began amidst the thunderous roar of racing engines. His family's home, just a mile from the Hanger Straight at Silverstone, was the perfect vantage point for the British Grand Prix. This early exposure to the world of racing would shape his future in ways he couldn't yet understand.

Max grew up in a comfortable home with every spare space containing huge stacks of old Motor Sport, Autosport, Motoring, and Motorcycle magazines. Little wonder that in his early years, he thought motoring was the real world...the rest just seemed strange.

His mother said his first word had been Mummy; in fact, it had been money.

Even at this young age, Max knew that if he wanted to be a racing driver, he would need lots of money.

With unwavering determination, persistence, and a dash of skill, Max follows his dream to becoming a successful racing driver. His journey began with motorbikes, then transitioned to racing cars. Always on the move, jetting off to the next race meeting, never lingering in one place for long. But when the last racing engine fell silent, he always found his way back home.

Max enjoyed the taste of victory in many races, but his path was not without its hurdles. A constant shortage of funds and some colossal crashes prevented him from reaching the pinnacle of the sport. Yet, his resilience and unwavering determination to succeed in the face of adversity is a testament to his character.

A few times, he has tried to retire from racing, but his addiction would always drag him back to the sport he loves.

Today, Max resides in his workshop in the East of England, surrounded by his trophies from past victories and the remnants of broken racing cars.

Despite the challenges he's faced, he remains an unwavering optimist, always looking forward to the next race with the belief that this time, he'll emerge victorious.

His motto is " Where's the next race, I'm going to win this time"

I hope you have enjoyed this work of fiction,
if so, remember there are
Two more books in the series!

Steve Bradley – a.k.a Max.M.Power

Printed in Dunstable, United Kingdom

76840637R10228